WHIRLIGIG

WHIRLIGIG

MAGNUS MACINTYRE

MARBLE ARCH
PRESS

**MARBLE ARCH
PRESS**

Marble Arch Press
1230 Avenue of the Americas
New York, NY 10020

Originally published in Great Britain in 2013 by Short Books.

First Marble Arch Press trade paperback edition August 2015

Marble Arch Press is a publishing collaboration between Short Books, UK, and Atria Books, US.

Marble Arch Press and colophon are trademarks of Short Books.

For information about special discounts for bulk purchases, please contact Simon & Schuster Special Sales at 1-866-506-1949 or business@simonandschuster.com

Manufactured in the United States of America

10 9 8 7 6 5 4 3 2 1

Library of Congress Cataloging-in-Publication Data has been applied for.

ISBN 978-1-4767-3048-6

ISBN 978-1-4767-3049-3 (ebook)

Cover design: Leo Nickolls

for Lucie

whirligig, n.

1. A mechanical instrument or toy that whirls or rotates.
2. A fickle, giddy or inconstant person.
3. An instrument of punishment or torture.

Nimble Men, Blue Men and
Green Ladies

'What can I be, then?' he said.

The girl paused, looking at the boy. They stood there, blinking dumbly at each other. Her eyes were sky blue, his mud brown. They had been alone in the glade for only a minute so far, and the rules of the game had not yet been established, except that she was Princess of Land-under-Waves.

'Um...' She hooked her finger in her mouth. He was tubby and awkward, this boy. An ill-fitting, thick-knit jumper barely covered his round tummy. His wellies were too big and had no mud on them, and he had on an alarmingly yellow cagoule. She would not have chosen this boy to play with, but he was the only other child for miles around. Anyway, she was curious about his tight curls of bright-orange hair. She had rarely seen such electrically ginger hair, and she had lived in Scotland all her life.

'You can be Black Pig,' she said at last.

The boy squinted at the girl, wondering what to do. He didn't play much with girls. At school he stuck very much to the weed-strewn edges of the playground, consorting only with the fat and the spastic. Of that group, he could be the leader. This girl was younger than him by two years, but he felt somehow junior. She was pretty with her long black careless hair and red corduroy dress, and it was her grandmother's house. The girl had taken charge of the game as soon as the grown-ups had gone back towards the vast and imposing house with their gins and tonics and crystal laughter. He was frightened of the house. It was a castle, or very nearly, and had turrets that reminded him of bats. And he was frightened of the garden. It was over-grown, huge, and drippingly moist even though this was summer. The girl was proprietress of everything here, but he was not going to be owned by her, and did not like the idea of being 'Black Pig'.

'Why can't I be The Man?'

'What man?' she said, pulling strands of hair from her eyes.

'That man you said.'

The girl continued to stare at the boy, her nose screwed up in confusion.

'You said there was a man,' he said uncertainly. 'And another man as well.'

'Oh!' The girl gave a patronising giggle. 'There are Nimble Men, Blue Men and Green Ladies. It's a Scottish story from the Olden Days, called a miff.'

'OK. Yeah.' He knew what a myth was, and chose not to correct her. It simply wasn't worth adding more incomprehension to the dynamic.

'Well,' began the girl, 'you can't be any of them, because you don't know how to reel.'

The fact is, as the girl explained to him, there is no point trying to teach an English boy who can't dance how to do so. At least, not when the boy is ten, and you yourself are eight. But she didn't want to hurt anyone's feelings.

'Black Pig is what they used to call the devil,' she went on. She stared again at the chaotic nest of ginger hair on the boy's head, and added, 'Come on, it'll be fun.'

The boy had to admit to himself that playing the part of The Devil did sound fun. But he did not like the imputation that he was less of a Scot than her. He was half Scottish, as his mother reminded him whenever they came on these trips to Scotland to rent a holiday cottage with Granny – although only then. His mother had, for her own convenience, dropped her Glaswegian accent some years ago. But he was reminded of his heritage every time he had to say his first name. 'Gordon' might be normal in Scotland, but in southern England it received a moment's hesitation. Just a stutter in the air. But it wasn't his first name or being 'a Jock' that got Gordon routinely bullied at low-to-medium intensity. Anyway, he thought, this girl could be no more than half Scottish. His parents had armed him with the knowledge that her father, an Indian man who now lived in America and taught people about Indian philosophy, had left her and her Scottish mother long ago. He knew that this was information he should not use. It might be *racialist*.

So Gordon knuckled down to the game, adapting his cagoule to become a diabolical cape. He even made her laugh with his impression of The Devil. 'Noo, har har!' he cackled, and swooped around the glade while she danced in the middle. This continued companionably enough for a while. But they both stopped dead when they saw the other boy.

He was tall and languid, with a shaggy thatch of blond hair, and he told them that his name was Harry in a way that made it clear he was already at Big School. He may as well have been a million years older.

'My name's Coky,' said the girl, and they smiled at each other, blinking in the sunlight.

'What's your name?' Harry had turned to the open-mouthed fat ginger boy at his elbow.

Gordon hesitated. He had never felt aware of his accent before. Compared to Coky's gentle tones, and Harry's soft Western Isles whistle, he felt that his English-English would grate. So he changed it, in what he hoped would be a subtle way.

'Moi name uss Goordun, so it uss,' said Gordon. Instantly he knew he had made a terrible mistake. If Coky and Harry had been cross, he would have understood. But their reaction was worse. They paused, both looking at him for a moment in the same distracted fashion, then turned to each other.

'We're playing a game,' said Coky, grabbing Harry's hand and dragging him to the centre of the clearing. 'I'm the Green Lady, and you can be the Nimble Man. Can you dance a reel?'

'Aye,' said Harry simply.

Coky gave Harry the additional title of King of Land-under-Waves. As they prepared themselves, Gordon asked, in his own voice this time, what Black Pig should do in this new game. He knew the answer before she gave it.

'Oh,' she paused, and bit her lip. 'Black Pig isn't really part of this game.'

Gordon squinted stupidly as the two other children

began to dance and sing. Intricate and deeply coded, this was dancing as Gordon had never seen it before. It had endless twirls, claps and steps that he couldn't fathom. It looked like it repeated, but just as he thought he knew what was going to happen next, it seemed to change. The girl tripped and skipped under Harry's careful hands, and they linked arms and twirled each other, and Coky's long black hair bounced and flicked, seeming to Gordon to dance its own jig. Then they sang together:

Where are the folk, like the folk of the West?
Canty and couthy, and kindly the best.

Gordon removed his cagoule silently, and it lay on the ground like the mangled corpse of a canary. He moved away behind a tree to watch a little more. They did not notice his absence and continued with their dance and their song.

Westering home, and a song in the air,
Light in the eye, and it's goodbye to care.

Gordon turned and slunk quietly away from the glade.

Used to being alone, he resolved to find something to do that was better than stupid old dancing. But he stomped his boots on the damp ground as he continued walking, to make some noise and give him some confidence in the face of the garden's dark and jungly presence. He pushed past odd and exotic trees and bushes, and swatted away fat flies, walking until he could no longer hear the laughter from Coky and Harry, and was lost.

13

As he wandered in the scary garden, it gave Gordon satisfaction to know that if he were killed by a tiger or an axe-murderer, the inevitable prison sentence the other children would serve would be justice for excluding him from the game. Nonetheless, when he emerged onto a patch of level ground and came upon a set of outhouses, he sighed deeply. Signs of nature being tamed by man came as profound relief.

The barn in the middle of the outhouses had a red tractor parked outside it, to which Gordon was automatically drawn. But as he came closer to the large barn doors, the sound of grown-up voices coming from inside made him check his ungainly stomp. There was something about the tone in the voices that made him cling silently to the wall as he approached. Crouching down outside the doors, he listened. No words were discernable, but he could tell that the man's voice was that of his father, speaking softly.

Gordon was cheered. His loud, fat, balding, ginger dad, who always made Gordon's mother laugh with his silly jokes, and drank whisky whenever he was home, was close at hand. Mostly he was Abroad, doing something with numbers that Gordon could not explain. It was the cause of much celebration in their suburban semi that his father was now being paid enough money for Gordon to be sent, next term, to a school with blazers where everyone called you by your surname. Apparently this was a good thing.

Gordon straightened, about to open the door and stride into the barn. Then there was a woman's voice, and he stopped. His mother's voice was always chirrupy, even when admonishing him – which was rare. This was a lower, soupier voice. Was this voice persuading? Denying? Gordon couldn't tell, but he could tell this was grown-up talk, and he turned to go. He would go and find his mother. Where there was Mum, there was food.

Walking around the back of the barn, though, he saw that there was a ladder with perhaps twenty rungs on it, propped up against a small window which would allow him to see into the barn. Gordon would dearly have loved to possess a stronger James Bond reflex but actual adventure seemed always to be defeated by inertia masquerading as caution. Now, though, he tested the ladder for strength, and it seemed secure enough, so he climbed it. Halfway up, Gordon had to steel himself. His legs felt wobbly, and he took a moment to decide to continue upwards to investigate what SPECTRE was up to.

At the top of the ladder, quietly humming to himself to ward off his unease, Gordon brushed away some of the cobwebs and dust on the window. At first he could see nothing, other than some pale shapes moving. He rubbed the window again, and through the smudges and the dust on the other side of the window he began to see more. He could see hay bales. He could see some large rusty farming tools, hanging menacingly on the walls. And he could see human shapes. The bald, gingery mess was certainly reminiscent of his father, but there was something wrong. That raw and constant laugh, like cigarettes and gravel, had stopped, and there was altogether too much pink in the hazy picture framed before his eyes.

Gordon rubbed the window once more, and he peered again. Then he saw something he did not understand.

--=◎=--

The grown-ups were sitting at a table on the thistly and mossy lawn, with a white tablecloth pinned down by many empty bottles. Present, besides Gordon's mother, were Gordon's grandmother, engaged in conversation with an old man with a white moustache, Coky's grandmother, looking as if she needed a nap, and a couple that Gordon took to be Harry's parents. His mother greeted him.

'Everything all right, darling?' she asked, and began automatically to make him a cheese sandwich.

Gordon muttered a 'yeah', but he squirmed when she tried to put her arm around him, aware of the gaze from the other adults.

'Can I have the Lotus Esprit?' he said, and slunk behind his mother's chair.

'All right, lovey. Here we are,' said his mother, dipping into her handbag and presenting Gordon with a white model car, the numberplate '007'. Gordon could feel, as he dipped below the tabletop, that he was being discussed with silent looks, and possibly with words being mouthed. He didn't care. He was acting shy because he did not want to be quizzed about why he was on his own. Not yet, anyway.

When Gordon had been there for a few minutes, his father and a dark-haired woman arrived at the table. He watched them carefully from underneath the table, examining his father for signs of injury or distress, but there appeared to be none. Gordon's father usually got a bit red in the face after lunch, and even more so when he went for a walk. The dark-haired woman sat breezily at the table. Gordon had never seen such hair: a mass of raven-black corkscrews that slunk gracefully about her neck and shoulders like seaweed in the tide. She gave a symposium on her views about the imminent demise of the Thatcher government in the upcoming election; a lecture on how the Soviets were going to invade West Germany; and news of her flirtation with Elton John at a social engagement the previous month, and the fact that she was, as a result, contemplating marriage to the long-haired pop star.

Gordon had not seen the children approaching. Harry and Coky were suddenly at the table. Coky had Gordon's yellow cagoule in her arms, and placed it on a chair.

'Who wants a 7-Up?' said Gordon's mother to the newcomers.

When the exotic fizzy drink had been distributed to all three children, Gordon's grandmother beckoned him over and whispered in his ear. He could feel the hairs on her upper lip and smell the sweet beige powder she put on her wrinkly face.

'Hello, piglet. Did the other children let you join in?'

Gordon looked at Coky across the table. She caught his eye and gave a tentative smile. He calculated that she could not have heard his grandmother's question and would not be able to hear the reply. Still, he hesitated to answer.

'I won't tell,' added Gordon's grandmother conspiratorially. 'I just want to know whether you got left out of the games again.'

He took a moment, looking reluctant, and calculating. Then he answered.

'It was both of them,' Gordon whispered to his grandmother. 'The boy tied me up and the girl kicked me.'

⊷●⊶

In the car, it wasn't long before Gordon's father began the lecture. Gordon was told that he shouldn't tell tales. He was also told that he shouldn't lie, which Gordon's father clearly suspected. And yet – and Gordon really couldn't understand this instruction because it struck him as such an inherent contradiction – he was also told to 'stick up for himself' and that he needed to 'toughen up a bit'. Gordon could never get the hang of the difference – and apparently there was one – between 'sticking up for yourself' and retaliation. Surely, if you wished to exact revenge, you had to use whatever means were available to you? Gordon decided silently to absorb the lecture, even though he did not regret his actions and had in fact achieved what he wanted to achieve extremely efficiently. Hadn't he?

He replayed what had occurred in his head.

Gordon's grandmother had immediately and utterly betrayed an explicit confidence by publicly accusing Harry and Coky of bullying. Appalled, Harry's parents had immediately weighed in with a series of questions for their son. Harry, nonplussed, had ably defended himself and Coky. But during Harry's defence of himself Coky had started to cry, making both her and Harry appear guilty. Gordon's father had then asked Gordon whether he was telling the truth. Gordon stuck to his lie, even embellishing a little by explaining where it still hurt. As a result of the pressure he was under, it was no great acting feat for him also to cry. All the adults then waded in with their opinions as to what had happened. When impasse had been reached, and both Harry and Gordon were red with indignation, Gordon's father had diffused the situation by saying it was getting late and that perhaps they should leave. While the adults were apologising to each other tensely, saying 'it was nothing', and 'please don't worry yourself', the children had stood glowering at each other. The dark-haired woman had prolonged the embarrassment by insisting on taking a group photograph.

Gordon now sat in the back seat of the Hillman Hunter, computing his victory while he watched the quickening rain. This hiatus was broken only when his mother silently smuggled him a boiled sweet. By the time the sweet was over, he decided that it was now time to clear up the other matter that had been niggling at him.

'Dad, why were you fighting that woman?'

Instantly, Gordon's mother looked not at Gordon, but at her husband. Gordon's father did not take his eyes off the road, and said nothing. Gordon was pleased to have gauged the mood correctly. They had clearly forgiven him for his misdemeanour enough to have a different conversation.

'How do you mean, Gordon?' asked his mother in a voice even higher than her usual one.

'I don't think the boy knows what –' began his father.

'Oh for goodness' sake, shut up, Geoffrey!' barked his mother with sudden and uncharacteristic viciousness. After a short silence, Gordon's mother encouraged Gordon to continue.

'Well,' said Gordon, sensing now that he was completely off the hook. 'You were in that barn with the red tractor, and she was fighting you. The woman with the dark hair. Had you had an argument?'

But there was no response from his father.

'Did you stick up for yourself?' asked Gordon.

That seemed to do the trick. His parents were silent again, and remained so for the rest of the journey.

With Death comes honesty.

The Satanic Verses, Salman Rushdie

Pink's, like many of the white-stuccoed buildings of St James's, is a private members' club. Some regard these clubs as not so much 'private' as 'secret', and certainly there are only two facts about Pink's which appear in the public domain. The first is that the club has recently inherited the bulk of the estate of the artist James Hoogstratten, R.A. This ran into millions, and the club's members have voted not to take the £30,000 each that they were due by the club's constitution. Instead, they ploughed the entire windfall into boosting the quality and size of Pink's wine cellar, and in acquiring van Gogh's *The Beech Tree*, which now hangs modestly at the bottom of the main staircase. The second fact that is known about Pink's is its strict dress code.

Wearing a suit and tie, in most lines of work these days, is a clear sign of a lack of seniority. But few men make the mistake of turning up at Pink's without the requisite garb. If they did they would be subjected to the special torture of being forced to wear something the club provided. This would be a jacket that bordered on fancy dress, and a tie of such luridness and unfashionability that it could only be worn by a fringe comedian, or a castaway looking to be seen from 35,000 feet.

There are many rules in Pink's. Many similar clubs have banned the use of mobile telephones, but Pink's also bans trousers without a crease, soft shoes, collarless shirts, children, personal computers, and the wearing of hats and swords beyond the cloakroom. Pink's considers itself rather *avant-garde* for having lifted – over ten years ago – its 240-year ban on women becoming members. But judging by the members present on the average hazy August afternoon, this happy news seems not yet to have been passed on to any actual women.

Peregrine MacGilp of MacGilp, one such member on one such afternoon, was perpetually irritated to have to smoke his cigarettes while standing in the street. But he used his time in the smoggy sunshine productively by simultaneously puffing and conducting an exchange of text messages with his niece. They had business to discuss.

'Lawyer phoned,' said the first incoming text. 'We only have a week. GC is realistically our last chance.'

Peregrine replied, thumbing the buttons on his phone with hesitancy, hindered by long-sightedness and lack of expertise. 'WILCO. REMINT ME WHAT WE NKOW OF GC?'

A minute later, his phone buzzed with another message. 'Rumour is he sold biz for big ££. Some sort of tech/media thing.'

Peregrine decided to tease his niece. 'GOLD-

LOOKING, IS HE? ALL YOUR FRIENDS ARE. TALL TOO, I SUPPORT.'

'Haven't seen him since we were kids,' replied the niece, ignoring the predictive text problems. 'Might be Scottish?'

Peregrine texted back. 'SOUND LIKE A MATTER OF THE UNIVERSE TYPE. BUSINESSMEN LIKE STRAIGHT TANKING. SHALL JUST BE MYSELF.'

It was just twenty seconds before the final communication.

'Strongly advise you not to.'

Smiling, but with a wrinkled brow, Peregrine tucked his phone away in a well-tailored pocket. He did not generally meet high-powered entrepreneurs, and was unaccustomed to business meetings in which he was not the one being sold to. He inhaled deeply on the remainder of his cigarette. But Peregrine would deal with this challenge as he did all others in life, by assuming that things would probably work out for the best. They always did. So he went back inside his club, there to order a pot of Russian Caravan, and put to the back of his mind the feeling that he would rather his niece were joining him for this meeting on which his fate, and the fate of many others, would be determined.

As Peregrine waited patiently for his tea, the man he was due to meet was standing just a hundred yards away on Piccadilly, sweating at his reflection in the broad window of an expensive shop.

Gordon Claypole was tubby, and only in the thorax. His short legs and arms, over which he had only limited control, were thin and weak. He was not 'a large man'. He was a fat man. This saddened him not just because of its genetic inevitability and the echo of his long-dead father, but because, having been a fat child, he had briefly been a normal-shaped young adult. At thirty-five, he was once again an egg with tentacles, and wished that he had never known what it was like to look anything other than odd. There was always something in his reflection to admonish, and inflict the persistent pain that, he supposed, dogs all people who are physically inadequate. He stared more closely at his reflection. Sometimes it was the beetroot bags under his eyes that struck him as ugly, sometimes the reddening bulb of a nose, or the collection of grey-green chins that hung from his jaw like stuffed shopping bags. Today, though, it was his oyster eyes and their network of scarlet veins that disgusted him. He also found time to loathe the dyed black hair that was losing the battle for influence over his huge potato of a head. And in these clothes – black suit, white shirt, black tie – he thought the entire ensemble gave him the appearance of a ghoulish and hard-living undertaker.

'Fuck it,' he burbled idly to his reflection as he stumbled on from the shop front and felt an ache in his chest.

Claypole was familiar with the other kind of private members' club. The sort that spring up like dandelions, and very often disappear again as quickly, from the streets of Soho. A short stroll from St James's, but a world away, the most octane-fuelled of the capital's media workers and their hangers-on collide in these other haunts on weeknights, bitching, bragging, gossiping and flirting, getting quickly drunk and lording it shrilly over the waiting staff. The older ones are tired and lonely, with the resources to destroy careers, egos or emotions as they choose. The younger ones fight among themselves for position, or fame, or money, and possess the joint characteristics of overconfidence and desperation, a combination only otherwise found in lesser-league football. Only the lucky few, for all the talk, find a decent price for their souls.

So, like Lewis Carroll's Alice trying to adjust to a new world, Claypole rubbed his eyes as he stepped through the small eighteenth-century door to Pink's. The size of the entrance belied the club's vast interior. It was stunning, too, in a faded sort of way. Like an ancient screen actress, it had former glory as an all-pervading memory, and it could not but impress even if it gave the impression that it no longer cared to do so. Shifting silently about, the members were, like the cool dark interior, old and rich. These men, in their fine suits, had never doubted their position and never wanted for anything. If these souls were for sale at all, they would be very expensive.

Claret-coloured and puffing from the walk, Claypole announced his presence to the moustachioed and liveried man at the front desk. Clearly ex-military, the man gave Claypole the same look of disdain bordering on disgust he gave all non-members. This was the look that allowed the club to charge its members a thousand pounds a year in membership fees. They didn't want ever to receive that look again. They wanted the other look the ex-military man gave, to members only: a slight but intensely respectful nod.

Moving slowly behind the ex-military gent into the main library, Claypole stiffened. He was trying to give himself the same air of unfettered, world-owning confidence he could feel coming from the members as they flicked through the pages of the *Daily Telegraph*, or coughed discreetly into a Scotch and soda. But he did not feel at home. A thousand pounds was what it cost you to belong, although it was a fee you got to pay only if you already belonged.

Using the arm of the old leather sofa for leverage, Peregrine MacGilp rose to an imposing six foot two. His silver hair, just a little long and fuzzy at the back but with a thick and immaculate quiff at the front, topped a remarkably unlined and square-set face. He looked like a Serbian war criminal in a burgundy corduroy suit and navy-blue sweater, but with boyishly excited eyes. Peregrine was the sort of old man – seventy, maybe, but with the gait of a fifty-year-old – that could grace a luxury yacht brochure until he was ninety. Claypole would become the other kind of old man – a structureless, cushiony wheezer with a baked-bean head. Claypole, should he still be alive at seventy, might look at home in the ticket booth of a funfair.

'My dear fellow,' said Peregrine in an immense baritone, stretching out a muscular arm and bristling with welcome.

'Hi,' said Claypole, and shook the old man's hand, but held his gaze for only the briefest of moments.

'Gordon, isn't it?' asked Peregrine.

'Just Claypole,' muttered Claypole, and gave him a challenging look. Peregrine smiled.

'Gosh. You mean you don't use your first name?'

'People just call me Claypole.'

'Oh... how marvellous!' Peregrine clapped his hands with delight. 'Like that left-wing chap with the dark glasses. What's his name? Bonzo.'

'Bono. Yeah,' said Claypole, narrowing his eyes.

'That's the fellow,' said Peregrine gaily, clicking his fingers. 'Or Plato, I suppose. He's only got one name, hasn't he? Or Liberace.' He smiled at Claypole with icy grey eyes, and added with unselfconscious non sequitur, 'What fun.'

'Brr.' Claypole cleared his throat, as he did habitually in company, like a man who has swallowed a sizeable fly but doesn't want anyone to know about it.

'Do have a pew,' said Peregrine, looking pleased and preparing to sit down. 'Do you fancy some tea?'

They both looked at a prissy brilliantined midget in a white mess jacket, who had appeared at Claypole's elbow.

'No, thanks,' said Claypole.

'Really? Or some sandwiches? Or something else? They have pretty much anything here... It was at that table over there that my grandfather once ate a record number of oysters, but, ah... A snorter, perhaps? Bit early to start opening the pipes, but be my guest if you...'

Claypole watched a nearby codger in a light-blue blazer being served something lurid involving prawns, avocado and aspic.

'Nah. Brr. Let's get on with it,' said Claypole, and barrelled himself into a red leather sofa opposite Peregrine. His intention – to make a proprietory gesture – was undermined somewhat by the fact that he bounced perilously on the unexpectedly well-sprung seat. Peregrine sat slowly, still smiling magnificently. They exchanged small talk as Claypole rehearsed to himself the chain of events that had led him to this place at this time.

Claypole had thirty-four Facebook friends. So when Peregrine's niece, Coky Viveksananda, who had 196 Facebook friends, requested to become number 35 some months previously, he was in no position to turn her down. She assured him in her message that their parents had known each other many years ago, and that they had met as children. He accepted her request and replied that indeed he remembered her, which he did not, and then examined her Facebook profile. There was a picture of a petite girl in shades, possibly of southern Asian origin, sitting on a lawn somewhere and smiling shyly. Her friends had names like Max von Strum and Felicia Hungerford and appeared to Claypole to be either smug or vacuous. But she listed her hobbies as 'necromancy and darts', and her job as 'Brigadier-General of Starfleet Command', and gave no other personal details, showing an amused disdain for the social networking medium that Claypole admired but could not bring himself to exhibit. No other communication had occurred between them until three days previously. Coky wondered – in a pleasantly un-pushy message – if he would be interested in meeting her uncle in regard to a business opportunity. So here he was, sitting opposite the laird of a desolate estate on the west coast of Scotland consisting of a bleak and bulky Gothic revival house, a few chilly cottages and a considerable chunk of... apparently nothing very much, according to its squire.

'Bugger all. It's useless,' said Peregrine, with simple sincerity. 'The Loch Garvach estate is some of the worst land in Europe. Three thousand acres of good-for-nothing floating bog.'

Claypole was surprised. He thought everywhere was used for something.

'Oh yes, indeed,' added Peregrine, driving home the point. 'You can't even walk on most of it.'

'Brr.' This was Claypole giving his usual cough, but this time it was nearly a laugh. Peregrine himself laughed unashamedly. It was loud, deep and used his full throat, even a bit of tongue.

'So what have you been up to, then? What keeps Gordon – sorry, *Claypole* – out of the alehouses?'

Claypole seemed to study his hands for a moment before speaking.

'I've been in the pre-school entertainment biz. Brr. Multimedia...' Claypole drummed the fingers of one hand on the other. 'I realised that phone Apps was the way to go. It's happened in everything. And I had this bunch of content – movies and text – which I converted to a kick-ass App. Content's about communities and fans these days, not...'

Peregrine was looking at him with bewilderment. 'By "movies", do you mean films?'

'Er... yeah.'

'American films?'

'No, just films. Cartoons,' said Claypole, blushing. 'Cathy the Cow, then Colin the Calf.'

Peregrine squinted. 'And by "text", you mean books?'

'Yeah.'

'For children?'

'Pre-school. Yeah.'

'Babies, in fact?'

'Er... yeah.'

'Right-oh...' Peregrine's incomprehension was not reduced. 'I have a mobile telephone, of course. But – and call me a Luddite if you must – I want it to... well, be a phone. Not another blasted computer!' Peregrine chuckled.

Claypole beheld the older man, eyeing him intensely. Here was the grinning MacGilp of MacGilp (for what possible reason could a man need the same name twice?), completely contented, and utterly comfortable.

Clearly he had been given the best that being British can offer. White, male and probably Protestant, yes. But also extremely privileged, classically educated, landed and moneyed, with the teeth of an Arab stallion. He seemed to be oblivious to modernity and more or less indifferent to the opinion of others. You couldn't learn to be like that, thought Claypole. You had to be born in the right place at the right time, and to the right people.

'Anyway,' Claypole concluded. 'Brr. I sold the company a month ago.'

'So you're free?' asked Peregrine.

Claypole sat back in his chair, and did his best Cheshire Cat.

'Well done,' said Peregrine, in a matter-of-fact way. 'I had a job in the City once, but I didn't understand it. Ballsed it up. If I hadn't inherited a fair chunk of lolly, God knows where I'd be.'

'Thanks,' muttered Claypole, chewing his jaw.

'Shall I talk a little about my proposition?' asked Peregrine freshly.

'Sure,' said Claypole. 'It's... er, making electricity from wind, right?' He watched the midget in the mess jacket glide past and regretted that he had not ordered a plate of cakes, or a pie. Peregrine leaned forward and explained the history of wind farming at Loch Garvach.

Two years previously, a company called Aeolectricity had paid Peregrine a small amount of money in the expectation that when the wind farm received approval from the planning authorities and was subsequently built and generating electricity, they would pay him a handsome annual rent. The gamble for Aeolectricity was that if planning permission were not granted, they would lose their investment. On the other hand, if successful, it would make them many millions over the twenty-five-year life of the wind farm. But Aeolectricity had gone bust even though almost all the work had been done, and the whole project now belonged to Peregrine. This had all happened in the last couple of months, and the planning committee of the local council was now due to make its decision on whether the wind farm could go ahead or not.

'It's madness,' began Peregrine in conclusion. 'Why they leave it to the little people to make these decisions, I really don't know. This and that sub-committee of Mr and Mrs McIdiot. They haven't got a clue about how to plan a power station. Why would they? They're not experts in anything very much, and they're certainly not experts in this.'

Peregrine finished his monologue and his grey eyes flashed at Claypole. 'Still. Pretty golden, eh?'

'Right, yeah,' said Claypole, looking across at the man in the light-blue blazer, who appeared to be falling asleep in front of his avocado mess. 'So you need money?'

'We need, more than anything else, a backer.' Peregrine smiled. 'A serious person. An *homme d'affaires*, if you like. Unpaid for the moment, but heavily rewarded if we're successful.'

This evasion, Claypole knew instantly, spelled danger. Everyone needed money.

'How much do you need?' asked Claypole, in as bald a manner as he could manage.

'As I say, it's not so much the money...'

'Yeah,' said Claypole, closing his eyes with irritation in the manner he had seen done by business hotshots on television when faced with yet another common-or-garden mendacious incompetent. 'How much do you need?'

'I really don't want your money, old chap,' said Peregrine, not letting up with his smile. 'I just need you to stand up in front of the powers that be and give them a bit of the old razzle-dazzle.'

'Brr,' said Claypole. 'You really think the plan stacks up? Profit-wise?'

'Oh yes. It's a gold mine. Thanks to the government.'

'There are government grants?'

'Not quite. It's cleverer than a straight hand-out.' Peregrine leaned forward conspiratorially. 'Because of these global warming do-dahs – you know, Britain has to reduce our carbon whatsits by such-and-such – anyone who has a wind farm can charge more for their electricity than someone with a coal-fired power station, or gas or whatever. A lot more. And there's a lot of other financial how's-your-fathers that make it even more attractive.'

Claypole scratched his nose.

'Speaking personally,' Peregrine continued, 'I'm not absolutely convinced that there is such a thing as global warming... Doesn't matter what I think, of course. Everyone else seems to think it's important, and so do the powers that be. It's the law.' Peregrine looked around him for spies. 'Don't tell my niece that I don't really believe in global warming, will you? She's a fervent believer.'

'Brr,' said Claypole, attempting inscrutability. 'But Loch Garvach is windy, yeah?'

'Oh yes. *Frightfully* windy,' said Peregrine.

'Blow your hat off?' suggested Claypole.

'Blow your face off,' corrected Peregrine. 'Honestly, it would carry you off to Ireland.' Then Peregrine was suddenly grave. 'If the wind were an easterly... which it rarely is.'

'Right,' said Claypole, also suddenly serious.

They fell silent for a moment. The old man in the light-blue blazer was slipping further towards his plate of avocado and prawn, and Claypole wondered whether he should alert someone.

'Do you go back to Scotland much?' asked Peregrine.

'Nah. Haven't been there for years. Used to go on holiday there till Granny died. I stay put in London mostly. Spain for holidays.'

Peregrine sniffed the air. 'Ah yes. *Italia para nacer, Francia para vivir, España para morir.* And of course you can't beat the dear old Prado.'

The two men stared into the middle distance, remembering their respective Spanish holidays. Of the two of them, only Claypole could see how different those memories would be. Peregrine, a floozy named Minty or Bella in tow, probably drank delicious rosé with cravat-wearing Spanish nobility in the olive groves of delightfully dilapidated castles. To date, Claypole's solo holidays had consisted of sleeping in the burning sun on plastic deckchairs next to tattooed plumbers from Brentwood with brattish children, and then trying to find somewhere in the evening that actually served Spanish food while he thumbed through a paperback.

Peregrine continued.

'The reason I ask is that you might have to... how shall I put it...? emphasise... no, *encourage*, the Scottish part of you, should you decide to go into this business.'

'Why is that?' Claypole leaned back.

'The Scots – the real Scots, not people like me who were educated in England – are terrible whingers.'

Claypole's brow twitched.

'Well, it's true. The silly buggers think they're a persecuted minority.' Peregrine wasn't smiling. 'It's incredibly childish. But I suppose being Scottish is pretty ghastly, so the only thing they've got is being more Scottish than someone else...'

The ghost of a smile crept into Claypole's expression.

'I'm serious! These people hate outsiders, especially the English, coming in and doing something clever which they should have done themselves if they didn't have their heads up their bottoms. Hence all this independence kerfuffle. Load of old tommy-rot.'

The two men nodded gravely – Peregrine to emphasise his point; Claypole trying to keep a straight face.

'It's politics, really,' Peregrine added, 'this last bit of the process. We've got all the paperwork, and nothing very much should stand in its way. We just need to gee everyone up a bit and get the all-clear from the busybodies on the council. I'm not awfully good at schmoozing – tend to get people's backs up.'

Silence again. Claypole struggled to think of what else he could ask.

'Is it an island? Garvach, I mean.'

'No,' said Peregrine. 'But it may as well be. You can only get to it by one road, and that goes over a tiny bridge over an isthmus that links it to the mainland. The isthmus is covered every few high tides, but mostly it just sits there being muddy and technically links us to the mainland. There's an old tale about the place, actually.'

Claypole stifled a yawn. Peregrine carried on.

'Saint Mungo, who wanted to marry the Chief of Garvach's daughter, went to the old Chief and asked for his permission. The Chief said Mungo could marry the daughter if he could get a boat to circle the Chief's lands in one day. The Chief knew it wasn't possible, but Mungo accepted the challenge. Mungo set sail, and got around the peninsula of Garvach in twenty hours. He then dragged his boat across the muddy isthmus and met the Chief at the other side. The Chief said he would still not agree to the marriage of his daughter.'

Peregrine sat back. Claypole was still waiting for him to finish the story, but Peregrine just smiled.

'Is that it?' said Claypole in disgust.

'Yes,' said Peregrine. 'You don't like it?'

'Well, it doesn't have an ending. You know, I mean… did Saint Mungo just go home and have a cup of tea?'

'Oh. Dunno. Probably killed everyone and took the land, I should think. That's the sort of thing those chaps did.'

Claypole wrinkled his forehead. Celtic stories always seemed to be rather peculiar, obeying none of the usual rules that stories tend to. He had studied the genre while at university. (Or rather, he had read half a book about it in the pub.) There certainly was little justice, and rarely a moral. Stuff just happened to the hero, and then he died. This heavy hand of Fate was, although in Claypole's view perfectly realistic, somewhat depressing. Claypole was not a sentimental man, but he liked a happy ending.

'What did Mungo get sanctified for?' asked Claypole. 'Services to disappointing narrative?'

Peregrine smiled neutrally. As he did so, Claypole could see light-blue-blazer man finally fall forwards into his prawn-and-avocado mousse and instantly wake with a start, his face a shambles of green and pink.

'Well,' said Claypole, stretching extravagantly and making the leather on the ancient sofa squeak. 'I don't think this is something for me.'

Peregrine nodded slowly. 'May I ask why?' he said coolly.

The light-blue blazer had wiped his face with a crisp linen napkin, and was gleefully eating what he had so nearly breathed in. Claypole took a moment, dropping his shoulders. He would have loved to reply honestly. 'Here are the reasons why I will not invest in your wind farm,' he would like to have said. 'One, there are no experts involved. Any business has to have experts. Two, if there were anything of any value there, the previous company – if they were professionals – would have sold it before they went bust. And, if they weren't professionals, the work they have done so far probably isn't worth anything. Three, it's not based on sound principles. Basing any business on the whims of politicians is too risky. Those bastards change their minds every three minutes. Wind energy might be in vogue today, but who's to say it won't be nuclear tomorrow, or wave power, or something else? Four, *you* don't believe in it. If *you* think that global warming is nonsense – which is the whole reason for the business to exist – why should anyone else? Five – and this is the most important – it doesn't have the feel of a business that should work. That's because for you it's not a business – it's a scam.'

But Claypole said none of this. Instead, he shrugged, and tried to look gently grave, as if telling a nine-year-old that their hamster has died in the night.

'Just don't fancy it,' he said. 'Best of luck with it, though. Brr.'

-->==◎==<--

Claypole's flat was in a mansion block in an area sand-wiched between a trendy and a stuffy part of west London. He had bought at the very top of the market, and the service charge was high, but Claypole had always considered it worth it, if only because he was greeted by a porter when he got home. Claypole wasn't entirely sure how to pronounce Wolé's name, having only ever seen it written down, and he calculated that it would be ruder to get it wrong than not to say it at all. Wolé was too shy to use anyone's name. So Claypole and Wolé nodded silently to each other this evening, as they did every evening, and performed knowing and manly winks.

The front door to his flat stuck against the letters and junk mail, and Claypole had to push his bulk against the door to force it open. He shuffled the assorted items into a deck, picked them up and puffed sweatily to the sitting room. Claypole had not decorated the place since buying it two years before, and had not even rearranged the furniture, also purchased from the previous occupant. She had been a woman of rather singular tastes. The purple and orange silks, the sheer curtains and lightshades, the ubiquitous African and Middle Eastern 'style' dark wood, and the overstuffed sofas with a thousand luxurious cushions gave it the air of a well-appointed Tangiers brothel. Claypole could not have cared less. No one ever came here, he had spent little waking time in it, and he neither cleaned nor tidied the place. Half his possessions were still in wilting cardboard boxes in the two unused spare bedrooms.

He hovered over the dusty dining table, leafing

through this day's paper doorstop. A freebie computer gaming magazine and *Didge*, a glossy rag for the technologically advanced media professional, were the periodicals. There was a bank statement, which he did not open, and a few bills of no apparent interest.

'Brr,' said Claypole, sweeping everything into the bin, save for one businesslike white envelope.

He examined his mobile phone idly for ten seconds or so and then put it back in his pocket. It was a conditioned reflex. He didn't really want to find out who wanted his attention. He just looked at it automatically, like someone who is not hungry looking in a fridge. Getting up with purpose, he took an unopened bottle of single malt whisky from his briefcase, saw that it was older than he was and sneered with pleasure. He also took a crystal tumbler from a shelf and a tray of ice from the freezer. He lined all these items up. He poured three-quarters of a tumbler of whisky into the glass and added six cubes of ice. Before putting his lips to the brimming glass, he squinted at the bottle and then at the remaining ice cubes. He calculated that he should put no more than four ice cubes in each glass, or he would run out of ice before he had finished the bottle. Satisfied, he sat back in his chair and drank deeply.

'Nyah!' he pronounced with exquisite pain, and bared his teeth.

Taking out his phone again, it took him four scrolls and two clicks to order his usual: one family-sized Krakatoa Special pizza with three kinds of sausage, extra chilli oil, extra chillies and extra cheese; two large tubs of Fatty Arbuckle's Famous Choctasmic ice cream; and four cans of different ballistically caffeinated and highly sugary drinks.

He leaned back in the chair with satisfaction, and looked sideways at the one remaining item of post. The white envelope. He took another massive draught of Scotch and crunched the ice. Then he poured himself another and drank it down. In the two minutes between drinking half a pint of whisky quickly and being drunk, his stomach burned unpleasantly and a high-pitched whine sounded in his ear. Claypole waited unblinkingly for these symptoms to be replaced with a warm body-wide buzz.

He picked up the letter, held it for a few seconds to his face as if about to sniff it and then opened it with undextrous violence. There were two pieces of paper. The larger one, with an embossed letterhead, he scanned and discarded. The smaller piece of paper was a cheque. Claypole regarded it without changing his expression. He put it on the table, facing him. Sipping Scotch all the while, he stared at it with unfocused grimness. He put his feet up on the table and picked the cheque up again. He put it down. He read it once more.

'Pay... Gordon Claypole... Sixty-six thousand one hundred and eighty pounds only.'

Claypole took another belt of Scotch, sat upright and refilled the glass again, adding four more cubes of ice. He looked once more at the cheque.

Slowly, Claypole started to cry. For a while, no part of him moved. Tears formed and ran down his cheeks, but there were no other symptoms. Then his shoulders started to shift rhythmically and the sobbing began, remaining constant – neither growing in volume nor intensity. But it did continue, whisky the only punctua-tion, for the next half-hour.

When the doorbell went, Claypole dried his eyes and

stumbled to the door in the full expectation that this would be the carbohydrate and fat delivery into which he could dive headlong with heavy-hearted abandon.

-2-

KING: Did we? Did we, uh...
LADY PEMBROKE: Your Majesty?
KING: Um, did we... Did-did, uh, did we forget ourselves utterly? Because, if we did, I should so like to remember, *what, what?*

The Madness of George III, Alan Bennett

Claypole lay absolutely still in an effort to give the Universe the impression that he was still asleep. No part of his body showed movement. They were all in on the ruse. His stomach was on fire but quiet, his lips parched but unmoving, and his bowels a tremulous but ostensibly dormant volcano. The pain and the nausea were as violent and as greasy as the North Sea, his heart was racing, and his teeth sang, but still he refused to acknowledge being awake. His brain, too, was trying neither to dream nor to think. Despite a sloppy tide of panic and shame rising, it was trying its hardest simply not to be. But remorselessly the questions came at him like the Viet Cong. How long had he been like this? A minute? A week? Where was he? If he did try to move, would he die, or vomit? (There could be no other outcome.) Could enough time pass lying like this for the horror to recede, or would he feel this bad for ever? Why did his hair ache? There were no answers.

Finally it was his eyes that betrayed him. The twin Judases opened falteringly, like cold neon lights flickering on. He now had no choice but to acknowledge that he was becoming awake. Immediately, other turncoats revealed themselves. His mouth twitched, and his dry tongue flicked over his lips, tasting flakes of noxious spittle. His stomach began to lurch and bubble, and his brain to rush. Violent and pestilential images rolled through his mind, and an anonymous paranoia pricked him mercilessly. As the actuality of the room came upon him, he tried to establish where he was. The curtains, not in focus but recognisable as the ones in his own bedroom in his own flat, formed a briefly reassuring backdrop. But in the foreground there was a sinister, dissonant presence that caused him instant angst. Something was in his bed that shouldn't be. He tried to bring the object into focus, but his pupils would not contract sufficiently. His nostrils twitched as they felt a distinct tang. The smell was acrid and intrusive. His eyes flickered and crossed uncomfortably. He closed them firmly, squeezing until it hurt, and then opened them again. There!

It was a bottle of whisky. Not the ancient and delicious single malt, though. This was one of those 'whiskies' which shared only flammability as a characteristic in common with the quality of Scotch Claypole usually drank. This sort of whisky tended to be popular in hot countries, labelled with lurid tartan and symbolised by birds of prey very far removed from anything that might actually be found in Scotland. Its top was missing, and when Claypole spasmed the bottle slopped a little more of its contents onto the sheet in the direction of his face. Claypole instinctively recoiled. Then he jumped. His left foot had touched warm human flesh.

So rare was it for him to have anyone else in his bed that Claypole instantly screamed, at first spluttering, and then hard and high. A moment after Claypole began his scream, scrambling his wispy legs and arms to panic stations and bolting upright, the other warm body in the bed squirmed and also sat up. Witnessing Claypole screaming, in all his crumpled and sweaty horror, his lank hair frighteningly distributed, the person sharing the bed with him – a woman, in fact – also screamed. Her scream was unlike his. There was less terror to it, and it contained more of a note of concern. This despite the fact that Claypole, with his arms waving about his pale-grey torso, appeared like nothing so much as an upturned woodlouse. For a couple of seconds Claypole and the woman sat shouting at each other, marooned on the bed. His surprise at being in bed with a woman was then overtaken by his surprise at being in bed with a woman he recognised as Coky Viveksananda, the niece of Peregrine MacGilp of MacGilp, and his thirty-fifth Facebook friend.

Her hair was thick and untidy, possibly self-cut. Her skin was a lighter shade of brown than it had appeared in the photograph on Facebook, and she was not as thin as that image had suggested. Her nose was long and asymmetrical with a curious knobble on the end of it. Her front teeth were white, but the rest yellow and the canines more than a little fanglike. Her upper lip had vestiges of dark hair at the corners, and her lips were thinnish and slightly cracked. Were it not for one aspect of her, she might have been described as conventionally unattractive. Her eyes, though, were extraordinary. A little tired-looking and quite deep-set, but of a violent blue – like a Mediterranean summer sky. Claypole had no time to decide that she was in fact unconventionally attractive, or to attempt to remember why or how she had got there, because he saw, with an extra fizz of panic, that she was wearing one of *his* t-shirts.

Except during his occasional and testy brushes with pornography, and when watching Wimbledon, Claypole had no time for thinking about sex. He was, after all, a fat, balding man, and very busy, so sex had no time for him. Women could not be expected to be interested in him, and if he had ever raised an enquiring eyebrow at one, disappointment (not to say rejection in the strongest possible terms) had been the inevitable result. Now though, as he found himself looking at Coky's breasts, bra-less but clothed by his own t-shirt, logic told him that these breasts must at some point have been naked in his flat. Sweat began to form on Claypole's upper lip and at his temples, and he suddenly felt as if he had too many arms.

'Guh. Brr,' said Claypole, and saw the expression of concern on Coky's face change to one of suppressed amusement as he coughed violently into a corner of the bedsheet.

'Hi,' said Coky Viveksananda. When he had finished coughing she added, 'Better now?'

Claypole shuddered as he realised that if he could not remember *whether* they had slept with each other, he could not have performed well if they had. Furthermore, he would no doubt have blown any chance of repeating the act. Equally, if they had not slept with each other, surely he would never again get the chance to do so. She would, unless she had some sort of mental problem, or was more desperate and weak than she appeared, avoid him from now until the End of Time. He had no choice but to find out from Coky herself what had happened the previous night. But he knew this much about women: he would have to make conversation first, lull her, and then discover the truth by stealth, employing the nearest approximation to charm that he could manage. Gently does it, he thought.

'Lovely,' said Claypole suddenly, his eyes frozen on Coky's breasts.

Had Claypole not immediately averted his eyes, he would have seen that she was, although surprised, smirking. But he buried his face in his clammy hands and muttered 'sorry' (meant for Coky's ears), and added 'what the fuck?' (in self-admonishment).

'I'll just go and...' said Coky, and stepped somewhat heavily from the bed, collecting a pile of clothes from the floor and moving towards the bathroom.

Claypole uncovered his face, hoping desperately that she had gone into the bathroom so that she did not have to see his shame; and, equally desperately, also hoping that she was in sight so that he could get a repeat view of her mostly naked legs. Was she tall or short? He could remember nothing.

She had disappeared, and Claypole sighed.

Then her head poked around the bathroom door. She was short.

'You really didn't remember that I stayed over?' she asked.

Claypole's jowls shook as he nodded vigorously, and his head pounded afresh. He looked away, and added, gasping from under a fresh wave of nausea, 'Course I did. I was just...' Then he shrugged weakly.

'Oh, well,' said Coky jauntily, 'Can't say I'm surprised. You were pretty wasted.' And her head ducked back inside the bathroom.

Claypole rolled out of bed and angrily threw a lot of clothes around in the vicinity of his porky body until he could be said, by all but the most rigorous standards, to be dressed.

He was gulping at a much-needed glass of water in his sparse kitchen when Coky appeared again, fully dressed and apparently without embarrassment. She spoke with a west-coast Scottish accent, tempered with a little of the plain-vanilla Londonish whine to which Claypole's ear was so used, and suggested that they go and get some breakfast elsewhere. He found himself agreeing heartily despite the fact that his body was pleading with him to be placed on the sofa and lobotomised in front of an entire Saturday's television.

Claypole refused to speak during the expedition out of his flat and onto the thrumming main street except to explain to Coky that he needed all his energy to remain upright and moving. Any resources used for talking might upset his precarious equilibrium. They seated themselves outside at one of those cafés that look forward to being a restaurant when they grow up, he in the shade, she in the sunshine. Having ordered a bucket of coffee and a meal containing the meat of many animals, both domestic and wild, he surprised himself by being the first to speak.

'What did we... brr... talk about... last night?' Claypole asked.

'This and that. I suppose I must have bored you...' She scowled at the table as she rolled a cigarette.

'Eh?'

'Well, I went on about climate change. I usually do. I'm told it gets in the way of good conversation.'

'Oh.' Claypole was finding it almost impossible to make sense of her words. But he decided, like an exhausted trout must do, to simply let the river take him where it may. Coky continued.

'I have this thing, you see.' Her speech was deliberate and thoughtful. 'It's like a mental groove. I can't help thinking... about the cost to the environment of whatever it is I'm looking at... or thinking of...' She frowned.

Claypole gaped.

'It's something of an affliction,' she said and sipped again. 'Not like Tourette's or motor neurone disease, but it gets in the way of life. You know?'

Coky explained that she could not catch a bus, look at a view, eat a meal or dream, without thinking of pollution or the carbon cycle. She had done her best to avoid it, she said. She had tried to be stupid. She had tried not to care so much, but was always dogged by insistent voices asking her constantly to weigh one action against another in terms of its impact on the environment. She explained that she was no eco-warrior and certainly did not always make the Earth-friendly choice, but that just made the voices shout louder. It was, she suggested, a curse as debilitating as Midas's touch.

The coffee arrived. Coky added nothing to her strong black. Claypole felt sick just looking at his mocha choccolatto, but added his habitual three sugars nonetheless.

'Sometimes I feel like an eco-accountant,' Coky continued. 'Just weighing up debit and credit... And when I was farting about in my rubbish job, I just thought: well, I'm not doing anything for the credit side, am I? Not exactly causing harm, but not exactly helping either... That's why I got involved with Peregrine's wind farm. Not that he gives a... I just thought I should take it upon myself to –'

Coky had stopped in mid-sentence, and Claypole looked up, realising that he had his head in his hands and was moaning gently.

'Sorry,' he offered weakly. 'Not you.'

'You must feel like cack.' She licked her cigarette closed expertly but did not light it. 'You kept the bottle of whisky I brought with me pretty close to you.'

Claypole tried to transmit shame, but just looked blank.

'I barely got a taste of it,' said Coky, but without resentment. 'Actually, you were quite... funny... when you did speak – which wasn't much.'

'Oh,' said Claypole.

'Yes. You kept going on about a "misfortune", but I couldn't work out what you were talking about.'

'Oh God,' said Claypole.

'I tried to cheer you up, and said it sounded like you needed a bit of time out. That...' Coky's eyes crinkled in amused recollection. 'That was when it got properly funny.'

'Oh God.'

'You just kept repeating "time out", "time out", "time..."' Coky paused dramatically, in imitation, '"... out". Like that. Then you *really* didn't speak much after that.'

'Oh God.'

Breakfast arrived and Claypole drilled into his meal like a starved hummingbird while Coky extolled the benefits of wind power between mouthfuls of Eggs Florentine.

'I mean it's clean, it's renewable. And the wind is free, so… what's not to like? And some people say they actively like the look of them. Beauty is in the eye of the beholder, and all that. And anyway, we really don't have much choice if we're going to reduce carbon emissions, right?'

Coky's cranberry juice silently shrank as she sucked at it through a straw. Claypole looked up from his plate briefly, his fat face full of protein. He wanted to show he was listening, even if he wasn't. She took off her shades.

'Mm-hm,' he said.

It struck Claypole now that Coky was unlike any of the girls he normally came across, who were for the most part arch, resentful, sly or picky. London girls. Indeed, it was not just that she seemed that most infrequent of combinations, confident *and* pleasant. There was something rare about Coky, and it wasn't just that she was breezily non-judgmental. Like her strange clothing with its scatty collection of strings, wisps and loose ends, she appeared guileless and unmodern. Despite being somewhat buffeted by concern, she seemed… free.

Claypole had finished his meal but felt no better. The meat and coffee were lapping at his tonsils and he had begun coldly to sweat.

'So when you came round last night, I was…?'

Coky lit her cigarette and told Claypole that when he had opened the door to his flat, he had initially been disappointed that she was not an enormous box of pizza. She was now gracious about this, and claimed to be amused rather than frightened by his drunkenness and his inept bumbling about the flat, 'tidying' for her presence. When the pizza did arrive, she had watched Claypole and made herself at home while he accelerated through the spicy, meaty feast. Then, with all the food thoroughly assassinated, they had sat about on Claypole's gaudy, dusty sofas. Coky had spoken of her uncle and his wind farm, and of having worked in public relations, or interior design, or something, here in London before returning recently to her uncle's Highland home for a 'career re-think'. But she revealed nothing about why she had come to see him, or indeed how and why she had joined him in his bed.

'Coky,' he said, his tone wavering just a little and the 'k' of Coky getting slightly hampered with spittle, 'what... er, happened then?'

She squinted at him, scrutinising. 'Gordon,' she began.

'It's just Claypole,' he said.

'Hm,' she said. 'What's the last thing you remember about last night?'

Claypole winced.

'I dunno,' he said helplessly, 'we were... talking... on sofas...?'

'You don't remember our last conversation, do you?' Coky nibbled her thumb while Claypole wondered what on earth he might have said to her. He put his hands up in extravagant protest.

'No. No, no. Yes, yes, yes. Yes.'

'Mm,' she said. 'You said you'd like to do a bit of... saving the planet.'

'Saving the planet?' Claypole was incredulous. He took out his recycling, bought organic food when it was available and didn't fill the kettle for one cup of tea, but he was preparing for imminent climate change by doing precisely what the majority of people were were doing: getting on with his life.

'Yeah. Wind farming is a Good Thing, right? Capital "G", capital "T"? You said you'd been wasting your time doing kid's TV, and... this wind farm is something that you and me can actually do to make a difference. To the big picture.'

Claypole closed his eyes and breathed heavily. Understanding whether he had slept with this woman seemed as far away as ever, and manipulating the conversation was becoming harder as his nausea developed.

'Right, yeah,' he said, and pinched the bridge of his nose.

'Of course if you were just being polite...' Coky looked at her fork with interest.

'No, but –'

'Oh. Good,' she said. He couldn't tell whether she was truly satisfied with his answer because she had put on her shades again.

'Good,' he echoed. It was time to grasp the nettle. 'But, brr... did we...?' He began. 'I mean, sorry about being so drunk and everything, but...' But that was all that he could manage. He was suddenly feeling very tired.

'Doesn't matter,' said Coky, relighting her cigarette. 'I did what I set out to do.' She smiled and blew smoke.

Claypole heard her words and immediately froze in panic.

No one had ever seduced him before, and he didn't like the idea. He went back over the facts as he now assumed them. Coky had come to his flat, drunk him under the table, talked him (or dragged him?) into bed, had her wicked way with him, and he didn't remember anything about it. Had she come to his flat with the sole purpose of sexual assault? This seemed so unlikely. A broad range of women – clever, beautiful, ugly, daft – had let him know that he was physically repulsive. Then, with a further grind of horror, he suddenly wondered if she had raped him in order to get at his money. Perhaps she had even used drugs to do so! That would certainly explain the memory loss.

'I mean,' Coky continued, 'you didn't exactly say yes, but you didn't exactly say no either.' And she smiled. 'At least we agreed that we should not talk about money. Not yet anyway!'

With this, Claypole's panic doubled and he wiped sweat from his forehead. He had heard of rich men being preyed upon by unscrupulous women. Trapped either by pregnancy or false emotion, these hapless chaps were forced into sham marriages, then blackmailed for their millions in divorce settlements. Was this what it was like being wealthy? He cursed himself. How could he have been so naïve? If he escaped this predicament, he would forever be on his guard against harpies and sirens. But might it already be too late?

'I told you I was boring about it. As you can tell, I'm on a bit of a mission.' She looked down at the smears of egg yolk on her plate. 'Peregrine's useless, and we really need a person who knows what they're doing. Someone to... provide a bit of leadership. And the crucial meeting is next week, so it won't take much of your time. Won't you please think about it?'

Claypole fixed on Coky's shy smile. It was not that of a rapist. At least, not that of a contrite one. Furthermore, he concluded, despite feeling overwhelmingly tired and fantastically sweaty, it was now clear that she was not talking about sex.

'I... Yeah,' he said, and blinked away the sweat.

She sighed and leaned back in her chair. 'Sorry, let's change the subject... How is your mother? I remember her as a very kind lady.'

Claypole hesitated. He shaped his mouth to reply. Immediately, nothing happened. He rehearsed the line he had meant to say in his head, just to be sure that it was not his emotions concerning his mother that were somehow blocking the synapses, and he shaped to speak again. Nothing.

At this point, Coky started to look concerned. There had, Claypole had to admit, been sufficient silence to cause concern to the average punter, let alone someone like Coky who might be expected to be more than averagely concerned about Claypole's welfare. Especially if they had just slept together, about which he was no clearer.

Claypole was just wondering if his body was once again conspiring to pretend to be asleep when something did happen. While still trying to say something and being inexplicably unable to, he began to feel a burning sensation in his forehead, as if a lit match had been flicked into his shapeless forelock. He moved his hand to his head instantly. At least, that's what he tried to do. But when his brain asked his hand to move, it refused. He asked his hand again to move, in any direction it chose this time, just to see if it still worked at all. It refused again and merely began to tremble. So he forgot about the hand and simply asked his lungs and voicebox to emit an exclamation. Any exclamation would do. 'Ouch', perhaps. Or 'argh'. Even a grunt would have been fine. But no sound came from his mouth at all, and Claypole began to panic as it dawned on him that something was seriously wrong.

His panic was undetectable except in his eyes, which were now wildly straining, desperate to be understood. The rest of his face and body could not do anything to show the world – and particularly Coky – that he needed help, instantly. Coky jumped out of her chair and came around the table to Claypole. He would have responded to this, but nothing in his body was working. The burning sensation in his head redoubled.

As Coky put her hand on his arm in concern and said something that he could not make out, Claypole began to slump sideways and off the chair. She moved instinctively to catch him, but had only limited success. His sheer bulk would probably have been too much for her to bear, even though she was a reasonably fit woman, without the added difficulty that there were, owing to his peculiar shape, no normal structures to hold on to. Claypole was not only heavy but spherical, and his thin arms and legs had turned completely to jelly. It would have been like trying to catch, with no warning given, an oversized beachball filled with water and with the tentacles of a dead octopus protruding from it. The two of them collapsed together in a deathly clinch, dragging the tablecloth with them. The plates, glasses and cutlery crashed and danced crazily all around them as they splayed on the pavement outside the café.

The last thing Claypole remembered before everything went black was Coky's face – near enough for him to smell her sweet coffee breath. His numb and burning head was next to her soft features. He beheld himself as a melting monster, and she as a picture of innocent, infinite worry. And his last thought – such a gentle one in the light of his parlous state – was that he still didn't know whether this unusual and pleasant woman was his friend or his lover.

-3-

> When a crop is so thin,
> There's nothing to do but to set the teeth
> And plough it in.
>
> 'A Failure', Cecil Day-Lewis

Coky had never been able to understand why so many people said 'I don't like hospitals' as if it were a revelation. Something to be marked and understood. Of course you don't *like* hospitals, she thought. Nasty things happen to you there. Maybe you had your gall bladder removed in a hospital, or you gave birth to a ten-pounder, or maybe you had to take a man there because he had a stroke while eating breakfast with you and you haven't seen him since they took him away in an ambulance. Liking hospitals doesn't come into it. You don't *like* a sewer, but you can appreciate what sort of a mess you'd be in if they did not exist.

At the reception desk of the fifth floor of St Paul's Hospital was a young and heavily made-up welterweight, who responded to Coky's businesslike 'hullo' with an expression that managed to be simultaneously blank and hostile, indicating that she was terribly,

terribly busy. It seemed to Coky that the woman clearly had nothing more urgent to accomplish than the eating of many sugary buns.

'Murble help you?' said the receptionist, not looking up from a half-demolished pink doughnut. Coky patiently explained to the top of the woman's head that she would like to visit Mr Claypole.

The woman tapped away at her computer, her long purple nails gingerly scratching the keyboard. She looked at the screen, puzzled.

'Is he dead?' the receptionist asked.

'Could...?' Coky gulped and covered her mouth with her hand. 'I...' She choked on her words.

'Says here,' the receptionist began, her fingers performing some more arachnid scuttling on the keyboard.

'Oh God,' exclaimed Coky, staring at the floor and blinking. 'He was...'

But that was as much eulogy as she could manage for the late Gordon Claypole. Who had he been to her? A childhood acquaintance with whom she had spent a few hours twenty-five years later. Even that had been a strange evening, during which he had got so drunk that he needed putting to bed and monitoring periodically throughout the night for continued signs of life. They had been, she thought glumly, friendly, but not yet friends. Her goal in going to see him had been to persuade him to be the spokesman for the wind farm. He wasn't perhaps the ideal candidate, being something in children's television, but she had asked every other person of her and her uncle Peregrine's acquaintance who might be in the least bit suitable, and every one of them had turned her down. In any case, she told herself, if you were successful in one sort of business, presumably you could be successful in another. But now that Claypole was dead she would have to do the job herself, and she doubted her own abilities. None of this entitled her to any grief, she realised, only dread for her own prospects. And yet, she had liked Gordon Claypole. He was an odd fish, but he had a worldliness that she utterly lacked. He was a drunk, yes. But she was hardly on strong ground to censure an addict. And now she would never meet him again. She looked up sadly. The receptionist was gawping at her.

'Yeah, Mr Cartwright is in the mortuary. Ground floor.'

'Clay-pole,' said Coky slowly, transmitting relief and irritation in carefully equal measure. This was lost on her audience.

'Gordon S. Claypole?' asked the receptionist. Coky nodded slowly.

As she made her way to the ward in which Claypole was recovering, she found herself wondering what Claypole's middle initial might stand for. Had his parents continued with the Scottish theme? Thus, maybe Stuart or Sandy? But perhaps they had gone cute (Summer?), or whacky (Sasquatch?).

⊶▪◉▪⊷

Since being admitted to St Paul's two days previously, Claypole's mood had veered between petulant and weepy, with little in between. Breezy or sympathetic nurses, bothersome wandering crazies and his doctor, the humourless Dr De Witt, had been his only human contact. It was no surprise for him to remain unvisited. But he was surprised to find Coky's face on his mind whenever he was not feeling sorry for himself. Perhaps, he thought, this was because she had been present when he had so nearly departed from the world. But it was possible that he was just grateful to her, and not just because she had paid the bill for breakfast. Dr De Witt had explained – several times – how vastly Coky's quick thinking had increased Claypole's chances of a complete recovery. Coky had identified that he was having some sort of stroke, obtained some aspirin from the first-aid box in the kitchen of the restaurant, crunched it up in a glass with some water and swilled it into his bubbling, panicking mouth. The vaso-dilatory effect thus ensured that his weak and punished heart could pump more oxygen to his brain, limiting the damage.

The Transient Ischemic Attack Claypole had suffered was dramatic, and unusual for a man of his years, but De Witt was cautiously pleased with progress. He told Claypole that if he could just improve the quality and reduce the quantity of his diet, get some exercise, drink plenty of water and much less alcohol, cut out stressful work and take his pills, his heart might not require surgery for another thirty years. (If I could manage to live like that, Claypole had thought ruefully, I wouldn't have had a stroke in the first place, you patronising Dutch hermaphrodite.)

In any case, it was not directly from the stroke that Claypole looked so dramatically bad. The problem was that he had, when he was on his way to the ambulance, regained consciousness and suffered a panic attack. In what were, as far as he was concerned at the time, his dying moments, he had thrashed and kicked, resisting all help from the paramedics, requiring them to restrain and finally to sedate him. As a result, Claypole had barked his shin, split his nostril, bitten his tongue, given himself a black eye, cracked a knuckle and a rib, trapped his little finger and given himself a blood-blister, banged his funny bone and – most dramatically – smashed his two front teeth out on the ambulance door and cut his lip badly in the process. A mass of other small cuts, bruises and scrapes decorated his person. De Witt had commented on the extraordinarily varied range of minor injuries his patient had sustained. 'For you, Mr Claypole,' De Witt had said in front of what seemed like fifty student doctors, 'I would prescribe a twice-daily course of salad, and a box of sticking plasters.' The doctor had then chuckled in the same mirthless way that northern Europeans reserve for laughing at their tasteless films. Claypole had nodded slowly, his piggy eyes darkly flashing.

Miserable and beached on his hospital bed, a mass of contusions, he could only be glad that Coky was not here to see him.

'Hello, soldier!'

And here she was, grinning at him with all those teeth and her gorgeously unarranged hair. For Claypole it was like having a torch shone in his face in the middle of the night. Coky's expression told him that the smile he had attempted was not well transmitted by his bloodied, mutant, toothless face.

'Oh, cripes,' she said, and failed to suppress a giggle.

Claypole said nothing, and raised his unbandaged left hand in greeting. She grabbed it as she half sat half perched on the bed. But the hand Claypole had offered was neither fingers down for a wrong-handed handshake, nor fingers up for a more intimate grasp. They grappled awkwardly for a moment.

'Oops,' said Coky. Claypole looked as if he was

thinking, and the moment hung in the air for a second. His mouth moved impotently.

'Oh, sorry,' she said quickly, 'I didn't realise you couldn't speak.'

She patted his hand. Claypole blinked, and then nodded slowly.

'Poor you,' she said.

Coky had expected – assumed – that Claypole would be able to talk at least a little, and silently cursed the doctor for failing to tell her on the phone that he could not. She would have prepared herself better if she had known.

'When do they...? Do you know when you might recover your, um, speech? If...' She swallowed.

Claypole, his expression hovering nowhere in particular, shrugged.

'I expect you've had lots of visitors.'

Claypole shook his head, but then nodded vigorously.

'Oh.' Coky was confused. 'My fault. Are you able to wink or something so we can have a conversation? Like that bloke who wrote a book while he was in a persistent vegetative state. Something about butterflies. You know, wrote it with his eyebrows or something. Amazing, really. Must have taken terrific pluck... No pun intended... Eyebrows? Pluck?'

Claypole turned one thumb upwards.

'Oh right. Yeah. Well, OK then. Do you want to write something down?' Coky leapt up and opened the drawer of Claypole's bedside table. As she did so, she did a lot of 'what-have-we-got-here-then'ing and 'hope-you-don't-mind-me-rummaging-about'ing. She found a pencil and a newspaper.

'Look, we could even do the crossword.' She placed

the pencil in Claypole's limp and clammy hand.

'So, I'll ask a question. Would you like to do the cross-word or would you like to have a conversation where you write down the answers to questions that I ask?' Coky smiled nervously at Claypole's utterly blank expression.

'Silly me. Still not clear. Would you like to do the crossword?'

Claypole hesitated, gripped the pencil and prepared to write. Coky jumped up to help him. Claypole watched Coky incredulously as she eased his hand over the blank space next to the crossword for work-ings-out and doodles.

'There we go,' said Coky, sitting down again, pained by the fact that she sounded like a bumptious lollipop lady but seemingly quite unable to stop herself.

Claypole pressed down on the paper and wrote. Then he put down the pencil as if spent by the effort and looked out of the window. Coky looked at the paper. 'NO' took up all the space available in a shaky script.

'OK,' said Coky, her cheery demeanour beginning to fade. 'Would you like me to ask you questions and you can write down the answers?'

Claypole looked back at her with a look of profound sadness. He took up the pencil. Coky got up to help him again, but Claypole swiftly raised his hand as if to stop oncoming traffic.

'Oh,' said Coky, 'you've got it, have you? Cool.'

She looked at what Claypole had written. He had put the smallest of ticks next to the massive 'NO' that he had written before.

'Oh.' Coky frowned. 'What about if you put your hand up when you want to say "no", like you just did, and you can put your other hand up when you want to say "yes". OK?'

Claypole raised the same hand he had raised previously.

'Ah, no. You mean "yes", so you raise your other hand, your left hand. Right?'

Claypole continued to keep his right hand raised. Coky sighed.

'Sorry, I'm not being very clear, am I? I said "right" just after I said "left", which didn't help. Come to think of it, I also said "no" and "yes" in the same sentence as well.' She paused and her shoulders sank. 'Sorry.'

To Coky's relief, a nurse appeared at her shoulder. 'How are we today, Mr Claypole?' asked the nurse.

'Fine, fanks,' said Claypole, and had just enough time to regret having spoken before Coky exploded. While she would have been justified in exploding with anger, in fact the explosion was one of laughter.

After they had spent some time apologising to each other, Claypole found the next ten minutes wonderfully relaxing. No one had talked to him for two days for any purpose other than the briefest of introductions before stabbing him with a hypodermic or to enquire with hasty condescension whether "we need a wee-wee". But this was a delight. Coky's enthusiasm for wind farming allowed him to concentrate on her face. He could just bathe in her gaze, unabashedly.

'It wasn't so long ago that it was still a novelty,' she was saying. 'But it's a mature technology now, of course.'

Claypole noticed again how fanglike Coky's incisors were. They flashed periodically when she smiled that nervous smile of hers.

'Of course, almost everything that could have been done to ensure a bad result from the council's planning committee has been done. My uncle is nothing if not a shoddy cheapskate, and Aeolectricity wasn't much better. The environmental survey is amateurish; the plans for where the turbines are going has never been properly settled; little thought seems to have been given to the requirements of the national grid, or the transport problems that will arise; and no plans at all have been put in place to actually buy turbines. We should delay it, really. But that costs money. And if the council says no, in theory we could take it to inquiry, but that would cost a million quid, and... well, same problem.'

Claypole's face held firm, attempting not to betray his incomprehension. Were 'turbines' the windmill thingies? Yes, probably. He knew vaguely what the national grid was, but the rest of it sounded too much like science and legal quagmire.

'But in a way, none of that matters,' said Coky. 'The biggest problem is that the local community is either suspicious or actively hostile. We have a PR disaster on our hands. That's the thing we'd like you to turn around.'

This was less difficult for Claypole to grasp. It sounded like very bad news, and very much as if his inclination to run in the opposite direction from this project as soon and as fast as possible was the correct one.

'Having said all that, it is windy.' Coky shrugged.

'I've heard.'

'*Really* windy. If we get planning consent, it'll make a fortune. You're getting two per cent, right? Did Perry tell you what that might amount to?'

Claypole shook his head.

'About £200,000.'

Claypole coughed, and a fleck of spittle arced towards his foot. To his relief this seemed to go unnoticed by Coky, who was staring into space.

'… And about £25,000 a year for twenty-five years,' she continued. 'Of course we're all interested in the environmental benefits. But it's going to make money too. I mean, that's the ideal thing, isn't it…?'

Her eyebrows also wrinkled and unwrinkled constantly, flicking between worry and brightness.

'… From your point of view. As an entrepreneur and a committed environmentalist. Good for the world, and good for your wallet…'

Claypole wondered what had happened in her life to make her so tense. She had presumably, like her uncle, so many advantages, and on top of the self-possession of her upbringing, she appeared so free. So why did she seem just a little bit… broken? Claypole wanted very much to puzzle her out.

'… Anyway,' Coky carried on, 'this project has been so amateurishly conducted that you couldn't possibly make it worse.'

Finally Claypole surrendered to the thought he knew he shouldn't allow himself, viz. how beautiful he found those eyebrows, those teeth, that peculiar clothing, so dark for a summer's day. And those limpid blue eyes. He had a sudden vision of the two of them in a Venice hotel bedroom. Having never been to Venice, he had to fill in the gaps in his knowledge with a lot of white muslin and soft focus, and the effect on his mind's eye was a bit too much like a 1980s pop video, but he enjoyed it nonetheless. After slow walks and long meals, they would… What would they do? Would they perform the act of love that they had probably not yet enjoyed? But might it be possible if he hung around her for long enough? Claypole had never in his life chased a girl, but assumed that all you had to do was put the hours in.

'... And it wouldn't be for very long... Anyway, now is the time to tell me if you can't do it. I mean, maybe it's not medically... well, for whatever reason.'

She stopped, and blinked at Claypole. With a jolt, Claypole realised that he should now respond, but he had missed a piece of her monologue and thus had no idea what he was responding to, so he just nodded sagely.

'Oh good. Great news. I'm flying to Scotland tonight. But you'll come and join me next week?'

They sat in silence while he licked his split lip and his tongue explored the gap where his front teeth had been. Then he prepared to speak, but she interjected.

'Oh yeah,' Coky said. 'What does the "S" stand for? Your middle initial.'

Claypole reshaped his mangled mouth with extra effort.

'I don' know why vey put dat. I 'aven't gorra miggle name.' He looked away.

'Oh. OK.' She played with her fingers. 'So, you'll come and help us out?'

Claypole thought. Coky was watching him so closely with those blue, blue eyes. Claypole stared across the ward. A small boy clutching a plastic beaker containing his appendix held Claypole with a malevolent glare. So Claypole looked away and out of the window. A pigeon reproached him from the sill outside as it unblinkingly shat.

The silence went on for so long that Coky thought

momentarily that her friend might have had another stroke, and she looked at him with concern. But gradually a smile broke across her face as Claypole spoke.

'I owe you my life.'

-4-

What lemmings are supposed to do when they get too many has become almost apocryphal, and the simile has been used often enough to prophesy the course of human behaviour by people who have no understanding of lemmings or their environment.

Wilderness and Plenty, Frank Fraser Darling

Claypole never ran. In fact he never even hurried. Nonetheless his gait certainly had an extra jaunty element as he trotted through Edinburgh Airport with a stein of strong frothy coffee in one hand, and in the other a gravid sack of muffins, croissants and other chocolatey treats from the same multinational purveyor. His tiny legs tiptoed and scuffled his bulky frame along, extra-heavy with a backpack and suited again for the first time since his meeting with Peregrine MacGilp. He told himself he was hurrying so friskily because the plane he had to catch was *his* plane, chartered for the purpose of flying to Loch Garvach, there to become the spokesman for a wind farm project. He would not admit to himself the possibility that he was jogging through the airport because he was, for the first time in his life, in pursuit of a woman.

Arriving at the private departure lounge, he saw Peregrine MacGilp, on the other side of a glass partition, who waved at him extravagantly. When Claypole had put down his backpack, and Peregrine had ordered champagne for himself and mineral water for Claypole, they immediately got down to business.

'Here it is,' said Peregrine, sliding a binder across a coffee table and pointing to the last page of a legal document. 'Fresh from the lawyer. Just plop a pawprint at the bottom, dear boy, and we shall be partners.'

'Brr', said Claypole. He took a minute to read the three pages that gave him ownership of two per cent of the Loch Garvach Wind Farm. It seemed like a straightforward document, and he saw that Peregrine had already signed it. 'MacGilp', said the signature, and underneath it in block capitals 'MacGilp of MacGilp'. Claypole made a rapid series of indecipherable scrapes and slashes, and underneath wrote 'Claypole' in capitals. Then his pen hesitated. He wrote again, and pushed the file over to his new business partner.

Peregrine looked at it. 'Claypole of Claypole,' it said.

'Congratulations,' said Peregrine, absent of glee, and put the binder to one side. They were silent for a moment, perhaps in lieu of celebration.

'Brr,' said Claypole.

'Do you know Edinburgh?' asked Peregrine.

'Been once. S'awright,' said Claypole, and while Peregrine made his own views of the city known, Claypole reflected privately on his only other experience of Scotland's capital.

In the summer after leaving university, Claypole had acted in a student production at the Edinburgh Festival

Fringe. It was a musical-comedy adaptation of *The Diaries of John Major,* entitled 'Not Inconsiderably!', and the performance had been reviewed by the *Scotsman.* The cast had crowded excitedly around the newspaper as they read together:

Beany Luckett, who plays Norma Major, manages to bring some gusto to her solo song, 'Does He Even Love Me?', but she punctuates every joke with a nervous, almost angry, glance at the front row of the audience. Tristram Jones, the writer, director, producer and star, plays John Major as a camp bodybuilder with minor financial worries – which may or may not be intentional. But really the only member of the cast with a possible career in show-business is Claire Pearson, whose Edwina Currie is played for laughs of the 'Carry On' type. I enjoyed her solo, 'Secrets' – but I enjoyed the striptease that accompanied it more. The part of Norman Lamont was played by Gordon Claypole. At no point were his lines audible, and he sweated so profusely that his grey wig kept slipping over his false eyebrows. It was only during the jazz dance number 'Black Wednesday' that it became clear why he he was also strangely reluctant to face the audience. Mr Claypole was maintaining, despite the black lycra, an all-too-visible erection.

Claypole's attention clicked back to Peregrine's monologue.

'The terrible thing about Edinburgh – Scotland in general, come to that – is that it could be such fun,'

Peregrine pronounced. 'It's cheap, drink is everywhere and it's awfully pretty. The problem isn't the place, or even the blasted weather. It's the people.'

'Oh yes?' Claypole asked, staring at Peregrine's glass of champagne.

'Posh Scots are horrible. Old rivalries and jealousies still lurk. Grudges going back to the Monmouth Rebellion of 1687. Further, really. At the drop of a hat they'll sing Jacobite songs and they'll damn you if you don't know the words. You have to be on your guard.'

Claypole glanced around the departure lounge. A man in baggy linen trousers and a tall woman with a ruddy complexion were earnestly looking at a laptop. Two men in suits of different shades of corporate blue talked intensely over expensive beer. This didn't appear to be a nation at war with itself. It just looked... busy. Peregrine leaned in conspiratorially.

'Religion still causes a ruckus too, absurdly. But worse is land. Did you know that sixty per cent of the land in Scotland is owned by just a thousand people? Scottish nobles' complicity to Union with England was bought with gifts of land in the early eighteenth century, and the place has never fully recovered. No wonder the poor hate the landowners. Not that I'm a nationalist. But Union has never really worked. Even under torture no Scot would admit to being British. He is a Highlander, or a Scot, even – God help us – a European. Never British. Only the English call themselves British.'

Claypole watched the bubbles in his mineral water as Peregrine glugged at his champagne.

'So is me being English going to be a problem?' Claypole asked.

'I thought you were half Scottish? No matter. The

important thing is to show them there's a new sheriff in town. And there are worse crimes than being English. Just don't be posh.'

'Right. Yeah. I couldn't... Right. But...' He took a sip of his water. 'Aren't you posh, though, Peregrine?'

'Yes, quite so,' said the older man. 'But we're not a unified tribe. Posh Scots absolutely hate each other.'

Claypole could not help but smile.

'It's true,' said Peregrine with gravity. 'When any two members of the Scottish upper class meet, they are mutually suspicious, and with good reason. There is the distinct likelihood that an ancestor on one side probably diddled, raped or killed an ancestor on the other side. Given all these ancient internecine loathings, it's a wonder we still marry each other. And we go through life being as loud and as weird as we like.'

Peregrine leaned back.

'Take my old chum Crispian Mount...'

Lord Mount, according to Peregrine, never left his monstrous, freezing castle in a flat and rain-drenched part of the far north, and his main entertainment was to threaten the guests at his strange dinner parties. 'Now then, Bubble,' he would bellow to the woman on his left and gesture to a man halfway down the table but very much within earshot, 'do you mind awfully if I bump off your fat friend? Never killed a fat man, see?' When informed that the man was in fact her husband, Mount would merely laugh and pronounce, 'Ah well, there's profit in the enterprise then.' The man in question, quartered alone in a chilly dungeon, would not sleep well. Mount himself was known to sleep in nothing but a cummerbund.

'Anyway, look,' said Peregrine, looking at his watch. 'I assume your great business brain is forming a plan as to how to banjax these blasted local councillors at this evening's meeting.'

Claypole's face registered confusion.

'At the community hall.' Peregrine frowned.

'Oh. Yeah.' But before Claypole could quiz his business partner further about this public meeting, a man wearing a luminous tabard was upon them.

'You the 4.30? Over to the west, aye?' The man had addressed Peregrine.

'That's me,' said Claypole.

Claypole had imagined his PR offensive – the new sheriff gambit, as Peregrine had put it – starting with disembarkation at Loch Garvach from some sort of jet, with Claypole kissing the ground and shaking hands with emissaries bearing chains of office. But emerging from the craft which he and Peregrine now beheld on the damp tarmac would not be so impressive. The four-seater plane was painted in two shades of brown, comically squat and of early 1970s vintage. But Peregrine was making up for Claypole's disappointment with boyish excitement as they squeezed into the tiny charter, courtesy of Claypole's credit card.

'I say,' said Peregrine cheerily. 'This certainly beats taking the bus.'

After an uncomfortable take-off, they banked and turned west, West Lothian opening up below them in bumpy fits. The engine was hard at work, and conversation was impossible, so Claypole pressed his head against the cold window and watched the world underneath them. They passed over Silicon Glen in the central belt of Scotland. Where once the economy of middle Scotland had mined coal and then made semiconductors, it now had call centres and Amazon.com. Claypole caught sight of a wind farm, looking small in the grand sweep of the landscape and snuggled next to a motorway. Just a few minutes later they winged over the vast sprawl of Glasgow – home of sectarian football, boiled sweets and fine art. Then further west, over the mountains of the Highlands, the purple and the green rising up as if to kiss the small plane. Coyly it reeled upwards and away from the embrace of the land, and then dipped down, teasing the ground to rise up again. Lochs, both the still, brown inland version and the inlets of the choppy, grey sea began to appear more frequently below them, interspersed with steamy pine forest.

Claypole almost never thought about Scotland. He classed anywhere that was ten Tube stops from Marble Arch as 'the countryside', and tried to keep time spent there to a minimum. This despite the fact that his parents – and after the age of ten, just his mother – had whenever possible bussed him from the southern English market town where they lived into what she called 'greenery'. Claypole had protested that all countryside was 'full of people who had failed'. (It was a line he had got from a newspaper columnist in pursuit of cheap Saturday morning laughs, but he had been happy to recycle it as his own coinage.) But relentlessly these excursions had continued. Creeping down the A303 at half-term to childless friends of his mother's in Cornwall, eating fish-paste sandwiches in the Hillman Hunter in front of raging seas, and the interminable summers in Scotland for as long as his grandmother lived. In those damp rented cottages, he had stayed moodily indoors, fitting together thousand-piece jigsaw puzzles of HMS *Victory* and mildly racist depictions of African scenes, openly wishing for a return to concrete and real life.

So, while he did not particularly look forward to being a part of the scenery he saw below him, at least being spokesman for a wind farm in the undeniably attractive Scottish countryside would be easy. The backwaters of Loch Garvach, after all, could not be remotely as shark-infested as the editing suites of Soho. The work, in any case, was a secondary goal compared to that of persuading Coky to…

Claypole felt a hand on his shoulder. He turned to see Peregrine with headphones on, offering him a similar pair. Peregrine adjusted the microphone in front of his mouth, flicked a switch and urged Claypole to do the same.

'Hello!' said Claypole.

Peregrine winced. 'These things are pretty good at picking up a normal voice, old boy. No need to shout.'

Claypole looked down again at the forests, incongruously neat green blankets of regimented planting lines in the rocky chaos surrounding them.

'So, what are you going to say at this meeting, old boy?' Peregrine asked.

'What?'

'Your speech. To the community meeting.' Peregrine smiled.

Claypole's eyes widened in alarm. In response, so did Peregrine's.

'What? You mean I've got to –'

'Christ! Don't tell me Coky didn't… She must have thought that I –'

'Maybe Coky did tell me. I'm afraid I…'

'Right.'

In wide-eyed silence, they both computed the crossed wires that must have occurred. Then they rallied.

'So. Well. I'll just, brr –'

'Yes. Just...'

'Talk the thing up a bit.'

'That's the spirit. Give 'em a bit of la-di-da,' said Peregrine.

'Right.'

'King Hal at Agincourt. Fighting spirit and all that. Good man. Terrific.'

The men looked out of different windows for a full minute.

'Ooh, hullo. Doors to manual!' announced Peregrine, and the plane began a steep descent into Loch Garvach.

-×-≡◎≡-×-

The reception committee at Loch Garvach airfield consisted of a man in turned-down black wellies and a bulky white sweater, a crew-cut youth with a clipboard and Coky Viveksananda, grimacing stoically against the wet wind. Claypole had so wanted to emerge from the plane – his plane – like a billionaire in the making, and doubly so now that Coky was watching. But owing to the minuteness of the plane and the tremendous size of his rucksack, he ended up having to get out of the plane in an ungainly bum-first fashion. Peregrine sprang deftly onto the tarmac like a rock star, lit a ciga- rette and bounced towards Coky.

'Darling!' he trumpeted and stooped to kiss his niece, a gesture she more allowed than participated in. Claypole dawdled behind Peregrine, hoping that following on the heels of Peregrine's kiss, he would be allowed to do the same. So when Peregrine moved aside, he began to lean in towards her. But Coky stuck out a hand for him to shake.

'Hey, Gordon,' she said warmly.

'Hey, Coky.' He reeled backwards. 'What an unexpected –'

'Claypole!' said Peregrine, offering the man in
wellies, whose thick white hair remained impervious
to the wind as Claypole's few purple-black wisps
danced manically. 'This is Tommy Thompson. Old
friend, stand-up chap, and importantly for us, a local
councillor and chairman of the planning committee.'

Of indeterminate age between fifty and eighty,
Tommy Thompson's face was a medieval field of lines
and pits, the colour of smoked mackerel. He looked more
like a fisherman than a politician, and his demeanour
suggested that he owed deference to no man.

'Tommy, this is Claypole. He's going to be helping
out with the wind farm.'

'Aye,' said Tommy Thompson, and fixed Claypole
with an intense look from under wiry salt-and-pepper
eyebrows. Claypole nodded and moved swiftly to
shake the hand of the boy with the clipboard, who
blushed instantly.

'That's an airport chap,' said Peregrine quickly.

'Oh,' said Claypole.

'Hullo,' said the boy sheepishly, and darted away to
minister to the plane.

'I have arranged a room at the hotel and a car for
you, Mr Claypole,' said Tommy Thompson.

'It's just Claypole,' said Claypole, and added his
thanks. As they set off towards the car park, Claypole
strode ahead of the party. He had read in a magazine
that the person with the highest status always gets into
a waiting limousine first. So he walked quickly and
hopped through the gate in the perimeter fence well
in front of everyone else, scanning the car park. There

was a Royal Mail van, a mud-spattered four-wheel drive with a child asleep in the back seat and a lorry which to judge by its livery contained a large quantity of crisps. None of these looked like a suitable vehicle for a visiting dignitary. Peregrine, Tommy Thompson and Coky arrived next to him.

'Behind the truck,' said Tommy Thompson as he pressed a keyfob and a shaft of orange light briefly lit up the gloom behind the crisps lorry.

'I thought you'd probably like something with a small carbon footprint,' said Tommy Thompson. 'What with you being a green.'

It was an electric car in a shade of aquamarine found only in lycra on the legs of Miami trophy wives. It was laterally squished as if it had been in a cartoon crash and clearly designed to carry nothing larger than a couple of anorexic seventeen-year-olds. Claypole was handed the keys, and the four of them walked around the car in silence, examining it as a school of sardines might regard a tin.

On the twenty-minute journey along the coast road to the town of Garvachhead, Peregrine and Tommy Thompson squatted in the back, their grey heads bent together and giggling like schoolboys. Coky was hunched in the front, dwarfed by Claypole's rucksack on her lap, and with Peregrine's brief-case cramping her legs. The car shook and twitched violently at even the tiniest gasp of wind, and Claypole sweated and strained like a fighter pilot as he drove.

A road sign said 'Garvachhead' in black, and '*Céann Loch Garbhach*' again in green. Claypole spoke to the rucksack next to him.

'What's with the Gaelic?' he said.

'For the tourists,' said the rucksack. 'Here we are. Opposite the hotel.'

A dim blue light shone outside a small granite building, and Claypole slowed. 'Police', it said reassuringly in 1950s script. Next to it, the community hall announced its presence with a red-and-white canvas banner lashed to the front of its breeze-block facade. Across the road, 'Loch Garvach Hotel' in austere letters across the front of a whitewashed building with black windows announced Claypole's residence for the duration. Outside it were half a dozen male smokers, stoically and silently puffing away. One of them, a dark-haired shambles in a donkey jacket, caught sight of them and tapped a lanky and bearded compadre on the shoulder. The two of them glared at the car with purpose.

'Who's that?' Claypole looked at the dark-haired man, who stared back. 'They look like Swampy's dad and Shaggy from *Scooby-Doo*.'

'Listen, Gordon,' Coky turned to him. 'Just keep it short, OK?'

'Ha,' he said. He thought better of telling her that he had no speech, and that therefore keeping it short would not be a problem. 'Brr. Piece of cake.'

'Don't underestimate them just because they're country people. Some of them are extremely good at getting what they want.'

'I suppose the wicked witch is coming?' This was Peregrine, from somewhere behind and above Claypole's left ear. Coky did not answer as she opened the passenger door and wriggled out from beneath the rucksack.

Inside the hall, Claypole was ushered into a seat on the first row of chairs in front of a wooden stage. Peregrine and Coky sat either side of him. The rest of the gathering numbered no more than fifty. Tommy Thompson positioned himself on the stage behind a long formica table, an efficient smile on his lips. On his left, sitting with her arms folded, was a woman in her sixties with a shelf-like bosom and half-moon spectacles. She was looking at Claypole with the curiosity a child gives a struggling beetle. On Tommy Thompson's right was a man in bottle-bottom spectacles, grey jacket and brown v-neck jumper. Tommy Thompson banged a gavel and the room settled quickly.

'Welcome, everyone. As most of you know, I'm Tommy Thompson, and I'm the chairman of the planning committee. The other members of the committee are also here: Helen MacDougall and John Bruce...'

As Tommy Thompson continued his introduction, Claypole turned around as surreptitiously as he could to scan the audience. All eyes seemed to be either bored or angry, but they were all looking at Claypole. He turned quickly back to face the stage.

'So, with no further delay, I would like to introduce you to the new spokesman for the wind farm, Gordon Claypole...' Tommy Thompson looked at the audience and added with featherweight amusement, 'from London.'

Abruptly, Tommy Thompson sat down. There were coughs and shiftings in the audience as Claypole rose from his chair. He turned and raised a hand in greeting and gave a clipped nod. His eyes found the dark-haired man in the donkey jacket. Mid-forties, the man was six foot of twisted steel cable with a woodsman's tan and an expression of disgust on his wrinkled smoker's lips. They met eyes, and to Claypole's shock, the man raised his forefinger and slowly drew it across his throat.

Claypole turned quickly to see Tommy Thompson

smiling and gesturing to the front of the stage. Claypole gathered himself and stepped slowly onto the stage, and then looked back at the audience. Peregrine was the only one smiling.

'Hello. Brr. I'm Claypole. I'll be... representing the wind farm.'

'Speak up!' said someone from the back of the hall.

'Right... brr,' said Claypole. 'Right!' Now his voice was raised. 'Now, you must all understand that I haven't had much of a chance to get to grips with the detail of the project... you know... but I'll do my best to...'

He thought for a moment and took a breath in an attempt to regain his disintegrated confidence. The image of the crusty drawing his finger across his throat kept replaying in his mind. He looked at Peregrine who was beaming beatifically. Agincourt, thought Claypole.

'We can all agree, I think, that global warming is the biggest threat facing the world in the next century. Brr. It's a... big deal. So we have to do something about it. Right? I mean we can't just... So, it's up to all of us to make a difference, and to make sure that we... save the...' He gulped. He couldn't help himself. Nothing else was entering his mind. '... save the planet.'

Claypole looked around the audience. Should he go on? He saw Coky, who was biting a fingernail, and remembered her advice to keep it short.

'That's it, really,' he said, and went to leave the stage.

'Thank you, Mr Claypole,' said Tommy Thompson. 'Perhaps you would like to stay up here for the moment.'

Claypole, who was halfway down the steps at the

front of the stage, turned around and went back up them. He stood, hands in pockets.

'Bonnie, you wanted to say a few words...'

While Tommy Thompson pointed to a spare chair on the stage and Claypole sat down, a woman in her early sixties drew out a typed script from a bulging bag and walked slowly to the front. With long curls of grey hair, she was heavily mascaraed, her eyes a moonlike expanse of white with small green pools in the centre. Green-suited, she wore no jewellery save for a leather necklace holding a single shark's tooth. She gave Claypole a severe look, flicked her voluminous hair back and began.

Bonnie Straughan's speech to the Loch Garvach community hall that afternoon was passionate, long and confusing. She had spent many hours writing it, but had denied herself the benefit of an edit. As a result she regularly became lost, which she covered by returning to certain stock phrases, more often than not 'so that's what I think', which she would follow quickly with 'and another thing I strongly feel', which was the only pause before another tirade. She railed broadly against the ugliness of modern life, the terrible toll that development of the countryside took on its inhabitants, and stressed how the natural world needed to be safe-guarded. In regard to wind farming, she referred only to 'these hideous machines', and spat the phrase 'scarring the landscape' often. In her view, wind power was a confidence trick perpetrated by city-dwellers and power companies and should be rejected wholesale. Eventually, she sat down to a short blast of applause.

'Are there any questions for Mr Claypole?' asked Tommy Thompson breezily.

'Ah, well, no,' Claypole began, but stopped in horror

when almost every hand in the audience immediately rose in the air. Tommy Thompson pointed to the second row of chairs and a woman stood up.

'Mary Hislop,' said the woman in a whisper. 'I have heard that wind farming requires more energy to make the windmills than is – '

'Turbines,' corrected Tommy Thompson.

'Thank you,' she said gracefully. 'To make the *turbines*... than they produce. Is this true?'

Claypole smiled. 'Nah. Can't possibly be true,' he said with confidence.

'But you don't *know*,' offered the woman.

'Well, I... It can't be the case, can it? Otherwise they wouldn't do it.'

'They?'

'Well, us. We.' Claypole coughed. 'Look, I'll... Brr... I'll find out and get back to you on that.'

The woman might have wished to continue the debate, but Tommy Thompson was pointing at a man with large spectacles.

'Will any of the wind farm be visible from Ballaig Point?' said the man.

'I... don't know, I'm afraid,' said Claypole. He looked at the smiling Peregrine, who seemed in no danger of intervening.

'Oh,' said the man, 'what about from the Giant's Table?'

Claypole smiled weakly. 'Dunno. Sorry.'

The man sat down. Many hands rose again.

'Kayleigh, you have a question?' said Tommy Thompson.

'I want to know,' said Kayleigh, a child of no more than ten, 'whether any buds will be hut by the windmills.'

Claypole could not disguise his confusion. 'Any

buds... will be... hut? I'm sorry, I don't...'

'Are there,' Tommy Thompson translated, 'going to be any avian casualties as a result of the wind farm?'

'Oh, *birds!*' said Claypole brightening, 'will be... *hurt...* I see. Brr... Look... Time out, OK?' He pointed at the child severely. 'I became a partner in this scheme only today. I don't know the detail yet.'

Claypole looked at Peregrine with wide-eyed appeal. Peregrine gave him a surreptitious double thumbs-up.

'The chair recognises Carrie McMichael,' said Tommy Thompson.

A pretty young woman stood and smiled at Claypole. 'I would like to know what Mr Claypole thinks are going to be the benefits to the community of the scheme.'

There were many mutterings of approval at the question. Claypole swallowed.

'As chairman of the committee,' Tommy Thompson began slyly, 'let me give some background to this.'

Claypole breathed out deeply as Tommy Thompson spoke. 'In a scheme of this kind, as with most developments, the local community is usually entitled to receive what is known as "planning gain". That is to say, some sort of amenity for having to put up with disruption caused by building works and the like. We, the planners, are not allowed to take such considerations into account, of course, but perhaps Mr Claypole has such a benefit in mind?'

Claypole closed his eyes and held his breath. He opened them again, and saw only expectant faces.

'Well, yes. Brr. Planning gain. Yes.' The tuts and fidgets in the audience had stopped. Claypole felt the sweat chilling on his forehead as he tried to remember the contract he had signed that afternoon, it being the only document he had read in regard to the Loch Garvach Wind Farm. The audience seemed to blink at him as one. The silence continued until suddenly Claypole brightened.

'Of course there is the 2,000 quid thing!' he said in triumph.

'What's that?' asked someone from the back.

'Well, you… the community… gets £2,000 per turbine…' Claypole hesitated. 'Sorry, £2,000 per megawatt…' He frowned. 'Maybe it *is* per turbine… or… rr. Well, one of them, anyway, ha ha… which will go to…' He was looking at Peregrine, who nodded at him encouragingly. 'It's a fund which you, the community, will… you know… *have*. So you can buy more pigs, or whatever.'

There were confused faces. Bonnie Straughan was scribbling furiously.

'I reckon,' announced Claypole brightly, 'that the question for you is not, "Shall we allow this wind farm to go ahead?". Instead you should be saying to yourselves, "How shall we spend the wonga?"' He beamed.

'What is it?' asked a voice.

'Sorry?' said Claypole.

'How much is it over all?' said another voice.

Finally, here was a question to which Claypole knew the answer.

'Ah, well. Here's the good news. It's a couple of hun –' he began, but Peregrine had sprung to his feet.

'I think it would be more appropriate if *I* answered that question, Mr Chairman.'

'The chair acknowledges MacGilp of MacGilp,' said Tommy Thompson.

Peregrine turned towards the audience. He spoke fast. 'It's prejudicial to project an exact figure, because of several factors. Accruals, depreciation and exchange rate fluctuations, for example.'

Some in the audience looked at each other. Peregrine smiled condescendingly.

'In other words, at today's adjusted, pre-construction prices, and what with overages, and with the eurozone as it is, one set of projected figures could be examined and even postulated, but in order to pre-finance the after-tax ratios, and based on estimates over several fiscal cycles, you would have to adjust for inflation and then amortise the results. I'm sure you understand.'

Peregrine sat again, leaving a black hole of silence.

'Put it like this,' said Claypole helpfully. 'If it was a small number, we wouldn't be doing it.'

He beheld only dark looks and tutting. So he tried again.

'What I mean is... we're in this for the money, and you could be too!'

There were gasps and one cry of 'shame'.

'I'm just saying,' said Claypole, glancing briefly at Coky and seeing her massaging both temples. 'There'll be plenty of dosh to go around, OK?'

Tommy Thompson quelled the harrumphing with an authoritative hand. 'We'll have one more question,' he said, and selected a young man with a notepad. Claypole vowed to answer more like a politician.

'Hullo, Mr Claypole,' said the young man.

'Hi,' said Claypole guardedly.

'May I ask what qualifies you to stand where you are?'

'Brr. Well, what qualifies you to ask that question?' said Claypole.

'I'm Kevin Watt. I'm a journalist with the *Glenmorie Herald*.'

'Ah,' said Claypole, 'right. Well then... good.'

There was silence.

'Mr Claypole?'

'Yup?'

'You haven't answered my question.'

'What was the question again?'

'What are your qualifications to be the spokesman for a wind farm? I believe you have spent your career in children's television.'

'Apps for pre-school... Well, yeah. Yes, I have. But, look. When Branson launches a line of Virgin underwear or whatever, he doesn't have any qualifications, does he? He's not a woman, or an underwear model, and he's never been in the schmutter business. Doesn't matter. He's Richard Branson and he can do whatever he likes... Right?'

The journalist squinted. 'Are you saying you're Sir Richard Branson?'

'No.'

'Are you saying you can do whatever you like?'

'No, mate.' Claypole gritted his teeth. 'I'm saying that I'm a spokesman, not an expert. You want an expert? Hire your own.'

The young man scribbled energetically.

'Thank you, Mr Claypole,' said Tommy Thompson.

'It's just Claypole,' muttered Claypole bleakly, and sat down.

While the audience burbled, Claypole brooded. He couldn't bring himself to look at Coky, and fixed instead on Peregrine's face, which still held a smile, although a somewhat fractured one. Tommy Thompson called for quiet again.

'Before I close this meeting I have two suggestions. First, that the Loch Garvach Wind Farm Company replies in writing to the questions asked here today. Second, that we have another meeting where we can ask questions on any points which we feel need further elaboration. Perhaps Mr Claypole will have had a chance to become more familiar with the project by then. After that, the committee will make its decision.'

To more hubbub, Tommy Thompson and the other two councillors conferred as Claypole left the stage and slumped into the seat next to Coky.

'Who,' whispered Claypole, 'is that vile woman?'

Coky's wrinkled brow told Claypole that she had not understood him.

'The harridan who wanged on about the bloody view and saving the badgers or whatever. Must be who Peregrine meant by the wicked witch.'

Again the wrinkled brow. Coky seemed to be ignoring him. But he was desperate to deflect attention away from his own disastrous performance, so he ploughed on.

'That one.' He waved his finger at Bonnie Straughan in frustration. 'Looks like she used to be a hooker.'

'Bonnie Straughan,' said Coky slowly, 'is my mother.'

'We're agreed then,' Tommy Thompson concluded, picking up a gavel and looking at his fellow committee members, who nodded gravely. 'We meet again at five o'clock a week today. Meeting adjourned.'

With a bang that sounded to Claypole like the last nail going into a coffin lid, Tommy Thompson brought the gavel down on the formica table.

-5-

Outside every thin woman is a fat man trying to get in.

Selective Memory, Katharine Whitehorn

'But you don't understand,' Claypole repeated as he danced around a moving Coky on the pavement outside the community hall. The cries of the seagulls above him were no less plaintive. 'I'm not just *sorry*. I'm really, *really* sorry.'

'There's no need,' she said.

'Stop,' he said.

They were outside the police station now, next to Claypole's horrible electric car. If Coky did not forgive him for his blundering remark, he might as well get in it and drive back to London.

'Listen,' he said, and held his forehead. But he did not continue. To his surprise her expression was not registering anger. This was sorrow.

'I'm not offended,' she said. 'The reason I'm upset is that I know she's a... what was the word you used? Begins with an "h"?'

'Hooker?' he suggested.

'No. For God's sake, Gordon.' She was trying to be

angry, perhaps. But the corners of her mouth were turned up in a smile.

'Harridan?' he suggested.

'Yes. Harridan. I suppose it hit a nerve.'

They both looked out over the harbour.

'Oh. Right,' he said.

Coky gave a shudder in the quickening evening breeze as Peregrine appeared next to them, lighting a cigarette.

'Could have gone worse,' Peregrine chirped.

Claypole turned to his business partner. 'Could it?'

'Well, the wicked witch talked a lot of bilge, but she didn't land any blows.'

'She's your sister, Peregrine,' said Coky. Her expression was pained.

'Hm,' said Peregrine, and blew smoke voluminously. 'Come on. All back to mine for a dram.'

'We'd better get your stuff from the car,' said Coky.

'Are we abandoning the car?' Claypole asked, cheered.

'Well, we can't take it on the boat,' said Peregrine.

Claypole gulped and smiled horribly, showing his lack of teeth.

'I think I'll drive it. If that's... Can you get to the house by car?'

'Oh, yes, but...' Coky was suddenly amused.

'Nah,' Claypole said, 'I just... Brr.'

Claypole did not want to appear scared of boats. Because Claypole was not scared of boats. What he was scared of was drowning. But he looked about the harbour to see if there was a boat that Peregrine might use to get around in. A skiff. Wasn't that the word for those little death-traps? Those tiny rowing boats that bobbed and ducked on the ocean until a wave or a whale came and tossed the thing upside down? Maybe it was a rig, or a dinghy. However you were meant to describe them, Claypole could see no such thing in the harbour. All he could see were fishing trawlers, pleasure boats and...

'Is that it?' Claypole's eyes widened.

'Yup,' said Peregrine proudly. There was a fifty-foot yacht, pristine white and appearing to gleam even in the early evening gloom. Along its side was emblazoned 'Lady of the Isles' and a trio of 'go faster' stripes.

'It's just a boat,' said Peregrine, his chest swelling gently.

'It's a bloody great yacht is what it is,' Claypole squeaked. Was this, he wondered, what old money did with itself?

'Posh people call it a boat,' said Coky. 'It would be very "Non U" to talk about your "yacht". Isn't that right, Peregrine?'

Coky was teasing her uncle, but he seemed not to hear. Claypole backed away.

'It's a very nice... boat. But I'll just...'

'Don't be silly. It'll take you ages to drive,' she said.

'Really, I... I'd better take... with my stuff in the car, and... It's fine. Really, I'll take the... Pfah, no problem.'

'OK, but you might need directions...'

'Got satnav,' Claypole called over his shoulder, already wrestling his things out of the foul luminous car.

⤙⟶◉⟵⤚

Claypole checked into the Loch Garvach Hotel and dumped his rucksack in his room – a minute paisley-patterned box that smelled damply of chemicals – and received directions to MacGilp House from the hotelier to which he paid almost no attention. The car was one of the generation of electric cars that was almost completely silent, before designers gave them an artificial 'car noise' to decrease the sense of eerie unease in the driver. The only sounds were the muffled swish of tyre on road, his own breathing and – most unnervingly for a driving experience – birdsong. He could find only one radio station that didn't crackle, and he smiled at the dedications. 'This one goes out to all the Kirkinpatrick Posse from Craigie T. He says take a yellow one for him, 'cos he's workin' on the rigs till Christmas. It's Runrig!'

He looked at his phone, but the satellite navigation system had become paralysed with indecision. There was no reception. He would have to busk it.

After a few miles, the road became a single track littered with foul municipal notices bearing the legend 'Passing Place' where Claypole had remembered black-and-white painted wooden markers from his childhood. He did not let up speed. If he was going to go wrong, he calculated, it was better to go wrong quickly so that he could double-back and take another go at it. Anyway, speed made it fun – like some sort of extra-verdant computer game. He saw a sign to 'MacGilp House' and turned down a lane. The track started to show signs of becoming a long driveway, with thistles and patches of grass growing in the middle, but Claypole was so pleased at having gone the right way that he let his foot drift down on the accelerator, sometimes reaching the vehicle's top speed of forty-two miles an hour. And that's when it happened. Stepping whimsically into the road, just over the brow of a hill, was a female roe deer. The hind had no time to react to the impending collision, owing to the near-silence of the car. Claypole himself had only a moment. In some drivers, the reaction would have been to stamp on the brake. In others it would have been to steer the car onto the verge to avoid the animal. Claypole was too shocked to do either. The only thing he managed to do was take his foot off the accelerator and close his eyes. It was thus at thirty-six miles an hour that he and his tinny car hit fifty pounds of startled venison full in the chest.

⋅╼══◎═╾⋅

Night had only just fallen when Claypole, ashen and shivering, approached the French windows of the library of MacGilp House. He might have approached many other doors of the house before these to try and gain entry had he not been guided to them by loud Wagner. Claypole saw through a gap in the heavy curtains that Peregrine was smoking and drinking whisky, a laptop computer open at a pine table in front of him. When the old man heard Claypole's 'tack, tack, tack' on the window, he quickly shut the laptop, killing the music. Drawing back the curtains and seeing who it was, Peregrine windmilled his arms in welcome before opening the doors with much unlocking and unbolting.

Claypole blundered in and headed straight for the fire.

'Ha ha,' piped Peregrine as Claypole rushed past him. 'You've taken your time. I nearly sent out a search party.'

'Nightmare,' was all Claypole could say by way of greeting.

'Good heavens, old boy. What happened?'

'Buh.' Claypole dragged his hands down his face as

he let the fire warm his thin-suited rear.

'Can I, ah, get you a drink?' Peregrine tapped his pockets.

Claypole's face emerged from his hands and displayed the purest gratitude. Peregrine poured a whisky and handed it to Claypole, who looked at it doubtfully for the merest moment before throwing three-quarters of it down his throat. He looked at his host's raised eyebrows.

'Don't wanna talk about it.'

Claypole watched Peregrine silently refilling the glass in his hand and heard the parting words of Dr De Witt echoing in his mind. 'You must eat better food, and no drinking. Exercise, also. Slowly at first, then getting more... *krachtig*.' Then the doctor had given a cruel smile. 'Otherwise you will die soon I think.'

While Peregrine fussed about in a hostly way, offering more drink (accepted) and to hang up Claypole's suit jacket (refused), Claypole had the opportunity to assess the room. The most striking feature of the library was a mounted and stuffed tiger's head, the sight of it these days offensive to all but the most ardent animal-hater, which hung above the door. Moths had attacked it, giving it a rampant case of alopecia and a mournful demeanour. As well as the many books, there were a couple of guns in a cabinet and fishing rods on the walls, and it was in some ways a very splendid room – an oak-panelled hug of a place. But then he saw beneath the pine table that Peregrine was using as a desk some carpet marks showing that until recently a larger item had stood there. Also, for a library that was clearly so old, it was unusual to see large gaps in the shelves.

Peregrine urged Claypole to a seat, and placed the

decanter of whisky on a surface within easy reach. When he had recovered his wheezing breath, Claypole spoke.

'Deer,' he said. 'Brr... I hit a deer.'

'Oh,' said Peregrine. 'It happens. I wouldn't worry about it.' There was a pause. 'Was it one of mine?'

Claypole looked darkly at his host.

'Just... didn't see it.'

'Yes. Well. It happens.'

'Took me an hour to walk here.'

'Ah,' said Peregrine with relief. 'Probably not one of mine, then.'

'Trashed the car.'

'Oh.' Peregrine furrowed his brow. 'Gosh. Are you...?'

'Brr. No. Just... you know...'

They sat sipping their whiskies in silence until the library door creaked open. There was Coky.

'Hello,' she said. 'Did you find us OK?'

A man will find it sexy to see a woman in her pyjamas if what he wants to do is sleep with her. It reminds him of bed, and of nakedness. The degree of sexiness doesn't normally depend on the bedwear in question. But Coky was wearing large, wasp-yellow winceyette pyjamas, an oatmeal jumper, huge checked slippers, and a pink velour dressing gown. It rendered her, to Claypole's relief because he couldn't deal with desire as well as everything else, about as sexy as a Womble.

When Coky had sat down and gauged the atmosphere to be one of stress, Claypole was forced to relate what had happened.

'I don't think... It wasn't the initial impact that did the damage. It was... Well, I was trying to do the right thing. Brr. You're not supposed to...'

He sipped his whisky, wondering whether he would be censured for his actions.

'What?' said Coky.

'I had to... gah, finish it off...'

Coky and her uncle exchanged glances.

'You did so, I hope.' This was Peregrine.

'Yeah. OK. Yeah. I reversed over it. Was that...?' Claypole's expression was pitiful. He had wanted to put the animal out of its misery and hadn't had a weapon to hand. Surely using the car had been the right thing to do?

Coky nodded. 'Yes, I think that was probably –'

'Several times,' said Claypole.

There was a pause. Claypole could feel their country eyes upon him.

'Seven or eight, OK?' he said with irritation.

Coky and Peregrine both raised their eyebrows.

'Maybe twenty. I think that's probably... The car's a bit...' Claypole went quiet again.

'Where is the car?' Coky asked.

'Ditch,' said Claypole sadly. 'I thought I should get it off the road, and it just... Brr... Upside down.'

All three sat in silence. Claypole had the uncomfortable feeling that if he had not been there, they would have been laughing. But Peregrine changed the subject, spending the next ten minutes trying to convince Coky and Claypole that the meeting in the community hall really hadn't gone so badly. As Peregrine spoke of his relief that Claypole had replaced him as the chief villain of the wind farm, a large and comfortable black labrador came and sniffed at Claypole. He noticed that it had three legs, and gave it a pat, whereupon it settled at his feet. In the soft embrace of an armchair with a whisky in his hand, and the fire in the grate raging, Claypole

was finding himself beginning to relax. He calculated
that the longer he stayed drinking whisky, the greater
the chances of being offered a bed at MacGilp House.
In his experience of staying in large houses – which
was very limited – he suspected it would be one of two
distinct experiences. Either it would be a delightful and
vast bed with Egyptian cotton bedclothes and devilled
kidneys for breakfast, or it would be a sleeping bag and
a camp bed in a mildewed attic, with vast spiders and
anonymous scuttlings in the wainscotting to keep him
fearfully awake. But anything was better than having
to go back to a bad hotel across open water, so he let
Peregrine's burbling stream of optimism drift over
him. Coky too seemed to be staring into space, and
eventually perhaps Peregrine realised that he did not
have a fully attentive audience and ground to a halt.

Silence had reigned for a short while, when Peregrine
barked again.

'What about a PR campaign?' he suggested.

'I think we're beyond that now,' said Claypole flatly.

'Mm,' Coky added. 'As far as I can see we have seven
days to get together written material that persuades
Tommy Thompson and John Bruce that the wind farm
should be given planning permission.'

'Is John Bruce the guy with the specs?' said Claypole.
Coky nodded.

'What about the other woman? Helen something?'
asked Peregrine.

'MacDougall? Dead set against,' said Coky. 'We'll
never convince her, so there's no point in trying. Almost
as anti it as my mother.'

'Ah,' said Peregrine, with heavy significance.

Claypole's eyes narrowed. 'What do you mean,
"ah"?'

'Well, we have to change Bonnie's mind, I'm afraid. At least… a bit.'

'I don't follow.' Claypole looked at Coky, but she too was frowning.

Peregrine explained. When Peregrine inherited MacGilp House and the Garvach estate, two parcels of land were reserved in his mother's will for his two sisters. A temporary right-of-way was required over those two parcels of land in order to get the huge turbine towers and blades to the construction site. Peregrine had already drawn up legal papers to guarantee his sisters a generous annual sum for the privilege of being able to drive HGVs across their land – which had no other use – but the two sisters had yet to sign. Without those signatures, there could be no wind farm.

'Oh,' said Claypole.

'Yes,' said Peregrine gravely. 'I rather thought that they might talk to you. I don't see Dorcas much, and I haven't spoken to the wicked witch for a year.'

Coky blushed.

Claypole was engaged with the subject now. 'And they know how much they are being paid?'

'Yup.'

'But you still can't get them to sign?'

'Nope.'

'So… do they want more money?'

Peregrine hesitated. 'Honestly, I think they're just doing it to piss me off. Silly girls.'

The three of them sat in silence again.

'I'm off to bed,' said Coky quickly, and left the room with such speed that Claypole wondered if he had done something to offend her. But Peregrine seemed not to have noticed, and ploughed on.

'I'll do all the paperwork that Tommy Thompson

wants us to do, if you'll just... Well, do you think you could go and have a word with them?'

Claypole thought. He knew he was not the man for any job that required diplomacy and tact, but all he really wanted at that moment was to go to sleep for a long time – and would have agreed to anything that would get him to a bed faster.

Claypole stood up and stretched.

'Yeah. Probably. Can I sleep on it?' he said, yawning as pointedly as he could without overacting.

'Sure,' said Peregrine, beginning to turn out the lights. As they walked through the door to the kitchen, the old man clicked his fingers. 'How rude of me...'

Claypole waited for the invitation to stay, which must surely now be coming.

'You're welcome to borrow the old Land Rover,' said Peregrine, picking a small key off a peg. He threw it at Claypole, who failed to catch it.

'She's in the barn,' said Peregrine, yawning and handing Claypole a small torch. 'Coky just retuned her, so she won't give you any trouble. I'm off to bed.'

'What if I...?' Claypole could hardly believe he was going to be turfed out at this hour, but couldn't summon the words to try and suggest otherwise. His eyes were heavy from tiredness and whisky.

'Don't use the accelerator in reverse, though. And I'd avoid second gear altogether if you know what's good for you. 'Night 'night.'

The light in the kitchen went off, and Claypole had no choice but to head out to the barn, torch in hand.

In the 1970s the company that made the Land Rover was still owned by Brits, and they were old-fashioned engineers to the core. They loved the Land Rover and were the guardians of its heritage. This meant that, when the oil crisis of that era really struck home and the price of petrol doubled within three years, they had two reactions. First, they said to each other, let's make the new model drink even more petrol. Second, let's make the windscreen wipers just slightly smaller. Thus, the Land Rover Series III – of which Peregrine's was an example – is what the Series I and II were before it: a cheap and nippy tractor that breaks down much of the time, but is extremely easy to mend. Essentially, if you open the bonnet, squint at it, fiddle with a few things and strike it firmly with a spanner, it works again. Nothing like the modern Land Rovers – all German plastic and Japanese electronics – the old Land Rovers are stubborn iron horses that seem to run better if you drag them through seventeen types of shit first, then cover them in salt water and give them ten years rusting in a barn with hens laying eggs on the battery.

Claypole's journey had started well enough. He had been surprised to have found and started the Land Rover with little fuss. The odour inside the cab was challenging – manure and sheep dip – but he headed down the long drive of MacGilp House with the imminent prospect of flopping down in his room at the Loch Garvach Hotel, there to be unconscious for as long as he needed to be. And he rather liked the old Land Rover. The floor was rusted away beneath the clutch, making it drafty, but it bounced about on the road in a cheery way and made Claypole feel rather macho despite how chilly he was in his thin suit.

The mist came first, which turned to fog as he

descended the hill away from the house. He tried using the wipers but they succeeded only in smearing the windscreen, cracked and mildewed as it already was. The headlights he also found to be interestingly arranged. When the headlights were in 'dip' mode he got a very good view of the road for ten feet in front of the vehicle. But if he put them on full beam he could see only the top of the trees some 700 yards ahead.

Four minutes later, the rain came. It was smeary and feathery at first, then in spits, then great gobbets heralded a loud and constant blanket of water. Claypole even had to slow the car down to a crawl to see the road, and to prevent slurry from spouting up through the rusty clutch-hole. At a three-way crossroads, which he thought he recognised from his walk to the house, he turned left, because that was what he had done when coming the other way. A few hundred yards later, he realised that this had been quite the wrong thing to do. If he had turned left coming the other way, then on returning he should turn right. So he made a fifty-three point turn in a lay-by. He would turn right when he got back to the crossroads. Then he doubted himself, and thought he might have been wrong. Turning round again, he went back to where he thought the three-way crossroads now was, but when it did not appear he realised with horror that he was utterly confused. He could not even retrace his steps and was blinking into the driving rain in baffled paralysis.

After eeny, meeny, miney, mo, he decided just to continue on the road he was on, and took a left at a fork in the road half a mile later. It must lead somewhere, he thought. At least if I meet any wildlife, it won't stop me in my huge, safe steel box. I'll just carry on, over the fields, if necessary, killing everything. He would find the way to Garvachhead no matter what. For, as long as he had petrol, he could just... He looked at the gauge. Oh. He tapped it hopefully. The needle sank even further towards the dreaded 'E'.

It was twelve fretful and desperate minutes later that the Land Rover ran out of fuel and sputtered to a stop in a lay-by, the rain thrumming on the roof suddenly the only noise. For the next minute, even in the deafening rain, and even a hundred yards away, Claypole might have been heard, in profound and pointless rage, levelling the basest language at, and thumping with all his tubby might on, an unyielding Bakelite steering wheel. But there was no one for miles around.

When he had stopped bellowing, his first instinct (other than checking that his phone still had no reception) was to look at the engine, despite the whipping, drenching rain. How this would magically locate more fuel, he didn't know. But it was the only thing he could think of. The bonnet of the Land Rover had a massive spare wheel on top of it, and was fastened down with two large clasps. They clipped onto the body with rusted bolts that took all the strength in Claypole's weak fingers to prise away. He struggled to get the bonnet up when he had freed it from the clasps, and then had to prop it up with a piece of driftwood which was supplied just inside the engine for the purpose. He stared into the blackness below the bonnet and squinted at the steaming, muddy engine. Of course, he had absolutely no idea what he was looking for, and gave up before his underpants became the only article of his clothing that was not wet through.

He got back in the cab of the car and spent seven minutes trying to find some internal lights, which did not exist. During this time, his body heat – and possibly the swearing as well – had steamed up the entire cab. He couldn't see a thing out of the tiny windscreen, or any of the windows. When it abruptly stopped raining he got out again and stared into the woods. Could he just take a walk through them and rejoin the road? Then he had a vision of himself, born of a hundred video rentals, stumbling through the woods pursued by a nameless horror, eventually to be terrified to death and eaten. He would not be doing any more walking tonight.

With the sincerest possible dread, and still lightly dripping, Claypole looked in the back of the Land Rover. It contained some wisps of straw and what he assumed was sheep shit, a jerry can of diesel (unhelpful, as the Land Rover had a petrol engine, but Claypole supposed that he could always set light to it if hypothermia was imminent), a broken garden fork, three empty feed sacks, a plastic buoy and – yes! – a dog's blanket. He knew now that he would have to be his bed this night, and he gave a little sob and a sigh as he remembered that in his rucksack in a grim hotel room that seemed like a palace at that moment were the pills he was supposed to take every night for his diseased heart.

He decided that speed was of the essence. It might rain again at any moment. Remembering something from a men's magazine about how to construct a shelter in the woods, he thought that bracken would serve well as bedding below him, and the blanket, rank-smelling and covered in dog hair as it was, would have to perform as his duvet. He walked towards the grass verge and immediately fell on his knees into a ditch. The muddy water instantly soaked his legs, and he scrambled upright in silent panic and fury. He squinted around him in the darkness and saw that there was indeed bracken within reach. He grabbed angrily at a handful and yanked. The fern slipped through his hand, tearing the skin on his palms easily and deeply. He bellowed in pain. Wiping his muddy and bloodied hands on his shirt, he cursed that mere foliage could do so much damage and more carefully began to uproot a few more plants, getting himself more wet and muddy in the process. When he reckoned that he had enough bracken to make himself some sort of rudimentary mattress, he gratefully stowed himself in the back of the Land Rover.

After making his 'bed' and lying entirely still for twenty minutes, he drifted into a shallow doze. Just as he was beginning to feel that sleep might be aided if his feet were lower than his swelling head, Claypole heard the swish of tyres on the wet road. He could not have got up in time to flag the vehicle down, so he didn't move. Remaining motionless and longing for sleep or death, he pondered as the car slowed and passed that it was probably the only car that would pass this way until eventually the police discovered his putrifying body the following spring.

It began to rain again.

-6-

VIKTOR: Cheer up, Mac. You can't eat scenery.
Local Hero, written and directed by Bill Forsyth

There is a theory that if a person walks through a forest, they are bound to find the one thing in that forest that is not forest. It is not, the theory goes, a coincidence. It is a rule of forests. Or rather, it is because it is in the nature of people. Human instinct is the same now as it was 4,000 years ago. Dwellings and other things important to people are found in hollows, by rivers, or at sites where a well can be dug with ease, or at points where the visibility is best. So when you are walking through a forest, you will find the old burial sites, and the houses, or places where houses used to be, or where people used to look out for their sheep, or kept watch for Vikings. Just so long, that is, as you're not really looking for them. If you were to use a map, or have any kind of plan, you might well go wrong. The modern will is more powerful than the ancient instinct, and in any case this principle has been a little confused since people have started to build houses where they shouldn't be: on the sides of hills with no water, on flood plains and so on. Deliberately testing the boundaries of technology and ingenuity, perhaps – but in the last fifty years more from lack of space or the desire for profit. If this theory is to be believed, then, it was a good thing for him that almost nothing was going through Claypole's head as he wandered through the Garvach forest.

He had woken with a swollen and aching head. Having provided no insulation during the night, the thin glass windows of the Land Rover had, after sunrise, quickly heated the inside of the vehicle to a temperature that Claypole calculated was probably sufficient to boil small rocks. Having emerged from the Land Rover and given it a hearty kick, he drank from and washed his face in a dribbling but icy-fresh waterfall and braced himself to be hungry for a while before setting off along the rough road.

It was a pleasant morning. Warm enough to dry his ditch-soaked trousers and erase some of the more nightmarish memories of the night. He felt like he hadn't slept, but the total length of time he had lain awake wishing he were dead did not add up to the six hours which had elapsed. It struck him, as he gloomily stumbled along the road, the flies beginning to buzz around him, that what was clearly needed on one's wrist in the countryside was not a watch, but a distress flare.

He had been ambling uphill for about twenty minutes when he realised he was no longer on a road, but on a track which appeared to be narrowing. When the track became such that normal vehicles could clearly not pass along it, he considered turning back, but couldn't really see the point, even when the path just became gaps in the trees. He wasn't, after all, looking for anything in particular. Just some sign of civilisation.

Then he saw a house. At first heavily obscured by trees, as he quickened his pace he could see that it was whitewashed save for the black door, and that the Virginia creeper growing up it was huge but neat. The bowing roof was slated long ago but there were none missing, and as he got closer he saw that the house had two sash windows downstairs, either side of the door, and three upstairs, all with four panes of old and wobbly glass. It was a child's drawing of a cottage. He tripped uncomfortably down a bank and onto a road by the side of the house, hoping to find an entrance. Some sort of path up to the door, or a fence to guide you there. But there seemed to be none. All there was was garden. And what a garden. Vast swathes of untidy but clearly very productive vegetable patch was how he might have described it at first. But as he got closer he could see that the vegetables were not all vegetables. There were herbs and weeds and bushes too, all jumbled in with what looked like a thousand varieties of fruit and vegetables. Raspberries climbed over peas which stood over potatoes. Honeysuckle was trying to throttle a pear tree, which was partly shading a small patch of damp, shiny lettuces, untidily distributed between carrots and garlic. Great fat beetles nestled on the patches of wild flowers, reeds and grasses that towered unmown between these small oases of food, and bees hummed all around as Claypole stood marvelling. A hen clucked from beneath a juniper hedge, and Claypole jumped as he realised that he was just ten feet away from a pair of heavily breathing and watchful pigs, the other side of a wicker fence. It was as if the BBC had come in and spent a fortune on setting it all up for its biggest and baddest Jane Austen yet.

It was perfectly pretty, gloriously ancient, and surely impossible.

'If you want to talk about Jesus, you'd better come in!'

Claypole swivelled on his dusty heels. Heading towards him from the side of the house at a brisk pace was a woman of about seventy, with white hair in a tight bun and wearing a painter's smock and blue jeans. She smiled.

'I'm not –' he began.

'Oh, crikey,' said the woman.

She sniffed as she looked him up and down from a vantage point some three inches taller than Claypole. He was crumpled and filthy, his shirt bloody, his face dirty and his suit torn and stained. A mugged bank teller. He had no desire to have a conversation about Jesus, but if that's what it took to be able to make a phone call and get back to his life, then so be it.

'I –' he began, 'I'm… I'm not a… I'd be happy to have a chat about… If that's what you…' The woman looked aggressively healthy and her eyes were twinkling in a friendly and amused way. Claypole dropped his shoulders and said earnestly, 'I'm really lost.'

'Oh good,' the woman smiled, revealing some gold fillings among a fine white set. 'It's only ever the postie or Jehovah's Witnesses who make it up here normally. It seems rude not to talk to them if they've come all this way. But really,' she tutted. 'Poor fools. I expect you'd like some tea, at least.'

She pointed to the house and Claypole nodded grimly, clutching his back.

'Come along, then. There's some kedgeree too if you fancy. I'm Dorcas.'

As he drank two glasses of water and wolfed a

ham sandwich, they established that she was Dorcas MacGilp, older sister of Peregrine, and that he was Claypole.

'Ah. The wind farm chap.' Her tone was neutral.

'Yeah.'

'Is that your first name?'

'No.'

The air remained still.

'What *is* your first name? Or would you rather I called you *Mr* Claypole?'

Dorcas said this with a note of condescension. Even posh women, Claypole thought, might be expected to be a little wary of fat men in suits who come bumbling out of the woods. But she exuded the usual supreme self-confidence of her class.

'It's just Claypole,' he said.

To this, she reacted most unusually. Most people, in Claypole's experience, silently judged him when he said this, whether as a fool or a poseur, he did not care. But Dorcas just looked him in the eye, deep in scrutiny.

'Oh. Oh,' she said slowly. Claypole became uncomfortable with the length of time she was taking to examine him. 'How very curious,' she added.

Perhaps she detected his discomfort, because she snapped out of her close examination of his face and almost squawked at him, 'Tea first, or do you want to take your clothes off?'

Claypole's expression of alarm turned to confusion as he saw Dorcas's politely enquiring face. Then she giggled and punched the air near his arm.

'You silly arse. I meant do you want to get out of that poor, knackered suit? I have some men's clothing somewhere.'

While the kettle was boiling, and she was upstairs fetching him a change of clothes, Claypole examined his host's kitchen and living room. The kitchen was small, dark and cluttered. Dried flowers, copper pots and garden produce fought for space with various dishes covered with ancient tea towels atop a scrubbed pine table. The smell of baking bread pervaded, and the overall impression was one of wholesome chaos. The living room was equally batty, but in a way that Claypole had never seen before. There were books everywhere. Not just everywhere in the way that a normally literate person has books everywhere – shelves bulging, and shelves on most of the walls. The books in this room covered every available surface, including large swathes of the floor. Indeed, books *were* every surface. In places they were piled two feet, four feet, high. He did not have time to examine them before Dorcas returned through what must have been a stairwell, but looked like a hole in the books.

'Brr… Perhaps I could just make a phone call?'

'By all means. But who are you going to telephone?'

'Well,' said Claypole. 'I thought a… taxi?'

'Pff. Don't be daft. I'll take you wherever you need to go. Now sit.'

As he ate a large portion of blackberry and apple pie, he was presented with an ancient shirt for a man very much thinner than he, a woman's fleece (judging by the pastel pink colour and the faint floral aroma) and an old pair of jeans which had once belonged to Peregrine. The jeans would have to be rolled several times at the bottom, and the top button left undone. Dorcas presented him with an old Etonian tie as a belt with which to disguise this last necessity.

That made sense, he thought as he changed in the

downstairs loo. Of course Peregrine had been to Eton. All the old Etonians Claypole had met divided into two types. First, there was the wiry, ascetic, intellectual sort. They tended to run government departments, banks and embassies. They had clever but blunt wives called Clarissa. The second sort were generally good-looking as the result of the parental union of money and beauty, falsely demotic for the first twenty years of adulthood and snobbish thereafter. They also exhibited arrogance, apathy, and addiction in various proportions. Peregrine was Type 2.

When dressed and washed, Claypole took a moment to examine the photographs. There were many of Coky, and some of Dorcas herself, including her own retirement party from 'Garvachhead and District Arts Council' in which she was the only one not smiling. There was a sepia photo of a grim-looking couple – he in wartime RAF uniform – on some church steps. But most seemed to be of various chirpy and solid-looking women in anoraks at the top of hills. There was one of Coky at about seventeen – shyly laughing. But there were none, he noticed, of Bonnie Straughan, or of Peregrine.

Before going back to his host, Claypole stopped in front of a small mirror. He leaned forward, pulling back his wispy forelock. There was ginger showing next to his scalp, making the thin black strands of hair look almost purple. He needed to get hold of some more dye. He must betray his roots.

'I hope you don't mind, but I simply must have the Dubai Championships on,' said Dorcas as he entered the living room again, and she turned a knob on a television of deep antiquity nestled among the books. Before Claypole could wonder which sport was being played in this strange desert paradise-cum-hell, the TV came to life. It was snooker. He remarked pleasantly that he didn't know that the Dubavians were fans of snooker.

'I know some people find it boring,' she said. 'I think it's the best game in the world. Tension, tactics, natural talent that can only come good with a strong mind, and...' Dorcas gave a slight pout, 'young men in tight, shiny clothing. I think it's rather a shame that they don't wear black tie any more, but you can't have everything.'

As she made tea, Claypole picked up one of the many books that made up the coffee table. It was *The Essays of Michel de Montaigne*. He had heard of the man, but never read any of his work, and was having trouble placing him in any particular century. The spine was worn and the pages well thumbed. He picked up a volume of Dirk Bogarde's autobiography, with a post-card marking a page. The postcard was from someone called Terri, thanking Dorcas for a wonderful weekend and hoping that she enjoyed the 'naughty chocs'. Another was a reasonably reputable-looking biography of Michael Jackson, with biro in the margins. 'Thriller – showing violence + repressed homosexuality,' said one of the notes. 'Earth Song not messiah complex, but father complex,' said another. And with an increasing sense of unease, he picked up another book. It was seventeenth-century Persian poetry, with a translation into French. Dorcas came back into the room.

'I can't bear books on shelves. Too ordered. They just sit there, fossilised. One forgets about them. I like to have them around me all the time. Like friends who might surprise me. Is that pretentious?' She looked up and to the left, as if examining the ceiling for some lost item. Claypole wondered whether he should fill the silence. But she continued. 'Yes! Yes, it *is* pretentious. Of course it's a bugger to hoover. Perfectly good reason to invent the bookshelf.'

She put Claypole's mug of tea down. It teetered dangerously on a paperback of Thomas Hobbes' *Leviathan*.

'Ignore me. I'm an old fool,' she snorted in disgust. 'Do smoke.'

Claypole said that he only smoked at weddings. She nodded sadly.

'I gave up fags when John Lennon was shot. Can't think why, really. Just seemed like a good idea to mark it in some way.'

They sipped their tea and chatted. Claypole explained that he had broken the Land Rover somewhere over the hill, and told her, to clucks of sympathy, about the night and his bed of bracken and feed bags. Dorcas assured him that she had spare fuel for the Land Rover, and that they would head over there at some point. Claypole relaxed and said he was grateful.

'Oh, don't be. In fact, there is something you could do for me.'

Claypole was about to say that he would be happy to help in any way he could, but Dorcas was suddenly focused on something in the middle distance. Claypole felt uneasy.

'Yes!' said Dorcas, whacking her thigh. 'Jamie Daldry's just got through to the semis.' She sat up. 'He's my favourite. Drinks a lot, I think. He's got that skin.'

Following Claypole's gaze toward the fruitcake she had put on top of a Gore Vidal novel, Dorcas cut a slice and put it on a commemorative Edward VIII Coronation saucer. She turned off the television.

'Help yourself to more,' she said, and relaxed again into her faded purple easy chair. She flicked a switch and a footrest catapulted her feet upwards, and the back of the chair sloped backwards with a thunk. She was practically horizontal. She smiled at Claypole. 'Now then, dear,' she said. 'Who are you?'

The question was so direct that Claypole nearly choked on the sizeable portion of cake that he had just put in his mouth. She's lost her marbles, he thought. Living in the middle of nowhere, it was no wonder. He rallied as he dusted his fingers.

'I'm Claypole. I'm helping Peregrine with the wind farm.'

She cocked her head on one side. 'I know that. But who *are* you? Perhaps I should say… *why* are you doing that?'

'Well, I…' Claypole was flummoxed. But there was something irresistible about Dorcas MacGilp's manner that forced him to search for a non-evasive answer. 'I want to do a bit of good for the…' He almost choked on the word. 'Brr… planet.' He shrugged.

'Right.' She was impassive.

'I was asked by Coky Viveksananda – brr, your niece, in fact – to come up and be a sort of spokesman. Just for a bit. While I'm not doing anything else.' A fly was thinking of diving into Claypole's tea. He wafted his hand above the mug.

Dorcas tapped her lip with a forefinger. 'When I was a girl there were still tinkers – gypsies, you might call them down south – living in caves up here.'

Claypole's bewilderment was taken by Dorcas to be incredulity.

'Oh yes! They lived all up and down the peninsula, working on farms in the summer. And caves were the perfect place. There are lots of them along the coast. You can't be moved on from a cave, and they were otherwise unused. But it was a bleak existence, I'm sure. *They* had beds of bracken and straw. I'm pretty sure they would have dried the bracken out first, though. I expect that's why your back hurts.'

Claypole nodded. She pressed a button on the side of her chair and shot upright again. She stared at Claypole.

'Are you a bit of a gypsy, Claypole? A bit of a wanderer? Or are you just... as you said, lost?' Claypole's eyes widened. 'What are you doing this afternoon? Shall we have some fun?'

Claypole now wondered whether he could run faster than Dorcas. He was fat, and she was a pensioner. It might be close.

'Because,' she continued, 'if you're just farting about with my oafish brother talking "wind", then I have better things for you to do. I've got some manly stuff that needs doing around the garden, and it strikes me that you might need to connect a little. Up for it?'

Claypole smiled uncertainly.

⊸━●═━⊷

Dorcas's garden, as Claypole learned over the following eight hours, was organic. She had developed, over the thirty-five years she had been in the house, her own fusion of the biodynamic method and the principles of permaculture for growing her own food. Claypole had heard of neither. By the time they were sitting down at supper, he had heard all about it and, much to his astonishment, he hadn't been bored for even a moment.

The day had gone by quickly. Claypole had ineptly dug a drain and lugged the pigsty from one corner of the pen to another. He had then been seconded to duties requiring less muscle, and they had worked together. They had picked raspberries, during which she taught him which insects were helpful and which she encouraged away from the raspberries by putting something nearby that was more attractive to the bugs but inedible to humans. The same detail had been given about the vegetables, and the other fruit. The same principles of balance, with none of the destructive artifice of what Claypole thought of as normal gardening, seemed to apply easily to everything in the garden. All he could remember now were a few phrases that stuck in his mind. 'There's no such thing as a weed. Just a plant in the wrong place'; 'Nothing in a garden should be wasted. It's all useful for something'; and 'Don't get between a pig and his supper.' This last after Claypole had been catapulted into the mud, accompanied by Dorcas's throaty laughter.

The dinner itself was his reward, served to the accompaniment of Bach. They sat at her kitchen table in the warm evening light, eating pheasant and ham pie with dauphinoise potatoes, vegetables and two salads (carrot, raisin and pine nut; avocado, lettuce and cheese). The pheasant had been shot by Dorcas, and the pig (a half-sister of Claypole's sparring partner) raised on delicious slops from her kitchen and fruit from her trees. Almost everything else had been grown by her. Even the raisins were from her vines, and the avocados (small and nutty as they were) from her greenhouse. The cheese was from a farm across the loch, swapped for chutney. This was food as Claypole had never experienced. The tastes so fresh and bottomless, the smells so electric. He was relieved when she had dismissed the idea of going to get the Land Rover with a stern 'Tomorrow. You take the sofa.' He was delirious with physical tiredness and the purity of the indulgence.

'Gardening is done all wrong by most people,' said Dorcas, waving her knife about with a fig on the end of it. 'They priss about with flowers and chemicals, use too much equipment and additives bought from garden centres. And they *worry*. My God. Why would you *worry* about which plants are going to succeed and which will fail? It's all predetermined by the genetics and strength of the plant, the condition of the soil, the weather and the chaotic rules of natural selection. It is not your fault if your spuds have blight. It just happens.'

Claypole was nodding as he savoured a mouthful of powerful creamy cheddar with quince jelly, washed down with warm, dry cider.

'There's not much point in trying to prevent it or mend it – you'll just do more damage to something else – usually the soil. Just move on, as they say. Have a turnip instead.'

'Mm,' said Claypole, not doubting that Dorcas's cooking could turn even the tedious turnip into ambrosia.

'The key to gardening is to do as little as possible. I know we've worked hard today, but really there's no point in growing your own fruit and veg if it's a ghastly slog and a tyranny. Just weave ten minutes of it into your day. It should be like cleaning your teeth. If it's four hours on a Saturday, it's going to wreck your back and ruin your week.'

'I *am* a little stiff,' Claypole remarked, but he held no grudge.

'Generally gardening actually saves me time.'

'Nah. Really?'

'My word, yes.' She leaned back in her chair. 'Look, most people do a weekly shop for food, right? They come back from a soul-pilfering supermarket exhausted and irritated, and an awful lot poorer, with fifty plastic bags of over-engineered rubbish in vast amounts of packaging, and the whole thing has taken three hours and however many litres of petrol. I spend not more than two hours a week sorting out my food, and it's twenty yards from my back door. Keeps me fit, it's fun, and it... connects me with my plate.'

Claypole stiffened with doubt.

'That sounds a bit ripe to you? Well, let me tell you, you have no idea of the joy and fun involved in eating a tomato when you've reared it yourself from a pup.'

'I wouldn't know,' said Claypole.

'It's not just food – it's like a cosmic swallow of one's own effort. It's laughing at Time.' She was stabbing the air as Johann Sebastian stuck his spurs into the orchestra to giddy them up a bit. '"Yah!" you say. "I got you back!" For this moment, as I chew on this carrot, I defy the cosmic forces and I laugh at Death. I have ingested my own labour. I haven't exploited or inconvenienced anyone, I haven't had to give any of it away in taxes, or paid any heed to the Man. It's mine.'

Claypole watched as she refilled both of their glasses.

'I know I'm a mad old goat, but it comes down to this...'

She paused, sipping gently. He watched her lips, as his mind drifted.

'The environment is complicated. It's complicated, and it's very messy. But if you care, you have to get involved. Like you're about to do.' She pointed at Claypole's chest. 'You can't live in a city and hope everything's going to be OK. You have to go to the countryside, get busy and make yourself part of it. There is no such thing as *the* environment. There's just parts of it.'

'Yeah,' he said. Now Claypole was looking at her hair. She had taken it out of its bun, and it was spilling down her neck, jigging and bobbing – as animated as she was.

'Is that what you're doing here, Claypole, old bean?'

Once again, he didn't know how to answer.

'Because if it is, you have chosen an excellent place to do it.'

Mr Bach finished his work wisely and poignantly, and they sat for almost a minute without speaking.

'What the world needs,' said Dorcas gently, her eyes almost closed with thought, 'is a heart attack.'

'Eh?' said Claypole. The sinews of Dorcas's neck were straining back and forth as she spoke, creating valleys of soft flesh.

'Well, they say that people who have survived heart attacks tend to live longer than they otherwise would because they sit up and pay attention to their lifestyle. The world has had an economic heart attack, and everyone is rushing around trying to solve the problem. If the climate had a heart attack – say, five years of drought in America, or the whole of Antarctica suddenly melting – we'd all sit up and pay attention. But the fact is, few people have really suffered yet from climate change.'

'Mm,' said Claypole, distracted by the realisation that he had not taken one of Dr De Witt's pills for forty-eight hours now.

'No one we know, anyway. We all still eat and we pay our mortgages, and life goes on. Some poor farmer drowns in Bangladesh and nobody gives a ... Are you unwell?'

'Yeah. No.' He sat upright and blinked. 'Just a bit...'

'Shall I open a window?'

'Brr. Thanks.'

'Better still,' she said, picking up her glass and slapping the table. 'Let's go and watch the snooker.'

In the living room, the cider drum by his side, and surrounded by all the printed wisdom of the polymath Dorcas MacGilp, Claypole kept his eyes fixed on his host. While she was pronouncing at the television about the virtues of some older player's safety play, he wondered what older women think when they come across a younger man. They've seen all the idiocy before. They might find it charming, and they might not. But at least an older woman wouldn't take it personally and would recognise that it is just the way of the world. He looked at Dorcas's profile too as she watched the television intensely. There was more than the remnant of good looks there. She had preserved herself very well, on top of what he suspected were a genetic hand of cards that it would be hard to match. The lairds of Garvach had no doubt picked the prettiest and strongest girls on Loch Garvach for hundreds of years, and the result was Darwin's wet dream.

'Are you a lesbian?' blurted Claypole. This surprised both of them, and they fixed eyes. There was a pause.

'I was a late starter,' she said quietly. Then she smiled. 'My first was at twenty-nine. Harriet Marriott. Stupid name. Lovely woman. Had a slight moustache. I think that's what I first liked about her. The moustache. We rented a cottage near Penrith and read each other poetry. No sex, of course. We assumed that couldn't be done. This was the sixties, after all, and nice girls didn't know about that sort of thing. We just cuddled, made elderflower champagne and didn't think beyond the weekend.'

The room had taken on an atmosphere of breathless intimacy. Claypole waited a discreet moment, and then asked how the affair had ended. Dorcas gave a sigh before answering.

'I thought I missed my previous boyfriend. I said I was going shopping in London and didn't come back. I wrote her a letter. Pretty cowardly really. The letters back from her dried up after she married a widowed diplomat called Charles Petty and moved to Corfu.'

The room breathed out. Dorcas continued.

'Must have been a relief to change her name, I suppose. But Hetty Petty isn't a vast improvement.'

Claypole decided to remain quiet.

'There were others. And men too... I'm too old now.'

'Surely not. You're a very...' Claypole's sentence got caught in his throat. She looked back at the snooker. He took a sip of cider and shook his head. 'What about... May I ask you about Coky?'

Dorcas didn't look at him.

'Well, she was gay for a while...'

'Oh, I didn't mean...' But he trailed off. 'Really?'

'One or two terms at university, I think. The only thing she could say about it was "women are no better at having honest relationships with women than men are." I agreed. She's been out with a few men in the past, but... She doesn't seem to be able to get over her natural caution. She was careful only to pick nice ones – but then none of them were very interesting. I suppose lots of girls have that problem these days.'

'These days?'

'Well... in my day, girls just fell in with some chap who didn't look like a waiter when he wore a dinner jacket, and if they discovered that they both had a fondness for red setters, that was that. I didn't go that way, obviously, but a lot of my friends did.'

She looked into the fire as she continued.

'They were all so young when they got married. So young. By the time they realised that there's a big old world out there, they couldn't remember how to be on their own.'

'Brr.' Claypole too was staring into the fire now, cuddling his cider.

'With her parents, it doesn't surprise me that she's...' Dorcas trailed off.

'Yeah,' said Claypole, trying to scoff. Then he asked, 'Why? What are her parents like?'

'Her father is a yogi in Los Angeles. Never sees her, and hardly ever has. Too busy imparting the benefits of being unmaterialistic to Californians at 200 dollars an hour. Angus Straughan, Bonnie's husband, died some years ago. He was a thoroughly nice, very dull man, and sweet to Coky. Can't think what he was doing with my sister.'

'I've met her,' said Claypole, his face registering disgust.

'Yes, well, there you go,' said Dorcas.

They sat for a while, the snooker greenly flickering.

'Right,' said Dorcas, and clapped her hands together as she sat up. 'Martin Chang's playing like a dick. High time we watched something improving.'

Claypole had seen *Braveheart* once before. He couldn't remember a great deal about it except that some of the later scenes were quite gory. Dorcas claimed to have seen it over a hundred times.

'Mind if we skip the first hour?' she said. 'The battles are the best bits.'

Claypole shrugged.

'So. William Wallace has rallied the Scots against the English oppressors. He's taken it personally because an English soldier killed his rather simpering wife. The Scottish nobles are divided, and while they dither he has a vision of justice for Scotland, which appeals to the common folk enough for them to fight for him. Or rather, as Wallace says, to fight for themselves. Battle scene coming up.'

She pressed play on an old VHS recorder, and they watched.

After a few shots of hillsides and men with weapons gathering together and making flippant remarks, Mel Gibson, mulletted and woden, rode a skittish nag up and down a line of mutinous Scots. Claypole glanced at Dorcas. She was transfixed, her eyes wild and moist. He smiled and placed his head back on the armrest of the sofa. He was almost horizontal.

'Everyone in Scotland has seen this film,' she said quietly as she watched. 'It made a big impact when it came out. It's one of the main reasons people vote for the Nationalists.'

Gibson was now bellowing in his Australian-Scots accent, swivelling his horse to and fro in front of the blue-faced hordes.

'They may take our lives,' yelled Mel, his voice taking on a stagey quality, like a man who knows that if he were actually to shout as loud as he wishes to give the impression he is shouting, his voicebox would splinter into a thousand pieces. 'But they will never take...' Here a pause, hardly discernable – the length of time it

takes a man to swallow an emotion. '… our freedom!'
The mob roared and rattled their weaponry.

A lone tear burned its way hotly out of Dorcas's eye.
She wiped it away quickly, and did not turn her head
from the television.

'I'm a silly billy,' she sniffed. 'But it gets me every
time.' She dabbed her eyes again. 'Anyway, that'll do.
Time for bed.'

Dorcas looked over at her guest and got slowly up
from her seat. She hovered over him, staring, for a
moment. Then, covering him with a duvet, and before
she turned the lights off and went to her own bed,
she whispered in the direction of Claypole's sleeping
form.

'Celibate,' said Dorcas quietly. Claypole stirred,
but did not wake. 'That's the word I was trying to
remember. Coky's decided to be celibate.'

-7-

Tha dragh anns an t-saoghal.

There is trouble in the world.
Teach Yourself Gaelic, Robert Mackinnon

Claypole woke among the silent books and the dusty sunlight in Dorcas MacGilp's sitting room and stared at the ceiling. He wondered whether he had ever spent so comfortable a night. The sofa's old springs and cushions had cradled him perfectly. The duvet that Dorcas had given him was vast and thick, excluding all draughts. But above all he had been *physically* tired. The echo of this novelty – the faint buzz in the limbs and the heaviness in his back – was still there as he got up and tried in vain to restart the fire in the grate. Frustrated that he would make such a poor arsonist, he went into the kitchen feeling instinctively that he was alone in the house even before he found the note.

While Claypole slept on sofa bed,
His broken truck was fetched and fed.
Niece Coky now suggests he come

123

And find the beach known as Glen Drum.
Behold! The aunt has drawn a map,
That he may find it *sans* mishap.
But first we must insist he break
His fast. Therefore, consume this cake.

Claypole read the note twice, and then put the map and a slice of fruitcake in his pocket. Although it was a little breezy for a day at the beach, there was a frisson of mystery in the note that he could not resist. Why had Coky summoned him to the beach? Might he get to see her in a swimming costume? He appropriated one of the many preposterous hats that hung in the hall of Dorcas's cottage and headed out to find the old Land Rover, keys inside and fuel a-plenty.

Cajoling the Land Rover along at a more sedate pace this time, he felt more than anything like optimistic flotsam. He thought a third disastrous journey in a row statistically unlikely and was almost cheery. He found Glen Drum using Dorcas's excellently drawn map and guided the Land Rover down the pitted and difficult track that would have tortured and killed any normal car. Walkers heading in the same direction had to stand out of his way, all carrying bags and cases of various kinds. They regarded him with what he initially thought might be suspicion, but soon realised was envy. So he offered a lift to a pregnant woman walking alone, and struck up a chat in the hope of finding out what was going on down on the beach.

It was a festival of sorts, but for just 150 invited souls. It had even been given a jokey name, Lochstock, in emulation of or homage to the first great music festival in New York State in 1968. Drinking, dancing and music would be taking place in the evening, according to the pregnant woman. But until then there would be food and chatting, with games for children, and swimming and fishing in the loch.

'It's just for locals,' said the woman, glancing sideways at Claypole. 'Lachlan doesn't want it to become a big thing.'

'Who's Lachlan?' asked Claypole.

The woman – nose-ring, rainbow-patterned sweater, name of Jade – described an interesting-sounding figure. About forty, Lachlan Black had no family other than the half-dozen or so friends and floaters he gathered around him at his encampment here on Glen Drum beach in a fluid sort of commune. Some would just come for a month, but others had been there for ages. When someone left, whether for work or to go surfing in Spain, they would always be replaced, although there were never more than half a dozen camper vans there at any one time. But Lachlan was the constant. He was there all year round, and had been for two years.

'I thought the guy at MacGilp House... I thought he owned this land,' said Claypole, not wanting to appear too friendly towards Peregrine in case Jade were hostile to him, or to ownership in general. She looked like she might be.

'He does,' said Jade, and proceeded to dish some first-class gossip, with some relish.

Peregrine had regarded the encampment initially with amusement. He openly regarded the campers as indolent, damaged and weird, but essentially benign. But when he learned that they collected somewhat cultishly under the wing of this Lachlan Black, he asked them to move on. Lachlan's response was to take two bottles of wine up to MacGilp House one rainy afternoon and request an audience. He emerged late that night with an understanding from Peregrine that they could stay on the beach as long as they didn't have wild parties or cause any litter or destruction. Lachlan's campers were immaculate, and the beach was in fact cleaner than it had been for decades. But they were keen on celebration. Thus, one wild party later, Lachlan had had to perform the same trick following a threatening letter from a law firm in Edinburgh stuck to the windshield of his camper van. This time, Lachlan knocked on the door of the big house with a bottle of cask-strength whisky of great vintage that had cost him a hundred pounds, and a bag of intensely transportative marijuana, and reprieve was again granted. To his camp-mates' surprise, Lachlan himself also began working for Peregrine, performing menial jobs on a part-time basis. The work became more skilled in nature as Peregrine discovered that Lachlan was both a competent mason and an excellent carpenter. But the bargain wages remained immutable, and Lachlan knew that becoming indispensable was the key to continuing the ad hoc tenancy of the beach.

Claypole wondered aloud how the woman knew all this.

'Oh,' she said, 'I live here.'

'Ah,' said Claypole.

'And also,' she said with pride, 'Lachlan is my lover.'

'Ah.' Claypole had never known anyone refer to their 'lover', and felt as bourgeois as life insurance.

'So… if you don't know Lachy, how come you're here?'

'Coky,' he said. 'Coky Viveksananda?'

'Oh,' said the woman, and stared straight ahead.

They came to a hand-painted sign that read 'SLOW

– Children and Daft Hippies', and Claypole drove at a crawl over the last hill before the grand sandy sweep of Glen Drum beach came into view.

Claypole had been to the Glastonbury Festival only once. He seemed alone in his generation in having put off going there for the first time until he was thirty. Many of his contemporaries had been going every year since they were at school. He had gone with some ex-colleagues from the BBC, and the enjoyment was rather muted. Not that any of them disapproved of taking drugs and getting drunk. They worked in television, after all. But the senior BBC people insisted on referring to it as a 'bonding experience', rather than a good time – which made it neither. Claypole had spent many hours talking to a bosomy Senegalese poet called Dolly, but she had moved off with a lot of men called Julian who barged into people when they danced, barked about how 'arbsolutely wickud' their yurts were, and worried publicly whether yobs were going to break into their 4x4, clearly under the impression that this was their own private party. He felt choked, not by Dolly's rejection, but by the volume of people, the overpowering smell and the very public brand of fun that everyone else seemed to be so effortlessly enjoying. Claypole concluded that he didn't like festivals. Mass humanity and shared experience might be a thing of joy in theory, but in practice it was a pain in the neck because it shared space.

Lochstock was not Glastonbury. There was music and food and bustle, but the people were utterly dwarfed by the landscape. The beach held the choppy loch as if in the vast head of a spoon, and was itself made to look small by the surrounding wilderness. On one side was low but dense forest, on another side peaty bog, and behind was rocky heathery outcrop. It was low tide, and there were many expanses of pure yellow sand. Claypole glanced around the horizon. There were no houses visible, no roads and no signs of technology save for the half-dozen camper vans, a few clusters of tents and now his Land Rover. The sea too was an empty green, sparkling in the sun. No human could possibly stumble across this scene unless they had been invited to come. This was an intimate party, but one conducted in infinite space. Claypole looked at the faces as they drew nearer. None of them was doing anything other than smiling. The musicians were smiling; the children dancing in front of them were smiling; the people cooking food over open fires were smiling; and even people aimlessly milling about were smiling. There was no fashion, and certainly no uniform. Some of the women were wearing luminous lycra, some long floating dresses, and some were wearing wellies and raincoats – there was even one in a wetsuit. The men were no more homogeneously dressed – there were some in jeans and jumpers, others in safari shorts and sweatshirts, and one man in a boiler suit. Claypole felt that here, even in ill-fitting cast-off jeans held up by a tie, a pink fleece and a flat cap of vivid green checks with a large fishing fly attached to the side, he would not stand out.

He pulled the creaking handbrake up on the Land Rover and was pleased to see Coky approaching.

'Hey, Gordon,' she called. She was wearing, to his disappointment, a large poncho and a black skirt down to her ankles.

'Heigh-ho,' he said, jumping out of the car. It was not something he was used to saying. In fact it might have been something he had never said before in his life.

'Heigh-ho yourself,' Coky chirped mockingly. Then she caught sight of the woman in the passenger seat. 'Hi, Jade.'

'Coky,' said the woman, who promptly got out of the vehicle and wandered off. Claypole noted that Jade had not thanked him for the lift. He was about to comment to Coky when he received a shock. Arriving at Coky's side was the dark-haired man who had made the threatening gesture at Claypole at the community hall in Garvach. Claypole took a step back. But the man was smiling in greeting.

Coky said, 'Claypole, this is Lachlan, chieftain of the beach. Laird of Lochstock.'

Lachlan thrust out a hand and Claypole took it with caution. The grip was firm to the point of violence.

'Hullo,' said Lachlan with a glower.

'Oh, I... Yes, I gave your... wife a lift down here...' Lachlan's face was blank. 'Across the fields...'

Lachlan's smile turned slightly sour. 'She's not my wife.'

Coky smirked, but left Claypole to dig himself out.

'Oh, no,' said Claypole. 'She said... That wasn't the word she... Congratulations on the baby...' Coky was almost grinning now.

'Aye.' Lachlan looked into space. 'Not mine.'

'Right. Brr. Anyway, I've... Nice turn out for the...' Claypole gestured at the partygoers.

'Mm-hm,' said Lachlan. 'We have a party here every full moon. But this is the biggest yet.'

'Oh right. Is that a religious thing?' Claypole tried to sound sincere and credulous. Lachlan looked at him with amusement.

'We just find we can see better. After dark.' The pause drifted on as all three looked at their feet. Then

Lachlan said quickly, 'Excuse me. I've got a lot of tofu to defrost,' and Coky and Claypole watched him leave.

'He was at the meeting the other day,' Claypole began in an excited whisper. 'He...'

But Coky wore a puzzled expression, and Claypole thought better of explaining the finger-across-the-throat gesture.

'He's fine,' she said defensively. 'He doesn't approve of the wind farm. But this is his party, and he won't spoil it. He's far too polite.'

'Brr,' said Claypole.

'Hey. Enjoy yourself. Do you want me to guide you around? Introduce you to a few folk?'

Claypole scratched his head and squinted at the sun. 'I'll just drift around for a bit, and come and find you when I'm...'

'Oh. OK,' said Coky, and began to retreat awkwardly.

'I met your aunt,' he called after her.

'Yeah,' she said. 'She liked you.'

For the next four hours, Claypole drifted about, determined neither to be bored, nor to resort to seeking Coky's company. He began ill at ease, but tried some tentative conversations. He talked to the man in the boiler suit about oyster farming, and a blonde in an anorak who informed him how to convert a diesel generator to run on chip fat. Then he had a chat with twin brothers. One made drystone walls, and the other was a forester, and they talked over each other. All of them, on hearing of his business in Loch Garvach, gave him their opinions on the subject of wind farms. Then he helped the couple in charge of the barbecue with the logistics of getting 150 people fed, which occupied the time nicely. They were called Joy and Evan, which

Claypole refrained from making a joke about. For that, and for his efforts at the grill, he was awarded a venison steak in a bun and licence to make free with the home-brewed beer. Evan came and sat next to him.

'How was the venison?' asked Evan.

'Delicious,' Claypole enthused.

'Normally these parties are strictly vegetarian. But this was roadkill, so we allow it. Found it on the road. Some idiot had driven over it a lot, but we still got some meat off it.'

As Claypole drank a sea-cooled beer, he watched some children playing in the shallows of the loch. They had invented a game that was a cross between football and water-polo, and it was fun until a girl of nine cut her foot on a razorfish shell. He was relieved when Coky found him again, but tried to appear nonchalant.

'Hi,' she said. 'Do you like mushrooms?'

He said that he didn't object to them, but he had just had a venison burger.

'No, no,' she said, lowering her voice. '*Magic* mushrooms?'

He said he didn't know, having never had any.

'I don't do them any more, but don't let that stop you. Milky says these ones are brilliant.'

In a green camper van, Lachlan was sitting over a calor-gas stove examining a gently boiling saucepan of dark liquid. He did not look up when Claypole and Coky entered. Also staring into the pan was the tall bearded man who had been standing with Lachlan outside the Loch Garvach Hotel. He gave the man a guarded nod.

'That's Milky,' said Coky.

'Claypole,' said Claypole.

'Come on, Milks,' said Lachlan, 'chop chop.'

'It's ready,' said Milky gloomily, and began to dole out the brew into plastic beakers. Lachlan pressed a button on an old stereo, and an ominous and heavy bass beat filled the van.

Claypole looked around for a seat, but opted for leaning against a cupboard. He was presented with a pint or so of black steaming cocktail. He sniffed and recoiled.

'What's... what's in it?' he asked, as nonchalantly as he could.

'Mushies, red wine, cloves, honey and brandy,' said Milky. 'My own recipe.'

'What kind of red wine?' asked Claypole, and wished he hadn't. Not losing face was going to be difficult. He was nervous. He had smoked dope a few times at university, and found himself being hopelessly giggly and then sick. He had also taken a tab of ecstasy once but it had turned out to be a dud.

'Doesn't matter,' said Milky. 'It's boiled.'

Claypole looked at the cup again. He saw something bobbing about in it, and dipped his finger in to try and retrieve it, wondering if he could demur from drinking. It was at once slimy and gritty. He looked at Coky, who smiled reassuringly. Then he saw Lachlan trying to suppress amusement. This instantly angered him. Why should this impudent beanpole, this crusty wood-sprite, have knowledge that he did not? How dare he assume the position of superiority? Claypole had drunk champagne with an ITN newsreader, for God's sake! Thus, with a mental holding of the nose, he drank. He didn't quite know what he was expecting – instant transportation to Narnia? – but he definitely wasn't expecting it to taste nice. And yet it did, almost.

A sweet, alcoholic, musty mud. His eyebrows saluted appreciatively.

'Not bad, eh?' Milky showed his crooked and blackened teeth.

'It's... awright,' agreed Claypole, giving his own toothless smile.

They all swigged and appreciated the brew. Then Lachlan looked at his watch.

'Anyway,' he said. 'it's a party drug. We need to be outside, with people.' And the men all drank up.

Outside the van, night had not yet arrived, but the sun was doing no more than lurking somewhere out of sight. The children had mostly disappeared, and it was now the adults who were running about and laughing. And there was dancing. The four of them – Lachlan, Milky, Coky and Claypole – headed instinctively for the bonfire, which now raged and lit up the rocks and the grass. The vans and tents had miraculously formed a circle. If there were Injuns to repel, Claypole mused, it would be done.

He sat on a bale of hay and watched the fire and the dancing. Coky placed a fresh beer in his hand, although she did not have one herself. The dancing was free-form, with head-waggling and twisting open palms that told of the influence of *bangra*. But there was also a Scottish twist to what some of the dancers were doing. There was the occasional clap, and some were twirling each other, or jigging briefly with their arms in the air and their knees pointing east and west. This was an echo of something more structured – a nine-teenth-century formality that seemed out of context. It reminded Claypole instantly of something. Some scene of distant pain, but he couldn't fix the memory in time or place. His head was beginning to feel light.

'You like that stuff?' he asked Coky.

'What?'

'It looks like Scottish country dancing,' he said, and sipped beer nervously.

'Uh-huh.' Coky was swaying to the music, but she looked very sober.

'You know how to... do it?' he said, and looked at her.

'Yeah. Love it. But it's tainted,' Coky said sadly.

'Eh?'

'Class.' Coky was now looking at Lachlan, who had suddenly thrown himself into a dance with the chip-fat-van woman Claypole had met earlier. There was no sign of Jade the Lover. 'Only posh people know how to dance, because only posh schools kept teaching it through the seventies, eighties and nineties. Then the Nationalists realised that only English people knew about Scottish culture, and all Scottish kids knew about was American culture. So they started teaching the Eightsome Reel again in primary schools. But anyone of our age who knows how to dance a Reel of the Fifty-First is immediately identifiable as posh. Or English. I'll teach you some time.'

He smiled, terrified.

'Ach,' she said, her Scottishness leaking out. 'But not now, eh? Having too much of a good time!' They watched as a heavy man in a fluorescent witch's hat slipped on some seaweed.

'Do you think you'll stay here? In Scotland?' he asked.

But before she could answer, they were joined by Milky, who sat down on a hay bale.

'You're the windy man,' Milky said gloomily.

'Yup,' said Claypole.

'Lachlan doesn't like wind farms.'

'Right.' Claypole tried to will Milky away, but the man had no antennae.

'Says they kill birds.'

'Oh yeah?'

'Yeah. He'd like to get a proper job as an ornithologist. But... casual work is all he can get right now. Criminal record, see.'

Claypole's eyebrows rose. Coky patted him on the arm and moved off.

'Nothin' bad,' continued Milky. 'Bit of community service. Pickin' up condoms and Lilt cans off the A83.'

Claypole coughed as he watched Coky go. 'What did he... er...?'

'Motorin' offences. Didn't pay.'

'God. And they gave him community service for that?' Claypole was genuinely shocked. Was the system in Scotland so much more draconian than in England?

'Four hundred and eighty-three fines totalling £31,095.'

Claypole's brow crinkled. Milky sighed as they both watched Lachlan, who had stopped dancing and was now sitting opposite them, out of earshot.

'He had this scam. Dreamt it up in the pub. It was brilliant. He would say he was driving other people's cars and was responsible for their tickets. Speedin', parkin' and that. They give him the money for the fine, plus ten quid, or a pack of fags, and he'd take care of the fine for them.' He sucked his teeth. 'But he just kept the money. Never paid the fines. All caught up with him.'

'I...' Claypole didn't know what to say.

'Yeah. He's a genius, really.'

During the previous five minutes, Claypole had become aware of a gentle and tickling paranoia. He now had a feeling of light but unshiftable dread, and he realised that the drugs were beginning to take effect. As Milky talked about something or other, Claypole felt some physical symptoms begin. It started in his knees. They became tender, as if the patella and the joint behind it were still notionally under his control, but now had the consistency of a thin stew. This stage did not last long. Shortly, even Milky had stopped talking, and was just staring into the fire. Claypole was suddenly feeling warmed and chummy. He shifted on the hay bale and found that he was perfectly comfortable despite the slight chill of the wind. Incongruously, he found himself thinking of his first car – wondering where it was now. Then he looked around the fire, and decided that they were all quite nice faces and deserved more study. He stood up, then couldn't remember why he had stood up, and sat down again. He began massaging his eyebrows, then his ears.

'Oh yes,' said Lachlan loudly from across the fire, and closed his eyes in reverie.

The next ten minutes for Claypole were spent trying not to laugh at inappropriate times and trying not to wipe his face with his hands as much as he wanted to. He also found he had incredibly itchy shins, and was scratching them with ursine vigour when Coky arrived at his side. He stood up again and wobbled.

'Wotcher,' she said grinning. 'Got any colours yet?'

He looked at her with blind panic as he realised that everything was slightly purple.

'Oh dear.' Her voice was genuinely concerned. 'OK, sit down.'

He did so. She said something Claypole could not hear

to Milky, who came immediately to Claypole's side.

'Listen to me, and listen carefully,' said Milky. He was woozy, but emphatic. Claypole's eyes swivelled and focused on Milky's long, hairy face. 'You are now on a trip. You need to give in to it. If you fight it, it might cause trouble for you. Nothing very bad, but it just won't be any fun. Don't drink any more. Shoulders back, breathe deeply.'

Claypole nodded.

'No, I mean it. Do it,' said Milky.

Claypole breathed deeply and straightened his back. He was still nervous, but he did feel slightly better. So he did it again.

'You should be reassured,' Milky continued in a lulling monotone. 'People have been taking mushrooms for thousands of years. Egyptians, Romans, everybody. Nothin' bad happens. Or at least, nothin' bad will happen *here* 'cos I know what I'm doin'. Psilocybin, which is the active ingredient in the mushrooms, is a psychoactive, or psychotomimetic, substance. This means that it will alter your consciousness. If you are in a bad mood, or you resist, the consciousness that you are brought into will jar with the natural order of things.'

Claypole nodded, not able at that moment to register that he thought Milky to be full of crap.

'Good. Now that you are not in charge, does that make you feel better?'

Claypole blinked.

'You're confused. That's OK. Let's us… Let me put it another way…' Milky was beginning to slur his words. 'You are not in control of this. You can't be. The drug is takin' over. You're still you, but you're you… on a journey.'

Claypole shifted in his seat. His palms were sweating. He said nothing.

'So, on this journey... does it matter to you that you are not driving?'

Even in this state Claypole could understand that this was a metaphor. He nodded and shook his head at the same time. Out of the corner of his eye, he could see that Lachlan had started to rock back and forth.

'Or... no, wait... does it matter to you that you are not the car?' Milky seemed satisfied. 'You just, ay, um... get acquainted with the High. Know what I mean?'

Claypole nodded, his jaw now stupidly slack. 'Will I see things?'

'Nah. I doubt it. I haven't given you enough. No one needs pixies and elves running about the place. But it should be interestin'.'

It was now just the four of them – Lachlan, Coky, Milky and Claypole – sitting on these hay bales. Everyone else was dancing. Suddenly, Lachlan was on his feet.

'I am Lailoken!' he shouted. The others, including some of the dancers, looked at him with detached curiosity. 'I am the Merlin of the North!'

'Oh God,' muttered Claypole, and received a pat on the shoulder from Milky.

'I roamed the forests and the glens in the days before Union,' Lachlan intoned. 'Before the Tweed met the Powsail. Before the English came!'

Claypole whispered to Milky. 'Is this normal?' Milky nodded.

'I am the prophet, and I roam in penance for the battle I caused! When I meet Kentigern in the wilderness, he will forgive me!' There were sprays of spittle as Lachlan roared.

'Come on,' said Coky, getting up, and tapping Lachlan on the shoulder. 'Time to get you to a bed.'

'If Gwendolen shall marry again, I shall kill the bridegroom. I shall kill him...' Lachlan smiled manically and fixed his glare now on Claypole, who shuddered. '... with a stroke of the antler to his heart.'

Coky had put an arm around Lachlan to help him. Lachlan looked at Claypole and, unseen by Coky, gave a look of surprise. There was a note of something else. Was it triumph? Claypole pretended not to notice. Inside, he was burning.

"Night, Claypole,' said Coky. And suddenly, Lachlan and Coky were gone, stepping into Lachlan's van.

Claypole gawped dumbly at Milky, who was in the throes of discourse.

'Of course, with some kinds of 'shroom you're strapped to the front of the Starship Enterprise for a couple of hours. Take the Venezuelan Redcap, for example...'

Claypole sighed as he looked behind him at the Land Rover, and beyond it to the black fields that led towards civilisation, unlit by the hidden moon. He was incapable of driving, and there was no way he was going to walk, or spend another night in the reeking car. With another, deeper sigh, Claypole knew that his fate was to stay up with Milky, at least until dawn. And Milky droned on.

'... The Bavarian Blackbonnet is a very different sort of mushroom, though...'

Claypole's eyelids felt heavy. But his fate was as inescapable as the blackness of the night, and as tragic as stolen love.

-8-

It is not uncommon for a seer's prediction to come to be applied to the prophet himself... Legend is fluid stuff.

The Lore of Scotland: A Guide To Scottish Legends, Jennifer Westwood and Sophia Kingshill

On waking, Claypole rejoiced briefly that he was not too hungover, before gloom descended as he remembered Lachlan and Coky disappearing into the van. He struggled onto his side in a borrowed all-weather sleeping bag. The morning light had a washed-out quality, but still it stung his eyes. Bottles and cans lay in clusters by the fire, which was still smouldering in a shallow, grey pyramid with some blackened logs lying on its outskirts. Tents billowed in the breeze, and a few people were stirring, either in their tents in low murmurs, or bumbling about quietly outside – cleaning their teeth in the burn, or putting on boots and coats. A tall man in a clean green t-shirt approached the fire carrying a large pot. Claypole saw that it was Milky, still with his beard, but now with a shaven head.

'Porridge'll be a little while,' said Milky, and placed

it by the side of the fire. With an expert series of kicks and fumbles, he caused the fire to come back to life. Then he looked at Claypole and giggled.

'Oops,' he said, and nodded at Claypole. 'Chilly night?'

'It was awright, but –' Claypole had stopped speaking. He had run his hands through his hair, but it was missing. His head too had been shaved. Milky giggled.

'Did you forget?' he said.

Claypole was speechless, and took a minute to do anything. He took his phone out of his jacket pocket. No reception, three voicemails and a text message. But he wasn't interested in the communications. He wanted to see his reflection in the dark screen. And there it was. Ginger stubble patchily bloodied where someone had shaved him badly, but otherwise he was bald.

'What the f… Brr. Brr.' Claypole took a moment. 'Did you do this?'

'No, man,' said Milky, looking hurt. 'You did.'

Lolling backwards with a sudden ache, Claypole longed for London. He longed for the Metropolitan Line's stagnant and ancient pong, its rattling carriages and interminable delays. He longed for a latte with an extra shot of espresso and a vanilla and chocolate shot to catapult him into a humming and airless office with its mindless chatter and hateful lighting. He longed to be normal. To spend the day manoeuvring for a position he didn't want, and grasping more money so that he could spend it on frivolous crap at the weekend in order to dull the terrible sense that his life was rapidly disappearing. Oh to be sipping an expensive cocktail in Soho on a Thursday night, dodging angry addicts in doorways, and arguing with Somalis over the taxi fare home! He wanted the grey, humid lung that is London in August to breathe him in and never breathe him out.

Instead, his newly nuded head throbbed with dehydration and cold. His socks itched his feet from not having been removed. The sleeping bag was cold and damp on the outside, hot and damp on the inside. He wrestled himself upright and out of the sleeping bag. He breathed in a lungful of what ought to have been healthy sea air and got instead a heavy whiff of sheep shit and seaweed that made him gag. He put his hand in something damp and squishy in the mossy grass, cursed quietly and wiped his palm on what he thought was a patch of clean grass but was in fact something even more squishy and disgusting.

'Morning.' Coky's voice, far off.

Claypole followed Milky's gaze to the back of a camper van, from which Coky was emerging, her black hair tangled and delicious. He returned his gaze to the fire. He threw a nearby empty orange juice carton onto the ashes, and it swelled ominously before giving a heavy pop and fizzing into flame. Coky arrived at the fire, hugging herself against the cold.

'Porridge,' she observed, and then caught sight of Claypole and his shaven head. 'Oh.'

'Brr' was all that Claypole could manage.

'It looks... good, actually,' she said. Claypole said he didn't believe her, but he could not help being heartened.

Claypole helped Milky put a couple of heavy logs onto the fire, and they hauled a large wire mesh over the top of it so that the vast saucepan could be positioned on top. They sat, and Claypole examined his phone to avoid having to talk. He looked at the text message.

'WICKED WITCH AGREES TO MEAT U THIS EVE. COME 2 THE BIG MOUSE THIS MORN. MUCH TO FIR BURP. Peregrine.'

Familiar with the perils of predictive texting, Claypole stared at the alphanumeric keypad on his phone for a few seconds.

'Dis... cuss. Much to discuss,' he muttered, put the phone away and looked at his watch.

Coky was looking at him. 'Everything OK?' she said.

'Yeah,' said Claypole, not meeting her eye and groaning as he stood up. 'Gonna miss the porridge. Got work to do with your uncle.'

'Oh good,' said Coky. 'You can give me a lift up to the house.'

Claypole drove with a fixed frown and grunted monosyllabically to all her questions until she raised the subject of his meeting with her mother that evening.

'How did you know about that?' he said.

'I... had a hand in setting it up.'

He remained quiet, so she riffed on the topic of Lachlan and Milky and the relationship between the two. Claypole let her talk. It was better than letting her know how much he wanted to strangle her and Lachlan both.

Lachlan and Milky had spent time in the city, Coky said. They had gone together when they were nineteen to Aberdeen to be pest controllers. This meant killing seagulls that nested in and on the municipal buildings. Milky, particularly, was fond of saying that he had never met a seagull that wasn't a total bastard.

Poisoning was deemed too cruel by the city authorities, and might cause damage to other birds or be a threat to human health, so they were each given a specially made bat with holes in it. The preferred method was for the operative to dispatch one or two of the gulls with a few swift and frenzied blows, and then to run for cover before the other gulls mobbed him. A couple of minutes later, the operative could return to the scene and do the same again.

'Milky stayed in Aberdeen for longer than was healthy. He still dreams about those birds, he says. Lachy left the job after three weeks, and a month later he was doing a correspondence course in ornithology.'

Claypole bristled at the term of endearment, and said nothing.

'Milky by rights should be angry with Lachlan for leaving him there,' Coky added. 'But they've been best friends since they were three. When they were twelve Lachlan got so sick of Milky's whining that he marooned him on a small island off Garvach Point for eight hours. Milky forgave him by bedtime. When they were fifteen, Lachlan set fire to Milky's sleeping bag on a camping trip and caused second-degree burns. Milky thought it was his own fault. And Lachlan's slept with Milky's sister on and off, and with Milky's mother once. But Milky blames the women, not Lachlan.'

'Yeah,' said Claypole, grimacing.

Coky shrugged. 'But when you grow up here... it's so remote, you can't choose your friends. You've just got to get along with whoever's around. Otherwise you've got no friends at all.'

Claypole chewed his lip as they approached MacGilp House.

'Now of course there's the question of Jade's baby. I

don't know whether even Lachlan and Milky can get over that one.'

Claypole had been gearing up to say something arch about some people seeming to be not so much tolerant of the defects of others as blind to them, but was distracted now that he saw MacGilp House for the first time in daylight. He had a strange sense as he took in its spooky towers and vast grey granite walls, and the lawn in front, that he had seen it before. He shook his head, putting this fleeting thought down to lack of sleep. Or perhaps he was still hallucinating.

Peregrine, wearing a pistachio-green sweater, greeted them from a sedentary position in a kitchen already thick with the smoke of many Dunhills. Coky immediately went upstairs. Peregrine suggested that Claypole make a fresh cafetière of coffee.

'Have we been with the naughty wood-nymphs?' asked Peregrine.

'I spent the night on the beach, yeah.'

'Tsk,' said the old man. 'Seems everyone takes drugs these days. Have you taken one that makes your hair fall out?'

Claypole ran his hand over his head and looked at the cigarette that Peregrine held delicately between his third and fourth fingers. Perhaps with the amount Peregrine smoked, nicotine was no longer a drug – more of a food group.

'Ha,' said Claypole. 'Just need a shower, and I'll be ready for work.'

During his two-hour bath, Claypole read a big chunk of the planning application for the Loch Garvach Wind Farm. He felt a little better informed, and he resolved to read the rest of it later in his hotel. He put on a shirt of Peregrine's that, while not to his taste, did very nearly fit him, and listened to his voicemails. There was one from his personal banker, and one from a credit card company. He deleted them without listening. The third message was from Kevin Watt of the *Glenmorie Herald*, which also got erased.

When Claypole joined him in the library, Peregrine was standing at his desk behind a large industrial document shredder, feeding it as a French farmer feeds a goose with corn. Owing to the noise of the machine – a high-pitched mechanical complaint, as if at any moment it might be sick – Peregrine did not hear Claypole's approach. Rather than shock the old man, Claypole called out when he was about ten feet away.

Peregrine reeled back in alarm and shouted. Both men clutched their hearts.

'For God's s-sake!' Peregrine stuttered.

Claypole looked at the pile of documents and back at his business partner. The two men watched as a large sheaf of printed material was chewed and swallowed by the machine. After a last grinding hiccup, the machine slowed itself to a whirr and Peregrine pressed the off switch. Claypole squinted at Peregrine.

'Love letters?' suggested Claypole, narrowing his eyes. The older man smiled naughtily.

'Just... yes, well... Things we don't need people to see. Let's have a drink,' said Peregrine, and proceeded to make a noise that sounded like language, but had so many glottal stops and hawkings thrown in that it could equally have been a death-rattle.

'What?'

'Knockenglachgach,' said Peregrine again. He held a bottle for Claypole to read. 'It's the name of the whisky.'

Claypole examined the dark-brown liquid inside the bottle. It had things in it. Some things were swilling densely about on the bottom; some of them floating on the top, dead; and some of the things, Claypole saw to his alarm, were actually swimming somewhere in the middle – as in, alive and doing the breaststroke.

'It's from Scapa,' said Peregrine, whipping the top of the bottle off and pouring a couple of measures into crystal lowballs. 'A windblown rock halfway to Iceland that you can only get onto using an arrangement of ropes and pulleys. Only seven people live there, but one of them makes this nectar. And it's very reasonable owing to being... not entirely legal.'

'Right,' said Claypole, peering into his glass. 'What were those documents, Peregrine?'

The older man sipped his drink.

'I think birds are overrated, don't you?' Peregrine examined his glass.

'Eh?'

'The RSPB is the richest non-governmental organisation in the country. Or something like that. Ten times richer than the NSPCC. Sickening, really. Sign of the times. Cheers.'

'I'm really not following you,' said Claypole.

'There's not only a lot of money to be made from this wind farm, there's also... it's a project that will... you know, save the planet and all that rot. And yet some people... some people who purport to have an environmental interest at heart, want to scupper it because a few birds might, *might*, get... um, damaged... I just think that's wrong. Don't you?'

'What's that got to do with...?'

'Mm-hm,' said the old man in frustration. He pointed to a sofa, and Claypole sat down.

'There are some birds on the bit of land where we want to build our little money-spinner. Not many. Just a few, really. But it could be damaging to our case if it... er... People get so touchy about our feathered friends. Especially birds of prey. I mean, what's so good about birds of prey? They snaffle your lambs and a lot else besides. It's not as if wind turbines kill that many of them. Birds aren't stupid. They get out of the way of twenty tonnes of steel and fibreglass rotating at sixty miles an hour... generally.'

He sipped his whisky again, and lit another cigarette.

'There was a survey done. Bit of an amateur job, really. Said there are some... merlins, and sea eagles. And some sparrowhawks. And a few hen harriers. And golden eagles. Total rubbish. Anyway, I've, er... made the report more... realistic.'

'So, so, so... Brr...' Claypole was having difficulty speaking, having just taken a draught of Knockenglachgach. 'So, so you've... falsified the report?'

'Of course not,' said Peregrine with a grin. 'I've made a few appropriate corrections to some poorly executed work.'

Claypole said nothing.

'We must think of the wealth that will be created.'

Peregrine had put a dark emphasis on the word 'wealth', and Claypole took a moment to think. He had often wondered what it would be like to be bribed. Television shows about cops usually had lazy plot lines involving a moral dilemma for some unfeasibly good-looking protagonist. Should he/she take the bribe and protect a friend, or reject it and put them/himself/ herself in jeopardy or jail? Occasionally the device was used well. He had always assumed, when wondering how he would act in the same circumstances, that he would accept the bribe, all things being equal. There didn't seem to be enough drawbacks to not doing so. If the money's there, take it – assuming it is enough to counter the risks. It's an awful lot easier to deal with the consequences of bad behaviour if you're rich. But now that he was being bribed, he couldn't help feeling defiled.

'Tell you what,' said Peregrine, judiciously changing the mood. 'Let's go and get some exercise. I'll go and get changed.'

Claypole was left in Peregrine's office, his attention drawn to the pile of papers next to the shredder.

⸺◈⸺

Claypole had been to a few golf clubs, although he had never joined one. He didn't particularly love the game, but some years ago he had fallen in with a crowd of beery entertainment lawyers who enjoyed playing nine holes on a Saturday morning and then getting drunk and complaining about their clients and their wives. Claypole found that it was as good a way as any of keeping a hangover at bay. He and his 'mates' noodled around perfectly maintained courses in south London and Surrey. Featureless carpets of green, they were, smelling of weedkiller and leather polish. Scotland being the birthplace of golf, Claypole had no reason to think that this morning's experience of the sport would be any different.

At the first tee, Peregrine was staring in the direction of the loch. All Peregrine would have been able to see, Claypole thought, even from six foot up, was a boggy patch of reeds. But it was nonetheless a wistful gesture.

'So what's the "S" for?' said Peregrine.

'What?' Claypole knew perfectly well what was being asked. He had been forced to produce identification in order to rent golfing equipment, and Peregrine must have snuck a look at Claypole's driving licence.

'What's your middle name?'

'Brr,' said Claypole.

'Can't be as embarrassing as mine,' said Peregrine. 'Peregrine Archibald Fincormachus MacGilp, at your service.'

'Pah,' muttered Claypole.

'You don't think Fincormachus is embarrassing?' Peregrine seemed almost hurt.

'Sounds magnificent,' said Claypole with a sneer.

'I suppose there is something regal about it. Fincormachus was a king of the Scots, as it happens. Fourth century.' Peregrine sniffed.

Claypole nodded.

'So, come on then,' said the older man. 'I've shown you mine. Now you show me yours.'

'Sorry. No can do,' said Claypole, and selected a driver. 'Now, who's going first?'

'Oof. You're peppy,' said Peregrine. 'Care to make it interesting?'

The first hole was a shock. Claypole had to cope with the ignominy of losing three balls, but this being matchplay he was only one hole down. The biggest shock was not that he seemed to have lost his touch and might be in danger of losing the hundred-pound wager. As he knew from even his limited experience of golf, the touch might come back at any time if only he could win the battle in his head. The shock was the course itself. The Loch Garvach Golf Course was a wild place. There were savagely twisting trees and vast rivers gushing through the middle of meadows you had to wade through with arms raised lest they attract snakes. There were thick forests between holes and down the side of them. Even the greens were barely mown mossy bogs in an otherwise jungly shambles. It was more Borneo than Britain.

At the third tee, Claypole turned to Peregrine. 'Is there a problem with the right-to-roam thing?'

'What do you mean?'

'The ramblers. They're going to want to walk all over the wind farm, aren't they?'

Peregrine narrowed his eyes. 'Over my dead body.'

'Why would that be a problem?'

Peregrine was suddenly animated.

'Because I don't want them to!' He cursed. 'Outrageous. Those ghastly bloody Labour people. What about my rights? Eh? What about *my* right to *my* property?'

'Well, brr...' Claypole smiled surreptitiously. 'They probably thought that everyone should be able to enjoy the... great outdoors...'

'Bah!' Peregrine was almost shouting now. 'It's *my* great outdoors, damn it!'

'Right,' said Claypole.

'Well, *Mister* Blair and all your Islington poofter cohorts...' Peregrine had gone quite scarlet. 'You can sodding well buy it off me! Then you can enjoy it all you like. I'd say you can have it for market price, which is about two and a half million smackers. But I don't want to leave, so it's going to cost you five. The good news is that I'll take a cheque.'

'Shouldn't it...?' Claypole knew he risked the wrath of his business partner. 'Shouldn't all this wilderness be for everyone to enjoy?'

Peregrine was now purple with indignation.

'Well, it isn't! It's mine, and that's all there is to it. You can take it off me with an army, if you like. But I'll raise an army too, and neither of us would enjoy what happens after that.'

Claypole snorted, and then laughed. Peregrine frowned at first, but eventually managed an embarrassed laugh.

The two men settled down and discussed the hole. Claypole was due to tee off first. He was two holes down, but felt he could still come back. This was a short hole, which in theory balanced the odds more evenly.

'I feel I can talk to you, Claypole, old boy,' said Peregrine, suddenly earnest.

'Yeah, sure,' said Claypole absent-mindedly, yanking a nine iron from his bag. He swung the club in the air, feeling its weight. Claypole turned to look at Peregrine. The old man's expression was puppyish. 'Brr. You were saying,' said Claypole grimly.

Peregrine looked out to sea again, and the only noise was birdsong as Claypole bent his fat frame over the ground and with a grunt inserted a tee into the sodden earth at his feet, balancing his Slazenger B51 on its head. Claypole lined up the shot and practised a swing. Despite the twinge in his lower back, he thought it went pretty well, and stepped closer to the ball to attempt the real thing. He breathed in and held the breath, preparing to backswing. Just then, Peregrine spoke.

'I have done some things,' began Peregrine, but sighed to a halt.

Claypole rested on his club and turned to his playing partner with irritation.

'Oh yes?'

'I've...' Peregrine began. He paused. 'No, it doesn't matter.'

Claypole settled into his shot again. 'OK, then.'

'I shouldn't have said anything.'

'Right.' Claypole tried a practice swing again, and settled once more to strike the ball for real.

'It's just that...'

In the middle of his swing, Claypole stopped. He looked at Peregrine, begging with his eyes for him to shut up. But Peregrine's focus was middle-distance.

'I've done worse things in my life than manipulate a few documents. Before I was... When I was young, I made a mistake. That mistake has...'

Perhaps it was Claypole's sudden interest that caused Peregrine to falter.

'Sorry. I shouldn't say anything. I shouldn't involve you...'

Claypole settled again.

'My sisters hate me.'

This time, Claypole dropped the club altogether, and was about to shout at Peregrine. Something like 'Are we fucking playing golf or are we not?' But then he realised what Peregrine had said.

'It's true,' Peregrine continued, perhaps thinking the dropping of the club was an act of surprised shock. 'Dorcas and Bonnie would probably be happy to see me dead.'

Claypole blushed. 'Brr.'

'I'm afraid so. You see, they think I... Well, they put a different interpretation on Mummy's death than I do.'

Claypole didn't know where to look.

'When Mummy died, and left the estate to me – except for those little parcels of land – they thought...

Well, they blamed me. Words were exchanged. They thought I'd, you know… got Mummy to change her will.'

'Oh,' said Claypole.

The two men stood in silence. Peregrine seemed close to tears. Claypole couldn't think of what to say. If Peregrine wanted to confess, perhaps Claypole should help him to do so.

'And did you… manipulate your mother?'

Peregrine looked as if he might speak, but then stopped. He turned away from Claypole, and simply walked off. Claypole thought about calling after him, but decided against it. The last thing Claypole wanted was a tearful toff on his hands. Anyway, Peregrine would forfeit the match if he didn't come back. A hundred pounds was, after all, a hundred pounds. Claypole would play a couple more holes on his own, just for the hell of it.

As he swished and bunted his ball along the third hole, the rain started, and he resolved that the next hole would be his last. But as he practised his tee shot, the rain came down faster. Suddenly, it was suffocatingly wet, and the sensible thing would have been to go immediately back to the Loch Garvach Hotel. He could become reacquainted with his own clothes, take one of the pills Dr De Witt had given him, have a short nap (although a long one would have been nicer) and prepare himself for his appointment at the house of Bonnie Straughan. He would need to be on top of his game for that encounter, and standing in the freezing rain whacking golf balls into the sea was not a constructive use of his time. And yet, he found himself at the fourth tee, and with the knowledge that he could not get any wetter or more uncomfortable, he became almost relaxed.

'Just one more hole,' he said aloud, almost laughing at the stupidity of it.

At the fourth tee, he selected a four iron and brought the club back to practise the shot. A gust of wind blew the club head almost out of his hands. He brought it down slowly, determined not to be defeated by these absurd elements. He steadied his feet. They squelched unpleasantly in the puddle he had created simply by standing there. He waggled the club head behind the ball, as if to show the crop to the horse. He saw the rain blowing sideways off the end of the club, but merely smiled to himself and eyed the horizon in the direction he calculated the pin to be.

He estimated the wind – probably a force 10 or 11 – and fidgeted around into it so that when he struck the ball the wind would compensate for the direction and the ball would travel in an arc towards the pin. Of course, this never happened in real life. But this was what you did as a golfer. He had read about it. You pretend you're going to hit the perfect shot, and you spend a lifetime trying minutely to correct your mistakes.

He heaved the club head back, and in the same movement took his swing.

For a moment, there was no rain. There was no wind. In Claypole's head, there was no weather. There was also no sky, and no earth. There was only him, the club and the ball. There was only dreamy sunlight, and Claypole's father was behind him, smiling. The birds twittered, and a full choir sang hallelujah. There was a whooshing noise as the club came forward to strike the ball and then just a neat 'tink' as it did so. Suddenly, though, as he followed the shot through, Claypole was back in the real world where the wind was howling and the grey-black sky was pouring forth everything it could to drown the world. But the shot had been taken, and the ball sailed forward in a silver streak. Claypole peered with a sense of panic into the pelting gloom. In a grand parabola, the ball went up, up into the air and sailed into the blackest of the black clouds above. As it did so, it also took the wind and began to head towards the green.

'Woof. Not bad,' Claypole muttered aloud. He gained a mouthful of freezing rain for the privilege of speaking, and was forced momentarily to turn away from the wind. Turning back, he glanced hopefully in the direction he had hit the ball and peered over the horizon, even hopping onto one leg to see further. But the ball was no longer visible. Oh well, he thought. It might be yet another lost ball, but hitting it had felt good.

As he put the club away, thunder rolled moodily not far away, clearly signalling the end of the game. He had heard of people being struck by lightning on golf courses and didn't fancy the idea. Walking next to the trees, he tried to remember whether you were supposed to walk under the trees during lightning strikes, or whether this was specifically not what you were supposed to do. He couldn't remember, and just plodded on.

Reaching the green like Sir Edmund and Tensing – with profound relief and similarly out of breath – Claypole looked around for the ball. He looked up the fairway and back towards the tee. He looked down the slope, as if he might have been mistaken about the quality of his shot and had sliced it. Nothing. He also looked up the hill in case he had hooked it. Nothing.

Standing in the middle of the green now, and some twelve feet from the hole, he was puzzled by the absence of the ball. Could it have sunk into the ground somewhere along the fairway? The ground was wet enough. Perhaps it had been appropriated by some larcenous rabbit? Ah well, he thought. Life's too short to look for golf balls when a hotel room is waiting. Walking past the pin, he just happened to glance into the hole. It was a gesture not of optimism – the shot could not have been that good – but of curiosity.

There was a ball. He didn't for a moment think it was *his* ball, so picking it up out of the hole was an act of surreptitious theft. He turned it round in his hand. 'Slazenger B51', it said.

In the black driving rain and soaked through, Claypole walked back to the Land Rover. No one would ever believe that he had hit a hole in one, but he didn't care. He wondered whether his luck might be changing.

-9-

Do I step on the brake to get out of her clutches?
Can I speak Double Dutch to a real Double Duchess?
'New Amsterdam', Elvis Costello

Meeting Peregrine's younger sister, the gorgon Bonnie Straughan, for dinner at her house was far from being a prospect he relished, but Claypole's joyous mood was not easily dimmed following his private triumph on the golf course. He even hummed as he skipped damply into the Loch Garvach Hotel and acquainted himself with his cramped room that now smelled of fried fish. He dried himself and put on some of his own clothes. Though there was no time to rest, he consoled himself that he would sleep in the hotel bed that night.

It had stopped raining when he emerged, and the evening sunshine blazed again on the damp street outside the hotel. With a skip, he hopped into the cab of the Land Rover and turned the key in the ignition. It made a noise like a rheumatic donkey, and then died. This evening, Claypole was not to be got down by the Fates. One quick 'fuckety fuck' was all he allowed himself by way of demonstrable irritation, and got out of the Land Rover whistling. A pair of hiking-booted tourists – German, if he'd been forced to guess – were watching him with curiosity. He gave them a 'good evening', and walked back into the hotel to order a taxi.

Bobby Henderson – he of the electric car hire – also ran Garvachhead's only taxi service. Claypole feared Henderson might know about the totalled electric car by now, and be on the hunt for Gordon Claypole. So under the name Barry Macbeth, Claypole called for the taxi to take him to Bonnie Straughan's house. Henderson, a garrulous pot-bellied Yorkshireman, refused to drive his Mercedes down Bonnie Straughan's pitted drive, and Claypole was forced to walk the last half-mile. Claypole swore as he walked along the gorse-lined track, and stumbled over rocks and fell into muddy potholes when his eye was taken from the track to the fabulous view across the loch. The green and light-brown hills rose up at a gentle gradient from the shore on the other side of the loch, which seemed a stone-skip away. The heather-covered mountains behind glowed a brownish purple in the golden evening light, and even Claypole, who never thought he had cared much for views, could not help but be impressed by the magnificence of the scene. But this uppish mood was destined not to last, for the sun was on its way down. The sun going down on a still, cloudless day at any point between April and October can mean wonderful sunsets in Scotland, and gladdens the heart of every visitor. But it also means midges, particularly in August.

It is very fortunate for the Scots, and any guests in the country, that the walking pace of an adult human, if they are reasonably fit and not doing anything to delay their pace (such as having a conversation, or admiring the scenery), is just greater than the flying pace of a midge. Even this is not enough to save you from being bitten occasionally, because the midges don't just follow you – the ones in front of you are also attracted to your scent, your heat, or the carbon dioxide in your breath (researchers are divided on their opinion as to which). In tests, the adult male going at a fair walking pace at dusk smacks the back of his neck, or flicks his ears with irritation, on average every fifty seconds. This is just tolerable. But Claypole felt none of the benefits of this lucky equation, because he was fat, urban and moving over rough ground. His was no greater than the walking speed of a heavily laden five-year-old. Within three minutes of closing the door of Henderson's Merc, he was being completely savaged.

When he finally saw a sprawling early-nineteenth century farmhouse with many messy and half-ruined outbuildings, he was therefore profoundly relieved, and yet also filled with dread. He never managed entirely to rid himself of the childhood fear of going to houses he did not know. This trepidation was doubled in the countryside. The inevitable lack of a doorbell forces one to go uninvited into the house, calling 'hullo' with a faltering voice. But his trepidation as he negotiated the gate to the courtyard, and listened hard for dogs and ghosts, was tempered by the fact that he was absolutely desperate to get indoors and stop being bitten by the infernal midges. If Bonnie Straughan did not answer the door, he told himself, he would have to get relief from the midges by running into the loch like a cartoon character running from a swarm of bees.

But there was Bonnie Straughan, answering the door

before Claypole got there. She was smiling uncertainly in a way that Claypole had seen Coky do.

'So,' she said, with the smile turning delinquent, 'are we to have the mutual respect of opposing generals?'

Claypole took a moment to decipher this elegant sentence.

'Yeah,' he said, 'no reason for it to be nasty. Brr.'

He followed her as she strode in silence to the large sitting room. On a grand sideboard stood a bottle of white wine in a cooler, and stuffed olives lay glistening in a bowl.

'Will you have a glass of Zinfandel?' she asked, and looked him up and down with a brazen sweep of her head. 'I'm afraid I have no beer.'

'Brr. Great,' said Claypole, and went to run his hand through his hair, only to discover afresh that he had none. He scratched his stubbly head.

'Were you *terribly* midged?' she asked with sympathy. 'I heard about your car, and I should have warned you that Henderson won't come up the drive. Big wimp. Will you be a poppet and open the wine?'

For somewhere with such bad communications, Loch Garvach certainly had an efficient bush telegraph. Everybody knew everybody else's business.

As he fussed to uncork the bottle, he examined the room furtively. There was a grand piano, and two sofas either side of a low table, on which were laid out Middle Eastern dishes of every hue and texture. Velvet throws adorned the furniture and kilims were piled overlapping on the floors as in a bazaar. The lushness of these fabrics in the dimly lit room made for an almost orgiastic feel. Framed photographs chaotically adorned one wall. Bonnie smiled toothily and flicked her magnificent hair. Claypole popped the cork on the bottle uneasily and sensed a stirring somewhere in the room. He turned and saw, rising from the floor behind the piano, the biggest dog he had ever seen. The animal lurched to its feet, as nimbly as a shire horse and not much different in size. Grey and white, it looked at Claypole and gave one thunderclap of a bark.

'What the...?' said Claypole, gulping.

'Zeus!' Bonnie admonished, and the animal swivelled its massive, stupid head towards her, its huge jaws spraying spittle twelve feet in every direction. 'Sit!'

The dog paused. It stared again at Claypole before flopping back down on the floor with a foundation-shaking thud.

'He's an English mastiff,' said Bonnie. 'Very sweet, but a bit nervy.'

'Wow,' was all Claypole could manage. He imagined the number of mouthfuls that Zeus would require in order to eat him, and decided that it was less than five. Bonnie continued.

'You're supposed to convince me about the wind farm. My brother is clearly too chicken to do so himself.'

'OK,' said Claypole neutrally.

She sat with poise on one of the sofas and gestured for Claypole to do the same.

'Brr,' said Claypole, having sipped the wine. He was no wine buff, but this tasted like dusty batteries. He vowed not to touch it again.

'I think the Loch Garvach Wind Farm is a dangerous mistake,' said Bonnie in the same shrill tone she had used in the community hall. 'Let's eat while we talk.'

Claypole sat dumbly looking at Bonnie, and she took this as her cue. As she spoke, he ate, and her thoughts seemed not to have evolved from those that she had chaotically outlined in the community hall. But to

Claypole's alarm she also posed him questions.

'Wind farms don't make very much electricity, do they?' she asserted.

'I don't think that's right,' Claypole began through a stuffed vine leaf, but found he could not follow up, and was subjected to another five-minute lecture. She then began a new topic.

'They only operate when the wind is blowing, of course. Don't you think that makes the whole thing redundant?'

'Well, brr... that doesn't make them useless,' he began, but was mown down once again.

'Why do they have to be so ugly?' she posed.

Claypole saw that further objection would be pointless, especially as he had no facts at his fingertips with which to deny her assertions. So she continued to list her every objection. Occasionally he managed to say 'I should ask someone whether that really is true'; 'I'd be interested to see evidence on that point'; or 'I bet that isn't entirely the case'. He even weakly muttered 'I'd heard that they aren't really that bad', but he was on quicksand and knew better than to struggle.

'They have to build roads to make wind farms, and they have to dig thousands of tons of earth out of the pristine hillside. Hundreds of tons of concrete get shoved into the ground; pylons get erected, buildings are built, and God knows what else. Lorries pinging up and down, emitting tons of CO_2. Does this sound like a boon to the environment to you? No, of course it doesn't.'

After half an hour, Bonnie had finished. Her final soliloquy, devoted to the qualities of nuclear power compared with the pointless hideousness of wind farming, ended with the question, 'So, why on earth would I sign Peregrine's silly old legal banana and let them drive HGVs over my land? You tell me that. Huh?'

Claypole looked at her and marshalled his thoughts. He had prepared nothing to say, so he made the only gambit he could think of.

'Money?' he said, and let the word hang in the air.

Slowly, a crooked smile ran across Bonnie's lips. 'Ha!' she said, and they sat in silence for some moments. Claypole looked at his watch.

'Tell me about yourself,' she said at length. 'Coky says I met your parents.'

'My father was Geoffrey Claypole. Mum Janice. Art teacher.'

'Your father's dead?'

'When I was ten.'

'Sorry to hear that,' Bonnie said, pulling her hair away from her neck. 'What did *he* do?'

'He was a spy,' said Claypole.

'Ooh, really?'

'No.' Claypole paused. 'Not really. But I used to tell people that. I wished he'd been a spy not just because it would have been exciting, but because if you're a spy and you die on the job the government really looks after your kids. No such luck for me, though. We got screwed when my dad died, and anyway, he was something much worse. Something much more cynical. One of the most morally bankrupt professions you can be in. It's viewed alongside arms dealing these days. With this wind farming, maybe I'm trying to... I dunno... Brr.'

Bonnie was looking at the houmous, suddenly quiet. Perhaps she was giving Claypole airtime for his unexpected confession.

'At the time, we were proud. Kids my age watched *Dallas* and thought that what he did was glamorous. They thought he was rich, or would be soon, and they envied me. But I can't even mention it now. You get hated before you've even opened your mouth if people know that your dad...' There was another pause. Bonnie's eyes were popping. Claypole smirked grimly. 'My father was in the oil business.'

Bonnie's eyes narrowed, and she studied Claypole intensely for a moment.

'I *do* remember your father,' she began. 'Yes. Geoffrey. Yes.' Then she looked up and laughed. There was something in her giggle that Claypole objected to. Bonnie played with the rim of her glass. 'Will you allow me to read your fortune?'

'Say what?'

'Tarot,' she said simply. 'I'd like to read for you.'

Claypole scowled, but found himself nodding.

Bonnie fetched a deck of cards, larger and more numerous than normal playing cards, and began, with no fuss or ceremony, to shuffle. She asked him to touch them, and then began dealing.

'What's first?' she said, and laid on the coffee table a picture card of a fat woman. 'Ah, the Empress. Known also as the Female Pope, and associated sometimes with the Virgin Mary. That's good, obviously.'

Claypole was already bored, but Bonnie was oblivious. She dealt again.

'The Three of Swords. I can't think that has any great significance, but you never know.'

She placed another card on the table.

'The Hanged Man. Another trump card, so we'll put that to one side. And, what have we here? Ah!' She sighed with deep satisfaction. 'The Fool. That's the best card you can get. The Fool – the forerunner of the Joker – is the most mysterious, and some say the luckiest, card in the pack.'

She picked the cards up with reverence and put them side by side. She turned and smiled at Claypole.

'What does it…? Brr. What's it mean?'

'Why don't you give me your interpretation, and I'll tell you whether I think you're correct.'

Claypole squinted sceptically. He had seen this before. As with astrology, the mind fills in the gaps in an attempt to locate meaning and attaches significance to images and words where there may be none, pulling together meaningless scraps of information to form a comfortable coherence. He could even feel himself doing it. In this atmosphere his sense of paranoia was building. He could see himself as the Fool, naturally. And whatever Bonnie said about the Three of Swords being insignificant, the image on the card was of violence, and he felt foreboding. But who was the Hanged Man? The image on the card was of a man with a twisted smile tied upside down to a tree by his leg.

Pah. It was nonsense, he told himself quickly, and he must not allow the charlatan Bonnie Straughan the satisfaction of him doing her work for her. Like a con artist or a poor psychoanalyst, she must be waiting for him to let his inadequacies and preoccupations show. Then she would reinforce them with her 'interpretation', making him feel as if this absurd charade had some meaning and she some dominion. She might even make a judgement or a prediction based on what she thought he wanted to hear – or possibly on what he least wanted to hear. He decided to sabotage the process by making something up about his feelings about the cards that was nowhere near what he was really thinking. If she told him he was right, he would get the private satisfaction of knowing she was a fraud.

'Well, I suppose I am the Hanged Man, and I think Coky is probably the Empress. And maybe Peregrine is the Fool.'

'Hm,' said Bonnie. She seemed doubtful. 'I don't...' She hesitated as if looking for inspiration. 'No. I'm not sure that's right. Although... the Hanged Man can mean a person on the horns of a dilemma. It doesn't have to be someone doomed, and it rarely means death. Are you in the throes of indecision about something?'

Claypole shrugged.

'I don't know that any of these other cards represent anyone specific,' she continued. 'You see, the presence of the Fool can confuse any interpretation. It rather depends what we turn up next. If it's the Ten of Coins, I think we can confidently predict riches. If it's the Seven of Cups, it might be a party. But the presence of the Fool can turn all that on its head. Do you see?'

'Pff.' Claypole was openly scoffing now. Bonnie's expression, irritatingly for Claypole, was one of infinite patience.

'Shall we see what the next card is?'

'Go on then.' Claypole looked at his watch.

Bonnie closed her eyes as if in a trance and lightly stroked the top of the deck with a long fingernail. Claypole took the opportunity while she could not see his expression to mouth the word 'idiot', but his eyes were drawn to the deck of cards nonetheless.

The top card was turned over slowly, and in Bonnie's direction so that she would see it first. She opened her eyes flickeringly. Then she stared at the card for some moments before saying abruptly, 'It's late,' and gathering the cards together.

Claypole's eyes were still fixed on the card on the top of the deck. Bonnie had seen it, and he had not. He did not want to give her the satisfaction of knowing that he was interested.

'OK, then. I'd better be going. Brr. Any chance of a glass of water?'

As soon as she was out of sight, Claypole darted forward out of the sofa and went to the Tarot pack. His hand hesitated above the deck as he listened nervously for Bonnie. Hearing nothing, he whipped the top card over. The picture on the card was shock enough: a grinning skeleton in a cardinal's cloak and hat, with one hand beckoning, the other carrying a short scythe. But below it was a single, simple word. 'Death'. He heard Bonnie's footsteps in the hall, whipped the card onto its back again, hiding it from his bulging eyes, and leapt towards one of the photographs on the wall. He made as if to study it. Then he *really* studied it. Then he picked it off the wall.

As far as Bonnie was concerned, Claypole was just looking at a photograph when she came back into the room holding a glass of water. Had she bothered to examine him more closely, or the photograph, she would have seen a lot more.

The photograph itself was nothing special. A group shot, clip-framed, it was fading. The colours were washed yellow, and the faces slightly fuzzy. But Claypole could see exactly who it was. For there, tucked underneath his father's arm, was Claypole himself. Aged ten or so, he was scowling. Claypole's mother was also in the group, as was his grandmother, and a few assorted others. The personnel had drawn his attention naturally enough, but what had frozen him to the spot was that next to his father, on the other side to himself, was Bonnie Straughan. Her cascading curly hair was jet black, and her smile broad. And around her hip, just visible, was Geoffrey Claypole's fat, cheating hand.

'I said, shall I call you a taxi?'

Claypole snapped to and nodded, but did not look at his host. Bonnie Straughan left the room.

By another door, so did Claypole, leaving the framed photograph on a sofa.

Claypole shut the front door of Bonnie Straughan's house as quietly as he could and wobbled across the darkening farmyard as fast as his jelly legs would take him. Beyond the soft fizz of the electricity lines strung over the yard, there was eerily little noise, and no movement save for a few twinkling stars. But Claypole's head was raging with noise. His head and heart pounding, he only gathered his thoughts halfway up the hill. He fished out his phone. One bar of reception. He dialled Henderson's Taxis.

'Hello,' said Claypole, breathless.

'Evening,' said Henderson.

'It's Barry Macbeth here. You dropped me off at the end of the drive of Bainhead House. Has a taxi been ordered to take me to Garvachhead?'

'Ah. Yes, sir.'

There was something sarcastic about the tone. Perhaps it was just Henderson's Yorkshire ways, thought Claypole, and he continued in a businesslike fashion.

'Great. I've set off walking from the house, and I'll meet you where you dropped me off in half an hour.'

'Certainly, sir. Would you like me to tell you how much it will be?'

Claypole assumed it would be roughly the twenty pounds he had paid for the outward journey, but he would not object if it were three times that amount. 'Sure,' he said.

'That will be £7,025.'

Claypole stopped walking. He knew what was coming, but his jaw dropped open anyway.

'Twenty-five pounds to get you to Garvachhead, you see, *Mr Claypole*... and seven grand for my car...' Henderson was now shouting. 'That you fucking *wrote off* and abandoned in a *ditch* without so much as a –'

Bip. Claypole had pressed the off switch.

'Bollocks,' said Claypole quietly. He sat on the verge, watching the silent house in the semi-darkness. Then he saw the light over the front door come on.

'Oh shit,' he whispered to himself, and for no good reason except instinct, lay on the ground. 'She's coming for me. With Zeus.'

The notion was unlikely, he realised. He had only been out of her company for two minutes, and she would still be assuming he had gone to the toilet. But when he looked back at the house, with a lurch of horror he saw that the front door was opening, and Bonnie was emerging from the house – with her vast dog on a lead, straining and barking madly into the night air. She actually did want him dead. This wicked witch – Peregrine could not have been more right – with her Tarot cards, her evil thoughts and her seduction of married men, wanted to hunt him down and kill him. With real fear now, Claypole looked for an escape route.

The road was not an option. Zeus would catch him up in a matter of moments. Could he run over the fields, and join the road further up the hill? It was nearly dark, after all. No. That was madness. If 'fields' were not the obstacle in the idea, then 'run' definitely was. Anyway, Zeus might hunt him down by scent even if he were out of sight. He found himself looking down the hill towards the shore, just a hundred or so yards away. He saw a small concrete jetty. Floating gently next to an orange buoy was a small rowing boat.

Claypole had not been in a boat since he was sixteen. At least, not one without a foghorn, lights, male and female toilets and parking for at least twenty cars. He had been sent by his mother on a sailing course on Lake Windermere for two weeks while she conducted an abortive relationship with a loss adjuster called Marvin. Claypole had hated every minute and feigned injuries and infections of all kinds in order to stay on dry land as much as possible. He had not learned to sail, but he had learned to row. Now, he figured, he had a choice. Conquer his fear of boats – or rather, of drowning or being eaten as a result of capsizing a boat – or die horribly under torture. And at her hands. *Her!* It must have been her. Claypole's mother had talked, long after his father's death, of an incident in Scotland, and a raven-haired temptress. It must have been Bonnie who had caused his parents to split up.

'Come on,' Claypole exhorted himself as he half rose from his crouched position on the side of the hill and waddle-crept along a fence in the direction of the jetty. The boat was uncomplicatedly moored, and he did not take long to untie the painter and jump in, his bulky frame and unaccustomed shoes conspiring to make him tumble into the craft rather than perform the neat leap he had imagined. The little wooden boat drifted unsteadily into the loch. With much scuffling, bruising and cursing, Claypole found the oars and placed them in the rusting metal rowlocks and sat heavily on the thwart. As he was taking the first pull on the oars, he looked back at the shore. He heard a car door slam and an engine start. He took three quick pulls on the oars to create some clear water between hunter and hunted. But when he and the little boat were some way out into the loch, he observed the eerie phosphorescence on the water disturbed by the action of the oars and visible in the stern wake. The blackness of the sea, and the bright green tinge to the disturbed surface made it all so horribly alien. He reminded himself that he was being chased, and he looked back to the shore again.

As he watched Bonnie's estate car, with Zeus squeezed into the boot, winding its way up the drive and away from the house, the thought occurred to Claypole that it was possible she did not want to kill him. It was, he had to acknowledge, just feasible that she was coming to offer him a lift. Or weirder, to apologise. It was a prospect even more dreadful than death that he might be forced – the thought filled his tightening throat to choking point – to forgive her. She might plead for forgiveness, explain some mitigating circumstances, and possibly even try to lay some blame for the incident at the feet of his father. He would have to swallow his pride and his loathing. For Coky's sake, if not his own. Then again, if her motives were innocent, why had she taken the dog with her? She must indeed, he concluded, require Zeus in order to rid the world of evidence that Claypole had ever existed. Claypole would be eaten by the hound, and she would thus get rid not only of a man who hated her, but the spokesman for a wind farm she objected to. That, he thought as he dug the oars into the water once again and pulled hard for the opposite shore, was the only realistic conclusion. All notions of turning back, small-voiced as they had been, were silenced.

The moon was behind a thin cloud, but he could see enough to estimate the distance to the opposite shore to be half a mile. What any of this would mean in terms of rowing time he had no idea, and as the sea became choppier the further out into the loch he went, he was reminded that this loch was not a lake in the English sense. This wasn't glassy, tame Windermere. There might be currents of hideous strength to take him directly out to sea. To his right was the mouth of the loch, which led eventually to some of the islands of the Inner Hebrides. He stared at the horizon. It looked particularly black and forbidding. Just beyond those islands, which one could miss as easily as a black cat on a dark street, was the Irish Sea. And should he have the misfortune to miss the coast of Northern Ireland some way to the south-west, there was 3,000 miles of nothing but chilly Atlantic Ocean until Canada.

He saw the lights of Bonnie's car coming back down her drive to the house. Then, with a lurch of panic, he saw that her car was not turning into the courtyard of her house, but was instead making its way down to the shore. His puny arms pulled on the oars again. As her car headed for the jetty, he wondered whether she could direct Zeus to swim out to him. If so, it would be a brief chase before Claypole's now wildly thrumming heart gave out. The massive dog would chew his boat to pieces, then to devour him with red-eyed cerberean slaverings. Now at the jetty's edge, Bonnie got out of the car and shouted something. She was angry, no doubt. But he could not make out her words. No dog was plunging into the sea, and Bonnie merely turned and got back into her car.

With a sigh, Claypole settled again to the task of rowing himself to freedom or to death, feeling the sinews of his chest tested in ways they were ill-suited to withstand. He thought momentarily of his heart pills, still in their bottle in his rucksack at the Loch Garvach Hotel. And after that, his thoughts turned, not without reason, to the day of his mother's funeral.

-10-

In the prison of his days
Teach the free man how to praise.

'In Memory of W.B. Yeats', W.H. Auden

From the moment he was woken stupidly early by his uncle Jerry, Claypole spent the day scowling. Jerry, a bumptious beardie who had lived in Australia for the last twenty years, had seen his sister, Claypole's mother, only twice in that time. Claypole was now an orphan, but there was no need to treat him like a child. Jerry was estranged from his own family because he was a total jerk, Claypole's father had been an only child, and all the older generations were already dead. It was just the two of them in the tiny suburban house, and the two of them would be the only relations present to cremate the remains of Janice Claypole.

A sunny day announced itself through the net curtains onto the pot-pourri as Claypole thundered out a slash into his dead mother's toilet. He wondered how many more times he would get to pee in that bowl before it was gone from his life for ever. He would have no reason ever to return. The house was rented and she left no legacy except a few bits of outdated furniture. Only Claypole would remain. All her toil, all the work she had done to send him to a fee-paying school, and every breath she had taken, would be memorialised only in him.

Claypole found the sunshine irritating. Couldn't he have been given a little pathetic fallacy? For once, couldn't he have been allowed some drama? His mother's passing from the world should have been marked by a chill in the air, or drizzle, or a wind blowing withered leaves around a bleak cemetery. But the crematorium had only municipal functionality to offer, and was glaringly cheerful with its gaudy plastic flowers. But he determined, as he walked uncomfortably in his black suit, white shirt and black tie, that he would display only dignified mourning. He didn't want to show how dismally empty he thought his mother's life had been. No one would know how much he wanted to scream. Who could he tell anyway? There was only Tiny Sue from orchestra; Sheila from the night class; one or two retired colleagues; and Uncle Jerry. The crematorium guy was a grey-skinned droop who ambled through the process of frying Claypole's mother as if she were just another job, which is exactly what she was.

Jerry was enjoying the whole funereal process, and being top gorilla. He patronised Tiny Sue, was flirty with Sheila and was way too cheerful with everyone. Would anyone have objected if Claypole had shoved Jerry, along with the coffin, through the sliding doors to hell? Claypole chewed the corner of the hastily photocopied order of service, of which he had laid out a pointless number on the not-really-pews.

There were no readings, but Uncle Jerry insisted on going through the biography of Janice Claypole née

McNair, managing to omit any reference either to her husband or her son. 'Then college, where Janice gained a life-long love of classical music,' he intoned. 'She moved here, and never left – teaching art and music to generations of children'; 'she set up her own summer school'; and 'in retirement, she took to macramé...' It was over pitifully quickly.

If Claypole had spoken, he would have told the assembled that Janice had had a rubbish life. It was full of drudgery and regret, and characterised by nothing but mediocrity. She was cheated on, abandoned and bereaved within eighteen months – triply betrayed by the garrulous fat man she loved. She was in turn used, bullied and then ignored by her son, who so resembled – without the cheeky grin – the man who ruined her life. She had worked hard to pay for an above-average education to be drilled into Claypole's below-average mind. The only things in her life that gave her solace were art and music, but she couldn't even share those things with her indolent, moody son. He was too busy sucking up every visual opiate that TV for his generation had to offer to pay her even a tenth of the attention she lavished on him. The generation before his had grown up watching all four channels, because there was nothing else. It was decent quality, and it was a shared experience. The generation after him had the internet with its billions of directions in which it could take you, its eclectic corners and wild frontiers. But his generation was caught in the middle. They all watched the gradually multiplying television channels avidly – MTV, Sky, Channel Five. And it was all crap.

The only thing his mother could service Claypole with that he showed the slightest passion for was food. But there too Claypole ingested only rubbish. Again,

Claypole had suffered from his particular time in the world. The generation previous to his had the benefits of a limited but balanced diet – the hangover of rationing. The generation after had prosperity and the resurgence of good food, with TV chefs preaching the use of quality ingredients. But his mother had served him what she had been told to by the marketeers of the eighties: processed food of the most dangerous kind, in as much quantity as her greedy son desired. She was told, as they all were, that these processes were technologically advanced and therefore good. Certainly her own arteries suffered: she had been sixty-five and a few days when the staff at Asda found that the last car in the car park contained an unmoving shopper.

Claypole would have told the thin assembly for Janice's funeral all that without hesitation. He would also have told them of the tawdry weight of guilt he felt now that she was gone. He had never treated her with any respect because she had never demanded any. But that didn't mean she didn't deserve it, and he felt desperately, desperately sorry. For her and for himself.

Uncle Jerry sidled up to him at the wake. Over curling fish-paste sandwiches and sherry, he wanted a man-to-man chat. Claypole stood stiffly and scowled.

'Gordon, mate,' said Jerry in the Aussified English accent that placed him precisely nowhere in the world. 'You should think about coming to Queensland.'

Claypole looked at his uncle with the blankest expression he could muster. Jerry winked.

'It's the golden land, you know. There's nothing a man like you couldn't do there. Forget the States. Oz is the real land of opportunity.'

Claypole stared at him. The thought of even visiting,

let alone living in Australia, had always filled him with horror. His father had always been disparaging about the place, largely because it was where Jerry lived. 'Hot, perilous, and full of cunts,' had been his father's assessment of God's Own Country.

'You could stay with me while you set yourself up. We'll have a laugh. And Aussie girls...' Jerry tried to elbow his nephew, but a surfeit of sherry caused him to miss Claypole's stomach and lose his balance slightly. 'They're the best, mate.' Then he added under his breath, 'Fit and fast, yeah?'

Claypole had looked at his watch. 'I've got to meet a man about a wind farm.'

Pulling his black suit around himself, Claypole had left his mother's wake early and made his way back to London, and to Pink's club on St James's.

--≈◎≈--

At first, Claypole thought the boat was being attacked from below. He had at least a hundred yards to go before the shore and did not expect to be running aground so soon. With the boat going nowhere, he attempted a few more strokes of the oars before he gave up. He sat panting as the boat gently pirouetted on a rock or sandbank and brought him face to face with the shore he had been striving for. The prospect of dragging the heavy wooden craft a hundred yards through the freezing shallows was grim. But he was at least relieved not to be heading for Nova Scotia.

He stood up in the boat and tried to survey the water. It was impenetrably black. The depth, he calculated, could not be more than a foot or so, for that was the draught of the little rowing boat. So he balanced himself on the bow and jumped out, his jacket in hand, and plunged up to his nipples in the black and terrifying sea.

He realised, as he gasped and slithered on the seaweeded rocks, that he probably should tether the boat, or drag it up the shore at least a little. But equally he knew, as the waves bumped it against him, that he did not care about the fate of the small boat, so he simply let it go, and it drifted away into the night. As he watched it disappear, he knew that technically he would owe Bonnie Straughan a rowing boat. She could whistle for it. Rapist.

Stepping gingerly between the rocks and up onto the drier seaweed at the shoreline, he glanced briefly up at the moon, which had emerged from the clouds. The moon he was used to seeing was dirty orange, like an eco-bulb. This was a bright hundred-watter, and every detail of the landscape was picked out. For that, if nothing else about his situation, he was grateful. He decided that treading his way back to civilisation in wet socks and wet brogues was not the way forward. He sat on a rock to take them off. Twenty yards later, he regretted it and put them back on again. His feet were still soaked, of course, and also now very cold. Shivering, he removed the damp clothing from his top half and replaced it with the only thing he had with him that was dry, namely his jacket. It felt strange having the lining of the jacket next to his salted skin.

Finding the fence, he followed it until another fence met it. He then climbed it ineptly and fell over on the other side. Clambering down and up a ditch, he saw that he was next to a road. He set about guessing which direction he should go in. He was suffering from the cold, and knew that he should get somewhere warm as soon as possible. As he stumbled along the road, he reflected that he hadn't spent this much time alone in years. At least, that was how it felt. The time he spent in London was generally solitary, but invariably accompanied by something: the telly, the radio, the iPod. In Scotland, though, and almost since he had arrived, he had been *really* alone. Time that would end soon, he was sure of that, and in grim ignominy. He would leave having failed on counts both professional and personal. For, how could he now gain Coky's love in the knowledge that her mother had seduced his father and precipitated the end of his parents' marriage? Perhaps, if he were honest, he could square the morality. But it was just so damned offputting.

Some way along the road, a path through the trees opened up to his right and away from the sea. Excitedly, he realised that he knew it. It was one of the paths that he had wandered along the morning after he had spent the night in the Land Rover. It would lead him to Dorcas's cottage in less than an hour, as long as he could remember the route. He whistled as he bounded along the path, feeling warmer. Just as he began actually to sing, he saw a flash of something light through the trees and stopped dead. He tried not to move, but his breathing was noisy. Through the trees, but unmistakeable, was a horse. Lit by the moonlight, its pale coat was given a bewitching sheen of silver. What was this unearthly creature doing? Why wasn't it asleep? Did horses sleep? Perhaps they slept standing up, and with their eyes open. Claypole had no idea. The belly of the horse seemed to be heaving, and its legs quivering. Was it ill? He took a step closer and saw to his horror that an object seemed to have been inserted into the back of the horse. Disgusted and intrigued, Claypole took a couple of paces forward better to see what the thing was. It looked like a transparent shopping bag containing something black and long, maybe an aubergine. He briefly wondered who could have done such a terrible thing to a poor defenceless animal when he saw the thing for what it was. With a dreadful thrill, Claypole realised that the object was a pair of spindly hoofed legs enveloped in a placental sac.

'Lady horse...' he whispered in surprise, 'having a baby.'

The mare looked directly at him. He ducked and averted his eyes. After a few seconds, he peeked back at the animal. Her gaze was fixed unblinkingly on him. He looked around him. The mare snorted again, the whites of her eyes luminescent in the moonlight. She must be in pain, Claypole thought. She took a pace towards him. He took a pace back, feeling that she might be about to attack. Then he looked at her unreproachful, gooey eyes, and wondered if the opposite might be true. Was she... (he gulped)... asking for his help?

He took a step forward, but stopped as the mare flopped onto the ground. A gush of amniotic fluid poured onto the forest floor. Claypole gagged and looked around him again. There was nothing but trees. No people, no houses, no lights. He looked back at the horse, which was unmoving. She must be dying, he thought, and he felt not just sympathy, but something he had not felt before. He felt a sense of duty, neither imposed upon him nor sullied by self-interest. The higher being's duty to help the lower. It was most ennobling.

Claypole took off his jacket and scuttled forward, half naked and crouching like a soldier. He made a cooing noise and muttered, 'There, there, horsey' to the mare, several times over, as he approached her gingerly. She seemed to encourage his presence with her eyes, so he carefully stroked her mane.

The mare twitched and heaved, but Claypole did not flinch. He looked towards the animal's tail. To his horror, more of the foal was beginning to emerge. He patted the mare's neck gently and kept his eyes fixed on her hind quarters with increasing wonderment. Knowing somewhere deep within him that he must help her, he crawled down to the business end. At considerable speed, and with great heaves from the mare, the foal was emerging. Claypole beheld the pliable damp sac through which he could see the foal's tiny thin head. It wasn't moving, and he reckoned he had to act quickly. Before he could stop himself, he was tugging at the foal's legs with both hands, aiding it out of its mother's womb. With a rush and a flop, the rest of the foal emerged. Claypole toppled backwards but kept hold of the foal, which collapsed half on him.

And there it was. A new life. In Claypole's quivering hands.

Bitumen black, the foal did not move. I must get it out of this bag, Claypole thought, but he possessed nothing with which he could tear the sac and allow the foal to breathe. He looked back at the mare. She looked knackered and gave him no guidance. Swallowing hard, he braced himself. He must do this, he thought. This animal is relying on me to act. There is no one else, and I refuse to be responsible for another death. So he knelt down and bit into the sweet and sour placental sac. It tore easily, and he ripped away the rest of the sac from the foal's face with his hands, spitting the foul taste from his lips. Still the creature did not move, so he ripped some of the sticky membrane from its body.

He looked down at his hands. They were pink with blood and goo, and his jeans had gone dark. His bare torso was steaming gently, also bloodied and sticky. He crawled away, disgusted with himself for being unable to commence the animal's life despite his sacrifice. He turned back to look, now sitting on the forest floor some six feet from the foal and the mare.

The foal craned its head and stood quickly, launching itself from a dead lump to standing in a second. Claypole's eyes widened. There it stood, its thin, shivering legs awkwardly splayed. It was like a chilly catwalk model in a tight black furry suit. To Claypole's delight, the mare got up and approached her progeny. She frantically licked the foal's face clean like it was covered in gravy. Claypole backed away again on his bottom, now at a distance of twenty feet. The foal looked at him and blinked. There was no fear in its eyes, and Claypole could not help smiling. It was not his normal smile – the guarded crinkle that barely ruptured his face. This was a real smile. His mouth was partly open, and his broken teeth visible. It didn't last long, though, because Claypole's mood was so confused. He found himself slightly annoyed because neither the mare nor the foal seemed to be showing him any gratitude. (Just a nod would have been fine. Even a noble glance.) But more importantly, and the real reason for the rapid fading of his smile, was that he found his bottom lip trembling.

At first he thought he must be cold. He was half naked, and misty rain had begun to fall. But these were not quite the symptoms of cold. Then, while sitting on the damp ground in the middle of nowhere, under moonlight and with two horses for company who were now oblivious to his incongruous presence, Claypole found himself weeping.

＊━━◎━━＊

Daylight did not so much break over Loch Garvach that morning as smear itself slowly over the land, taking an hour to do so. Claypole hadn't even registered that it was morning until he found himself shielding his eyes from the grey light as he strode with purpose over the brow of the hill that led to Dorcas's cottage. Sodden, sleepless, bloodied and bedraggled as he was, he was thoroughly energised. When he finally saw that the lights were on in the house, he would have broken into a run, were it not for the inextricable water in his shoes. He replayed the pictures in his mind of the foal's first steps. What joy to have helped it into the world! A life now existed because of Gordon S. Claypole. He skipped through Dorcas MacGilp's garden to find her welcoming him on the front doorstep with a cup of tea. She seemed unsurprised to see him.

After she had put his clothes in the washing machine and given him some more bizarre cast-offs to wear, he boasted of his recent bout of equine midwifery. It was not as satisfying in the telling as he had been expecting. Dorcas seemed unimpressed. She gave no more than one or two dutiful oohs and ahs, and Claypole found himself having to repeat what had happened in order to impress on her how heroic he had been. At length it was her turn to speak.

'You need a knife,' she said, fumbling in a drawer of the kitchen dresser. 'Everyone in the countryside has a knife.'

'Oh,' he said. She handed him a penknife. 'I suppose...

Yeah.' If he had had a knife, he would not have had to use his teeth on the placental sac.

'You can have that. I've got a few.' Dorcas sat down again.

'Thanks.'

'On one condition. You don't use it on any horses.'

Claypole stared at the floor. He felt upbraided, but was having difficulty understanding what for. There was a pause.

'My sister called me,' said Dorcas quietly.

'Brr,' said Claypole.

'She said you'd left her house in a huff, and she'd tried to find you to give you a lift. There was some tiff with Henderson's Taxis? She also said that you stole her boat.'

'Yes. Well. Brr. She deserved it.'

Dorcas paused thoughtfully before speaking.

'Gossip is vital in an area like this,' she began. 'It's a form of social grooming. If you don't see the other people in the community very often, you have to gossip fast and hard. It's how we guard against mental illness. If someone has hit the bottle, or is bashing their kids, everyone should know about it. Then we all chew over the allegations and the evidence, and act collectively. It's better than a social worker or a judge having to mop the whole thing up after it's too late.'

'Bit claustrophobic,' said Claypole petulantly.

'Oh. But surely it is cities that really make people feel claustrophobic.'

'Farmers are always... you know, offing themselves,' Claypole protested.

'Ah, well, yes,' said Dorcas with a sad smile, 'farming doesn't work so well any more. It used to be a communal activity. It used to take fifty people to do anything, and you'd be chatting away while you did it. These days it's just one chap in a tractor with his headphones on. No wonder they go bonkers.'

'Brr,' said Claypole.

'Oh, well, I... I just wanted to say...'

Dorcas seemed unwilling to finish her sentence.

'Huh,' said Claypole grumpily. 'I just need to get out of here.'

Dorcas drew a thoughtful breath and pursed her lips. 'I've been reading a lot about the Epicureans,' she said.

'Mm,' said Claypole, taking a mouthful of cake, neither knowing nor caring what she was talking about.

'It is said that Epicurus may have written over 300 books, on all subjects from music and food to fair dealing and love. Thirty-seven volumes on Nature alone. Probably the only philosopher you might want to spend an evening with. He not only liked fun, he thought it was of tremendous importance.'

'Yeah. Course. Fun. Brilliant.'

'Well, yes,' Dorcas began, with a cautious note in her voice, 'but who can say they are truly an expert in enjoying themselves? Not "partying", as the current parlance has it. God knows there are enough experts in that. I mean real joy. Long-lasting and profound.'

Claypole began to listen, if only because he detected that he was being patronised.

'Epicurus lived in a commune, and ate bread, olives and cheese, all produced in the back garden of his shared house, and thought about things all day. He had no wealth, and thought it illogical to seek such a thing, because it did not follow that wealthy people were happy. In fact, it seemed to him that the reverse was true.'

Claypole shifted in his seat and frowned. What was she driving at?

'You think you're an entrepreneur, don't you?'

Claypole was about to say that, yes, he did.

'Well, I've got news for you, Gordon. You're not.'

He was about to protest, both at the use of his first name and the accusation. But Dorcas ploughed on.

'And that's a good thing!' She waved at him approvingly with a teaspoon. 'Have you ever met a really successful entrepreneur, Gordon? Have you? They are arrogant, manipulative, selfish, planet-spoiling obsessives, often tortured by self-hatred and addiction, and more or less incapable of even basic empathy, let alone love. You almost have to be that sort to make a lot of money, I suppose. Now. I ask you... is that you, Gordon? Is that why you're doing the wind farm? Is it for the money, or for the good of the world? Or is it something else?'

Claypole blinked incredulously. This was an assault.

'It's a Good Thing, isn't it? Capital "G", capital "T"? Brr... a bit of everything, I s'pose.'

'Hm,' said Dorcas. 'Look, I know I sound like a crazy old goat, and I'm too much of a hermit. Epicurus would not approve. But I have found something important: the pleasure of being at one with your surroundings. The wax and wane of Nature is like a huge cosmic breath. The knowledge, while you are breathing in and out at such a break-neck pace until you run out of breaths, that something much larger and greater than yourself is also breathing, is truly joyful. Spring and summer in, autumn and winter out. In, out. Year after year for aeons. And Nature breathes with such complexity, some of it beautiful, some of it merely awesome.'

Claypole was silenced.

'There is a moment' – Dorcas spoke more slowly now, and drew a little closer to him – 'when the trees stutter in their breath. In fruit trees it's called June Drop, when the trees shed the fruits they know they cannot support and continue growing the ones they know they can. But all trees do it. It's at that moment in the summer when humans are rushing about wearing skimpy tops, or – in my case – just sitting down with a glass of lemonade at the end of the longest day. Everything stops growing, very suddenly, and takes a big breath. Like a child halfway through slaking its thirst with a glass of water. Like the child, the plants have concentrated all their energy on the task in hand and have spared no effort. Then, in the only pause since the first bud of spring, they take that much-needed breath before the final push. It is a moment of the most sublime pleasure when you know from the plants around you that it is happening. I feel like the parent of the whole world at that moment. I want it to succeed and thrive long after I am gone.'

Claypole was unmoving, gawping.

'Oh dear. You have no idea what I am talking about. You look at the discomforts and the strangeness of the countryside and think I must be talking out of my bottom. But I urge you to try and get to a state in which you know that moment, Claypole. Know it, love it, and experience it as many times as you can before you yourself stop taking breaths and cease to be for ever.'

Dorcas put down her tea and smiled. And Claypole, given a natural break in the conversation, leaned across the sofa to kiss her.

-11-

PASSENGER ONE: It's viruses and butterflies.
PASSENGER TWO: What is?
PASSENGER ONE: Life. Misery is like a virus. Once it gets hold of you, it uses you to multiply. Happiness is a butterfly. It arrives lightly, and leaves soon.

Overheard in Departures at Ibiza Airport,
July 2001

Scalded cats have been known to move more sluggishly than Dorcas MacGilp did when presented with Claypole's kiss-face, although there was no need for speed in this instance. Claypole's advance was in the nature of a romantic lean-in, not a lusty jump, and she easily ducked under his embrace and away from his quivering lips. 'Sorry. Oh. God. Shit. Did I...?' he said. 'Wow. Shit. OK. Sorry.'

They had another cup of tea just to pretend that things hadn't become weird, after which she drove him back to the Loch Garvach Hotel, by-the-by mending the Land Rover with an ease that was at once relieving and irritating. In his hotel room, an inspection of his mobile phone revealed it to be encrusted with salt water, and when he plugged it into its charger it was lifeless. So he picked up the hotel phone and dialled his answering service. He entered many numbers and passwords and listened to his messages.

'Good morning Mr Claypole, this is Hunter Chase Bank. We've been –'

Bip. Erase.

'Hi. Kevin Watt again here from the *Glenmorie Herald*. I just –'

Bip. Erase.

'Hey, Claypole. It's Peregrine. I heard you went to Bonnie's and it didn't go very well. Not surprised. Come over tomorrow for breakfast and we'll chew over what to do next. Toodle pip.'

Bip. Message saved.

Claypole slept for fourteen hours straight. He woke at two in the morning, strangely refreshed, and almost sprang upright. Making a pot of filthy coffee using an ancient teasmade, he set to reading the wind farm files. When he looked at his watch next it was seven o'clock, and as he drove the Land Rover (at ponderously slow pace) over to MacGilp House, Claypole knew that when he addressed the meeting at the community hall the following evening, he would have a great deal to say about the Loch Garvach Wind Farm.

At MacGilp House, no one seemed to have risen. Claypole reminded himself that it was early on a Sunday morning and had breakfast alone but for Peregrine's trio of ancient dogs. They watched him, perhaps waiting for the handling error that would release a piece of bacon or a sausage onto the kitchen floor. They would then all scamper to gobble the stray meat. But Claypole couldn't help feeling that the Labrador with three legs was scrutinising him for another purpose.

He had probably had too much coffee, but he imagined that the old dog wanted to know his intentions as regards Coky, whom it had presumably known since it was a skittering pup with all its limbs. He found himself addressing it.

'I don't have a plan, old fella,' he said. 'You tell me. What should I do?'

The hound beheld him with mournful disdain, so he chucked it half a piece of bacon. As he chased his bread around a greasy plate for the vestiges of egg yolk, he heard purposeful bootsteps in the hall, and Peregrine burst into the room carrying a shotgun.

'Ah. Ready to kill?' he barked.

Claypole swallowed, and suddenly the breakfast, so welcome moments before, began to sit heavy.

'We have to go to kirk before the shoot, I'm afraid.' Peregrine was unscrewing a large bottle of whisky. 'Just one of those things.'

'Shoot?'

'Yes.' Peregrine turned to look at Claypole. 'Bit behind the curve aren't you, old boy? It's the Garvach shoot today.' And seeing Claypole's further incomprehension. 'Grouse, man!'

'Right!' spluttered Claypole. 'Grouse. With guns?' He had of course heard of people shooting grouse.

'You can use a bow and arrow if you like, but I don't fancy your chances.'

'Do we...? Is it...?'

He was going to ask whether it was compulsory to actually fire a gun, but he had been stunned into silence by the sight of Peregrine MacGilp emptying the entire bottle of whisky into a huge silver hip flask. Peregrine eyed Claypole closely.

'You're not a *vegetarian*, are you?' said Peregrine.

'No,' said Claypole with indignation.

'Yes. Well. Stick with the ladies. Perhaps that's best.'

'Sure.' Claypole was cheered about the prospect, especially if one of the ladies were Coky.

'And you'll have to come to kirk, of course.'

'Kirk is... church?'

'Mm-hm.' Peregrine was now counting boxes of shotgun cartridges into a hamper.

'Why don't you just take the bottle?' Claypole nodded at the empty bottle of whisky and the hip flask.

'Ha!' Peregrine thought for a moment. 'Well, then the hip flask wouldn't save my life if I got shot, would it?' He inserted the huge silver beast into his breast pocket and patted it. It did indeed cover his heart as well as most of the rest of his torso.

'I've been reading the files,' said Claypole, 'and I think we should talk.'

Peregrine showed no signs of responding to him when the kitchen door opened. Both men turned towards it, and Coky stepped into the room, sending the dogs into a frenzy of excitement. They all charged at her with thrilled lurches and demanded to be fussed over.

'Hi!' she said to humans and dogs alike. Coky was wearing jodhpurs and tight leather riding boots. Claypole tried to get out of his chair, but his legs didn't seem to be working.

'Hello, darling!' Peregrine used the same soupy tone he used for the dogs. 'Now, you'll leave some of the birds for the guests this time, I hope?'

Coky blushed.

'Coky here's the best shot of all of us.'

She smiled modestly, and turned to Claypole.

'Ready to kill?' she said.

Having gone to a Church of England school that required a certain amount of time to be put in worship-wise, the teenaged Claypole had given some lazy thought to whether God did or did not exist. He had decided that, on the balance of the evidence available to him, it was more likely that the whole thing was a myth. He had made this calculation logically and rationally. Therefore, if God *did* exist, and was as forgiving as reputed, Claypole could not be blamed for drawing such a conclusion, and would therefore be excused at the Reckoning, should there in fact turn out to be such a thing. In the meantime, he was happy to abide by all the commandments except those that were clearly out of date or inconvenient. But he had no atheistical zeal, and had absorbed, even in the semi-waking slouch that he adopted during his religious education, some notion of the span of the Christian faiths. Scotland, he remembered, had various brands of Protestantism that ranged from the broad Church of Scotland to stricter and tinier sects, which were indistinguishable from large, gloomy families. He therefore went to kirk without any expectation except that of being bored. In any case, his mind was very much on other things. Coky had agreed to give him a lesson on how to fire a shotgun so that he might stand by her side at the afternoon's slaughter. He was by her side now, and that was all he wanted.

The Garvach kirk was no more than a whitewashed cottage, but it had a cute grace given it by dark leaded windows and a large arched door painted with that terracotta red you find on the underside of old fishing boats. The beach, just fifty yards below it, served as the car park, and there was storm-flung seaweed on the drystone walls of the cemetery. The rotting notice board, worn by time and sea air, had two fliers pinned inside it with rusty thumb tacks. One advertised a talent show and curry night three months ago, and one instructed the reader most sternly to 'Visit Norway'. Claypole was about to point this out to Coky, but the seriousness of her face stopped him. Her expression was, to his amusement and surprise, devout.

'Do you disapprove of shooting on a Sunday?' he asked, but she did not answer.

When they had filed into the kirk along with no more than a couple of dozen others, including Peregrine and Bonnie (studiously ignoring each other at opposite ends of one pew), a man in a dark suit stepped with serious intent onto a raised dais.

The Minister, Jim Fry, was a tall man in his fifties with eyebrows like poisonous caterpillars. Claypole watched him as he greeted each individual congregant very slowly with a furious stare. This look was intense enough to be very useful when rounding up sheep or trying to frighten children, but Claypole thought this was surely no way to greet consenting adults. He turned to Coky, but her face warned him against further flippancy.

'I shall now invite you,' said the Minister in a gravelly Glasgow accent, 'to sing hymn number 704...'

He coughed lightly to alert the organist and muttered the name of the hymn in her direction. The owlish organist was smiling pleasantly, but in a world of her own.

'Jeanie!?' barked the Minister crossly, and the organist grimaced as she bolted upright and squinted through her large tinted spectacles at the Minister.

'Sorry, pet,' Jeanie shouted cheerily as if they were alone in the building, and bumbled her way into the depths of the hymnbook in front of her, taking a long time to find the correct page. As she did so, itches were scratched and yawns were stifled in all of the congregation apart from two: Coky, who was desperately staring ahead, looking as if she were in terrible pain; and Claypole, who was open-mouthed and staring at the organist.

With a satisfied 'hurrumph', Jeanie folded down a page of the hymnal and immediately crashed her plump hands onto the plastic keyboard. The old organ howled in protest, almost quietly at first and then, as the loud pedal kicked and thrummed into life, suddenly at ear-splitting volume. Those near the speakers lurched backwards as a wall of sound came at them.

Claypole made his urge to laugh worse by suppressing it, and put his hand over his mouth. Coky was herself in the middle of trying to control her own rapidly building giggles, and they deliberately did not meet eyes.

'Sorry,' mouthed Jeanie as she squinted at the page in front of her. The organ continued with the melody, but was suddenly reduced to almost no volume at all. Jeanie's expression betrayed that she knew this wasn't right, but equally that she could do little about it.

Jeanie and the organ fought valiantly with each other as they wallowed through the first four lines of the hymn by way of introduction. Claypole had never heard the tune before. It was both mournful and chaotic. The other faces in the congregation seemed unconcerned, so Claypole cleared his throat with the confidence of a man who is going to mouth his way through a song he does not know while others do the work, in the knowledge that he will get away with the fraud.

But when the music started up again, Jeanie going back to the first line with an improvised flourish, several very different noises came from the congregation. One or two men growled an upward glissando, apparently fixing their pitch wherever the mood took them. One woman began with a soprano wail somewhere near Top C, and found that she had to stop and recalibrate more towards the middle of the range for *Homo sapiens.* Others seemed to pick a volume and a key that they knew suited them, and warbled uncertainly in the direction they imagined the tune was supposed to take. Had this been a rehearsal, a choirmaster would have stopped by tapping his baton on a music stand and bellowing 'No, no, no!', or possibly simply breaking his baton in two and walking off to become a postman. But this was kirk, and the momentum of the several different hymns they had begun was unstoppable. The Minister peered over his hymnbook with alarm, but carried on singing in his fulsome baritone.

Unaccountably considering what a bad idea they both knew it to be, Coky and Claypole met eyes. Instantly, they regretted it. Coky's nostrils began to quiver as she sang without volume, and her chin to shake. Claypole gave a 'ha!', but quickly pretended it had been a sneeze. Coky's eyes began silently to water.

Jeanie continued to thunder or whisper through the tune, cajoling the unruly organ beneath her flapping, tweeded arms.

As Claypole began to sing in a voice so small that the pitch and tone might be undetectable, Coky planted a finger firmly in the corner of one eye, her hand trying to hide the rest of her face, and she was partly doubled over. A generous assumption would have been that she had something very painful in her eye, and possibly osteoporosis as well, but Claypole could feel the bench shaking.

Eventually, the hymn ended and everyone sat. Coky gave Claypole a surreptitious flick on the arm, clearly blaming him for her hysterics. He retaliated with a playful punch on her thigh. They both stared straight ahead. Minister Fry beheld everyone individually again, pausing particularly to inspect the red-eyed Coky and the ashen Claypole. The Minister closed his eyes in reverence before starting his sermon.

'What...' he asked, with wistful cadence, 'do we find in the middle of the road... at night?'

He was staring at the congregation. After several seconds' pause beyond the merely rhetorical, to Claypole's horror one of the congregation piped up.

'Weeds?'

'No,' said the Minister definitively. He raised his magnificent eyebrows and cast around the congregation for other responses.

'A fox?' said another.

The Minister continued to look.

'Midges,' said a young girl.

'That wasn't what I was thinking of. No, *on* the road.'

'Horse poo,' said a boy of four, and some of the other children giggled. The Minister ignored them, and the congregation all continued to rack their brains. Claypole knew what the Minister was thinking of, and he knew why no one in the congregation would ever guess. They all lived in remote Scotland, and they all lived down single-track roads, rarely travelling on anything else.

'Cat's eyes,' he said, quietly.

'What? Who was that?' The Minister shot a look in his direction, and for one horrible moment Claypole thought he might be wrong, or worse, that he might have caused offence. But the Minister was looking straight at him, and he could not avoid repeating himself, this time more clearly.

'I just... Brr... Cat's eyes?'

'Aye!' shouted the Minister in delighted triumph. 'Cat's eyes.'

The rest of the sermon explored a clunky metaphor about 'lighting the way', and rounded off with a joke in poor taste about a dead cat. Claypole sat feeling the eyes of the rest of the congregation on the back of his neck while Coky dug him in the ribs, whispering 'swot' and 'teacher's pet' so that only he could hear. After some more excruciating hymns and a reading from a particularly gruesome section of Revelations, Jeanie struck up the organ with a Lloyd-Webber medley and they all filed out.

The Minister shook the hands of everyone as they left kirk, and Coky's smile as she greeted Jim Fry was of such joyousness that the Minister visibly brightened.

'I'm so glad you enjoyed it,' said the Minister to Coky, whose grin became even brighter. 'Have you come far?' Suddenly the Minister found himself shaking hands with the small fat man with broken teeth and a shaved head, and the striking Indian girl with the fixed grin had moved on.

'That was *spectacular,*' said Claypole gravely, and shook the Minister's hand like a long-lost brother. He and the Minister discussed the weather for twenty seconds, and Claypole caught up with Coky when she was halfway towards the Land Rover. He was expecting continued hilarity, but her mood had suddenly changed.

'That was... hilarious,' he ventured.

'Yeah,' she said, but her face said otherwise.

'What's the matter?'

'Did you hear what he said? "Have you come far?" Like he didn't know me. I've known him for twenty years and all he sees... *still*... is a brown face.'

'Oh.' Claypole didn't know how to react. They climbed into the car in silence. When they were half a mile or so away, Claypole spoke again.

'Is there... Do you get a lot of that sort of thing here...?'

'Yup,' said Coky curtly. 'Actually,' she said after a pause, 'it's not the prejudice I mind. At least prejudice is based on something. It has a certain ignorant logic. "I am suspicious of brown people. You are a brown person. Therefore I am suspicious of you." All the time I am assumed to be from somewhere else because of the colour of my skin. I'm not Indian, and I never will be. I'm Scottish. But never mind that. The thing that makes me cross is when people are prejudiced *after* they know me. Even people I've known for years still treat me differently. They ask me to order the curry for the carry-out; they ask me about yoga; they assume that my life is somehow like my genes: half Indian. I even had Lachlan asking me if I needed more clothing the other day, like I needed looking after in this cold climate or something.'

'Ah yes, Lachlan,' said Claypole with a sneer.

'Have you been listening?' He turned to look at her in surprise, but the irritation in her voice had gone as quickly as it had arrived. 'Ach, sod it.' They sat quietly for a moment before Coky spoke again. 'He likes you, you know. Lachlan.'

'Really?'

'Yeah. He said. You should give him another go.'

Claypole could not resist a jibe. 'You certainly did.'

Now Coky really was angry. 'Excuse me?'

Claypole swallowed, now regretting having raised the topic of Coky's night in Lachlan's van. 'The other night when you...'

Coky looked at him with horror. 'I did *not* sleep with Lachlan Black,' she said with a shudder. 'I helped him to bed because that's what friends do.' She huffed, and spoke almost to herself. 'God. Why does everything have to be so...?'

She trailed off into fuming silence, and Claypole was forced to reassess his assumptions about what had taken place on the night of the party at Glen Drum beach.

Arriving at MacGilp House, Claypole and Coky went immediately to the empty Victorian walled garden to practise firing a shotgun. Coky assumed that Claypole had fired a gun before. He didn't want to disappoint her, so he nodded sagely as she rattled through the basics.

'Well, here you go.' Coky handed him a twelve-bore shotgun with two cartridges loaded. 'Try and hit the can I've placed on that box hedge over there, and we'll see how your aim is.'

Claypole took the gun from her as if it were a day-old baby and then nearly dropped it from the weight. Then he raised it to the wrong shoulder and gazed uncertainly down the twin barrels. She corrected his grip and he aimed again. At the end of the barrels, and in between them, there was a helpful-looking bead of metal. But he found that if he focused on it, two cans would appear beyond, out of focus. Likewise, if he focused on the can, two beads would appear either side of it. But he said nothing, made his eyes go out of focus for everything as if looking at an Impressionist painting and lined twin cans somewhere near twin beads. He pulled the trigger. The gun recoiled dramatically, and the end of it shot up in the air.

'Ow,' he said. But then he saw that the can had been blasted from its position on the box hedge and it lay riven and mangled on the ground. He turned to Coky with undisguised glee.

'You'll be fine,' she said. 'I'll stick by you all the same.'

Claypole rejoiced. He had managed both to impress her and to cause her to be his companion for the afternoon. As they walked back to the house, he decided to capitalise on his success and ask her a question that had been nagging him.

'You're an eco-warrior, right?'

'Eco-accountant,' she corrected him with a smile.

'Yeah. Well, how do you square that with... You know...' He nodded at the gun she was carrying. He didn't want directly to accuse her of hypocrisy.

'Eh?'

'Um,' he continued. 'You like to kill birds, right?'

'Only grouse.'

'They're birds, aren't they?'

She looked at him with interest and amusement. 'Ah-ha! You're doing it!'

Now it was his turn to be confused. 'Doing what?'

'Weighing up an action in terms of its environmental consequence.'

Claypole sank into thought. 'Fuck me,' he said suddenly and stopped walking.

'Yeah, it's a real thing, isn't it? Very addictive.'

But Claypole's expletive had not been apropos of their conversation. He was staring at an old red tractor parked in a barn with double doors to it.

'What?' asked Coky.

'I'm having... Brr... It's a memory... or a déjà vu, or...' He stood and stared at the tractor, his mind turning over images from long ago that were by turns vivid and opaque.

'Never mind,' he said quickly, but frowned as he continued walking.

As they returned to the courtyard behind the house, they came across the shooting party, which was mustering itself in joyful chaos. There was Peregrine himself, several men of a similar vintage and class to him, a few women of ruddy and weathered demeanour, and a pair of American men. These men, in identical plus fours, woollen hose with loudly coloured garters, brand-new tweed jackets with shiny leather patches and worsted shirts, with their grey hair poking out from under extravagant tartan hats. It would be very difficult to describe to a Martian what it was that was different about their appearance from that of their host. Peregrine wore roughly the same gear, and even sported a ruby cravat, but something indefinable set him apart – and it wasn't just the kilt.

Coky sidled up to Claypole and whispered, 'The yanks look gayer than Freddie Mercury, don't they?'

Claypole nodded.

But Peregrine, although he was being loud, did not seem to be the master of ceremonies, and only appeared to be interested in making sure all the food and the booze were accounted for. It was Coky who quietly sorted out the guns and ammo and had quiet conversations with the beaters and loaders who, Claypole noticed, numbered Lachlan and Milky among them. People milled about, and dogs were everywhere, excitedly peeing on everyone's boots. Land Rovers began to start up. Claypole hopped into the one containing Coky and the two Americans. He was greeted in an overfamiliar fashion by one of them.

'I know old Perry's takin' me for a ride, but I don't care. Now my Ginny's gone I got no one to spend money on. I wouldn't be invited if I didn't pay, would I?' He winked.

'Oh. Brr...' Claypole flustered. 'Are you... a good shot?'

The man looked puzzled. 'I don't come for the shootin'. I come for the ceilidh!' And he clicked his fingers in a way that indicated that he had absolutely no rhythm whatsoever. Claypole smiled weakly, and the Land Rover lurched off.

It was after some twenty minutes of bumpy ride through woodland that the convoy stopped, and the party began to tramp across rough heather. In films of shooting parties there always seemed to be clouds of grouse, pinging in all directions and dying in Passchendaele numbers. This was certainly not the case here. The odd shot was fired at grey-brown streaks, but you could hardly call it action-packed. During the lulls between what Claypole thought could be described as other lulls, Coky chatted to him quietly about various aspects of gun safety without making him feel as if he were being babysat, although he clearly was. Once again he had cause to marvel at her ability to be kind and tactful.

'It's a good idea to keep the safety catch on while you're walking', she would gently suggest; 'If you're climbing a gate, you shouldn't really have your gun loaded'; and "perhaps you might like to keep it pointed at the ground," she would add intermittently, with a gentle hand on the barrel of his gun.

The shoot, it seemed from Peregrine's rapidly building temper, was not going well. His harsh voice, floating across the moor, could hardly be mistaken for that of a man having a good time.

'Where are all the bloody birds?' he shouted at Lachlan more than once, whose fault it could hardly be but who never left the old man's side and seemed to be his personal bagman.

'Slim pickin's, Perry!' said one of the ancient Americans with uncompromising honesty. 'Maybe it's divine retribution!'

Peregrine smiled thinly and fumed, muttering something that only Lachlan would have been able to hear. Lachlan did not smile.

'If Peregrine weren't so tight,' Coky whispered, 'he'd have managed the moor better.'

The party continued to trek further into nowhere in search of grouse. The midges became more intense, and the ground more intent on twisting the ankles of the unwary. But there were more birds, and Peregrine's hollering became more cheerful. As they walked further into the bleak hills, it seemed to Claypole that every time a dog bounded forward into the springy heather ahead of the line of guns, something feathery would fly up with a kerfuffle. With a short pause, the bird or birds would then be blasted at, and more often than not they would then cease flying and plummet to the ground with an ugly twist, landing on the ground with a deathly bounce.

Claypole spent his time tramping awkwardly through dusty heather, coughing quietly and swatting midges away from his ears, trying not to fall over. The first time he was allowed to fire, he raised his gun in a panicky arc and tried to locate anything in the sky near the end of the barrel. When he fired he had been holding the gun gingerly, and the butt had recoiled into his shoulder painfully. Of course, he had hit nothing. The second time, having been given further tips by Coky, he held the gun so tightly into his shoulder that he forgot to aim at all and the shot wanged harmlessly towards a lone cloud. The third time he squeezed the trigger and thought he might have been somewhere near hitting a bird, nothing happened because the safety catch was still on. He had just about got the hang of firing the gun when the last manoeuvre was announced.

'You're up,' Coky said excitedly. 'Whatever comes over you, you try and get the bead just ahead of it and fire. OK?'

Claypole knew that she had sacrificed her own shoot for his sake. She had allowed herself only six cartridges, and had bagged a grouse every time. He owed her some sort of victory therefore, and swore to himself that if anything coming out of the undergrowth had wings, be it owl, seagull or parrot, it would die. With gritted teeth and a bloodlusty squint, he leaned forward and raised the butt of his gun to chest height as she had instructed, adopting a stance like a keen pointer.

'Oh. Snipe!' said Coky. The snipe, a darting creature that had nothing of the fluttering grace of the grouse or its straight trajectory, came out of the heather just fifteen paces from them, and shot out at an angle, wheeling back towards them and up into the sky. Claypole raised his gun rapier-quick.

'Get it,' said Coky with excited insistence. Claypole

hesitated. He knew he was nowhere near being able to hit the thing, and he wheeled the gun about in the sky wildly, trying to line the bird up with the bead on the end of his gun.

'Go on, fire!' she said. But the bird broke its line and dived down again towards the horizon. Claypole pulled the end of the gun down to follow it. Just as he was preparing to fire, he took his focus off the bird. He saw other movement in his eyeline. Fifty yards away, staring in horror at Claypole, were Lachlan Black and Peregrine MacGilp. They both ducked instinctively as they saw Claypole's gun wheel in their direction, with the snipe between the end of his gun and them. Just beyond the bead of his gun, Claypole saw Lachlan barge Peregrine to the floor and cover the old man with his own body. It was not a feudal gesture, though – more of an instinctive reaction. In any case, it made Claypole hesitate, despite his avowed intention to murder the snipe.

'Go on,' commanded Coky, looking only at Claypole. He closed his eyes, tensed himself for the recoil, and squeezed the trigger.

There was silence for a moment, a wisp of smoke, and then pandemonium.

When he heard the shot pass a not-unworrisome six feet or so over his and Peregrine's sprawled bodies, Lachlan quickly got to his feet and shouted at Coky. It was a sentence too fearful to contain swear words, and too angry to be cogent. Coky immediately raised her hands in abject apology. Claypole just stood there dumbly shocked. Peregrine struggled to his feet. Lachlan turned to him with a worried look. Claypole could not hear what was said, but Peregrine threw down his gun and pushed the younger man twice, clearly giving him an earful. It was an argument conducted at contained volume, but vicious. Lachlan had to keep backing away and putting his hands up in placation. He did not raise his voice, but eventually turned and walked away, shedding various hampers and bags in his wake. Peregrine continued to mutter away to himself, even after he had picked up his gun and begun to head back down the hill for the long walk to the Land Rovers.

Claypole turned the incident over in his mind as the party sat on rugs and on tailgates, munching pâtés and cheeses and drinking warm whisky in the cool breeze. Claypole felt sheepish, and drank only water. But that wasn't what occupied his thoughts. Why had Peregrine reacted so badly? Yes, he had been pushed to the ground. But Lachlan's intentions had surely only been to protect his employer. Could Peregrine not see this? Coky was continually apologetic to her uncle, but the old man was inconsolable. He kept going on, not about Claypole's stupidity in letting off a shot that had endangered him, nor Coky's excitement getting the better of her caution, but about Lachlan's impertinence. If it had not been for the infectious delight of the Americans, kept unaware of how close death had been to visiting the party, there would have been ill-tempered silence instead of excited chatter about the evening's impending festivities.

Some distance away in a camper van, Lachlan and Milky were having a much darker conversation. They were debating the pros and cons of a crime for which it was possible to receive a life sentence.

'He nearly shot you, Lachy. That's got to be paid for.'

'Good enough reason, maybe.' But Lachlan did not hold a grudge for a near-accident at a shooting party.

He had other reasoning.

'You know what, Milky?'

Milky turned to his old friend excitedly. 'What?'

'We should kidnap him.'

LEONTES: Do't, and thou hast the one half of my heart;
Do't not, thou splitt'st thine own.
>> *A Winter's Tale*, Act I, scene. ii, William Shakespeare

'Claypole, there's someone I'd like you to meet,' said Peregrine in the hall of MacGilp House, all aftershave and bonhomie. It was six o'clock, and the shooting party was reassembling as a dinner party, with additional guests arriving by the minute. Some were in the drawing room, talking or flipping through old copies of pompous magazines. Some were still getting ready in their rooms – bathing, drinking, making themselves smart. And some were, as Claypole was, just hanging around waiting for the party to start, avoiding Peregrine's weapons-grade drinks. He felt the need to keep a clear head for the evening.

'This is Harry,' said Peregrine with laden significance, 'he's a *real* wind farmer.'

Since Claypole had last met Harry, the world had changed. The Berlin Wall was now landfill; New Labour had come and gone; and being a children's television star had gone from pinnacle to pits. Also, Harry had grown up and the fog of time had covered any recognition he might have had for Claypole from one afternoon twenty-five years previously. It might have been the same for Claypole had it not been for the half-memory brought back that afternoon by the sight of a red tractor. But Claypole felt a lurch of horror as he shook Harry's hand and sustained a violent coughing fit.

Once Claypole had regained his composure, he stood upright again and looked full into Harry's eyes, desperate not to find a hint of recognition. He found nothing but pity. With one ostensibly charming wink Harry managed effortlessly to say, 'It's OK, you are an idiot, but I forgive you.'

'Brr,' said Claypole. His eye level was at Button Two of Harry's expensive pink shirt. Claypole felt as if he were from a fatter and more troglodytic species.

'Hi,' said Harry with a manly bark. 'Pleased to meet you.'

'Awright,' said Claypole, now averting his eyes.

'I expect you two have a lot to talk about,' said Peregrine.

The men stood in silence.

Peregrine offered them cocktails, particularly pushing gin and Dubonnet with a jaunty 'if it's good enough for Her Majesty, it's good enough for me'. Harry accepted but Claypole opted for coffee, pleading that he required the caffeine. He went off at Peregrine's grumpy suggestion to make it himself, and bumbled around the kitchen, stepping around busy caterers and over reclining dogs, reflecting that all he had to do was get through the evening without making a fool of himself and stay fresh and sober for the meeting at the community hall the following day. At dinner, he said to himself, he would be as silent as he could possibly make himself.

Just as he took the first sip of the enormous bucket of coffee he had concocted, Coky appeared.

'Ah. There you are,' she said coyly. She was wearing a little black dress, a small black cardigan and high heels, and was carrying a brown envelope. He had never seen her dressed up or made up, and he was momentarily disorientated. She was showing by most standards a very modest amount of cleavage, but it was certainly different from the shotgun-wielding killer of the hills, and the transformation was intense. He tried to smile, but the hot coffee scalded his lips. She whispered, 'Come with me.'

Coky led a wide-eyed Claypole to a chilly room next to the kitchen. On the shelves were trays covered in linen cloths and many decanters of wine. She turned to him with a conspiratorial bent.

'I just want you to know,' said Coky excitedly, 'I think you're doing really well.' Her face was not more than six inches from his. 'And I've got something to show you.'

Claypole had so rarely been propositioned that he was ill-equipped to know whether the light in Coky's eye was as it might look if she wanted to kiss him. He swallowed and sucked in his stomach.

'Look!' she said, and smoothed the front of her dress. Claypole was appalled. He didn't want it to be like this. He wanted candlelight, and music. Coky slipping out of a negligée in a Venice hotel bedroom. Not this. Not like some back-alley barmaid type showing her boobs for a port and lemon.

'What...?' he managed.

Coky handed him the brown envelope, and Claypole drew out the contents, examining them in the dim light as Coky continued.

It was two sets of land release documents, as drafted by an Edinburgh law firm, one for the attention of Dorcas MacGilp and one for Bonnie Straughan. They were both signed.

'Dorcas's one had a note on it from her. It said, "If Claypole wonders why, tell him: because he didn't ask." But I can't imagine what you said to my mother to make her change her mind.'

'I didn't...' Claypole started, but couldn't think of what to say.

Coky leaned forward and kissed Claypole on the cheek. He felt himself blush instantly. Seeing this, the smile went from her face, and she backed away. The air between them seemed to freeze.

'Listen, Claypole,' she said, and retreated another step. 'There's something you should know about me.'

Claypole gulped. 'You're a cop?' Coky was not smiling, so he tried again. 'You're a bloke?'

'Oh, shut up a minute. This is important. I suppose I have developed a habit... The same way some people find themselves having the odd cigarette, then they buy a packet for parties, then it's two or three a day, and suddenly they are a smoker. That's pretty much how it happened to me...'

'Yes,' he said knowingly.

Coky looked puzzled. 'What?'

'I know,' said Claypole in condescending triumph. 'Don't worry.'

'Really?' Her puzzlement continued.

'Yes,' he said, 'I can see. It doesn't take a genius to work out your... little problem. Pretty obvious, really.

Your secret is safe with me.'

His smile was broad and understanding.

'Oh. Right.' She seemed almost deflated. 'OK then.'

'What was it? Smack?'

'I beg your pardon?'

'Weed, then. Or was it alcohol? I don't mind. I mean, I'm no saint, so...'

'What are you talking about?'

Suddenly, Claypole doubted himself. But it was too late.

'You're a... You've had problems with...' he began, but her expression was suddenly both confused and offended. He knew that he had made a mistake, but he could not stop his sentence from completing. '... drugs.'

'Gordon, I'm talking about sex.'

'Oh,' he said. 'Brr.'

'I started saying no to men, even when I liked them. I just... well, because I didn't want the complication, the embarrassment and the hassle involved in dealing with it all. When I found that it made me feel better about myself, I suppose I just got hooked.'

Claypole blinked several times. She was looking at him in a way that indicated that he should say something.

'Right,' he said.

'Yeah. Well. I suppose...' She looked at Claypole. 'I just thought you should know... My habit is the habit of not sleeping with people.'

Claypole made a noise like a tyre deflating. 'Pff. Yeah. Cool.'

'Great.' She smiled. 'Good. Come on. Let's stop talking shite and go and enjoy the party.'

And then she was gone. Claypole was left in the

pantry, holding a brown envelope in his hand, and with his dangerously weak heart dangerously close to broken.

-+=◎=+-

Some minutes later, Claypole was still dazed, but had allowed his legs to carry him to the drawing room. Peregrine grabbed him by the arm.

'Come in, my dear old thing,' he said. He had clearly had a couple of gin and Dubonnets already. 'All ready for tomorrow?'

'Yes. I've been meaning to talk to you about that,' said Claypole, trying to introduce a note of caution.

'Never mind that now. No shop talk tonight!' Peregrine yelled, dragging him into a circle of guests. Peregrine placed Claypole in front of a small woman in a red trilby and barked, 'This is Miko! She's a shepherd, and she also composes electronic pop for Israeli transsexuals.'

'Brr,' said Claypole, trying not to elbow the woman's drink out of her hand.

'Only *one* of my clients is a transsexual,' said the woman. Claypole wondered why she sounded apologetic. But Peregrine was introducing others.

'George and Vesper are funeral directors.'

A bald man in octagonal spectacles nodded, and a woman in pink raised her glass and smiled.

'We're, um,' said the man, 'we're wicker-basket and bury-you-in-a-field types, not the brass-and-mahogany sort.'

'Right,' said Claypole.

'And Harry Lightfoot you've met,' said Peregrine. 'Campaigner, businessman, saviour of the planet.'

'Bollocks, Peregrine. You're a silly arse, and you're embarrassing everyone.' Harry's tone was light, and Peregrine giggled delightedly. Harry winked at Claypole and continued his conversation, which seemed to be with everyone.

'You can't own pets and say you're an environmentalist. You just can't. Domestic cats kill about eight million birds a year in Britain, and dogs require an enormous amount of meat, which is incredibly unsound carbon-wise.'

Some nodded. Some sipped their drinks. Peregrine looked at Harry with pure outrage.

'But, but, but... dogs are the... cornerstone of the countryside!' Peregrine examined the faces of the others, hoping for encouragement. 'Everyone's got a dog, for heaven's sake! I mean, there's... shooting... and... hunting, and fishing... well, no. All right, not fishing. But I mean to say... You'll be saying humans eat too much meat next. This carbon doo-dah has got completely out of hand, if you ask me. I mean, what about breathing? Do you want me to knock that off too?'

'Hey,' Harry shrugged. 'Population is a problem too.'

'Well, ladies and gents,' said Peregrine clasping his hands together. 'That's just the hors d'oeuvres. Aren't you looking forward to Harry going head to head with our guest of honour over dinner? I know I am.'

Peregrine slapped Harry on the back before moving off, and Harry raised his eyes to heaven. Claypole was wondering whether he should introduce himself to the group when a large man in his sixties appeared at the door, and everyone's attention seemed to be drawn to him. In suede shoes and new-looking corduroy trousers, accompanied by a small woman in a pashmina with brittle blond hair, the man beamed at the room professionally. Peregrine fussed around the couple.

'Have you met Banfield Haines?' asked Harry, *sotto voce*. Claypole said he had heard the name but couldn't place it. Harry explained.

An averagely successful barrister before the current government, Banfield Haines QC had shared chambers with the Chancellor of the Exchequer decades before. The friendship had remained, although there were rumours that it was beginning to sour now that Banfield had been made Lord Haines, and had been given the job of Minister for Constitutional Reform. Haines and his wife, the reliably irritating political columnist Marian Pace, had a holiday home across the loch.

'It seems that he regards the job title of Constitutional Reform Minister as honorary. No reform need actually take place.'

This fiery streak in Harry Lightfoot, along with the ability openly to insult Peregrine and get away with it, was both unexpected and welcome. Claypole encouraged Harry to continue.

When he first started coming up to Loch Garvach for holidays, Banfield had appeared to be nothing more than an affable fogey – full of claret and good stories. But the government years had turned him into a puffy, meretricious bully. Claypole was just wondering idly if there was any merit in sucking up to Lord Haines to further the interests of the Loch Garvach Wind Farm, when Harry added with a snarl, 'and he absolutely *hates* wind farms'.

Claypole looked at Harry Lightfoot. He so wanted to hate him, with his vast mop of dishevelled sandy hair and his ramrod posture. But Harry was entertaining, vituperative, articulate and fabulously indiscreet. Far from being someone from whom Claypole wanted to hide, he might be useful to hide behind.

'Are you going to... brr?'

'Tackle them?' said Harry, draining his glass. 'Aye.'

Claypole looked across the room at Coky, who was talking to the Americans from the shooting party. She smiled at him, which just made him feel sadder. Claypole turned back to Harry and was shocked to see an unpleasant leer on his face. Harry was also looking at Coky, and winking. Claypole's blood turned to brimstone. But there was no time to kill Harry Lightfoot, because the gong for dinner sounded in the hall.

Dinner took place – or rather, was performed – in the grand old dining room of MacGilp House under the square dusty outlines where family portraits had once hung. The party wallowed in artichoke mousse and picked its way through quail, then hoovered up lemon posset. Claypole had been seated next to a woman who had recently come to Loch Garvach to paint and recover from a painful divorce. They were rubbing along adequately until she said innocently, 'It's so peaceful in this part of the world compared to London. You must love it here', and Claypole froze.

'Peaceful?' he said, and turned to her. Her innocent expression was broken by his incredulity. 'Brr. It is *not* peaceful!'

Her brow knitted, but he could not let it go. He spoke through gritted teeth.

'The countryside is appallingly bloody noisy. In every corner of every valley, and on every patch of grass and in every inch of tree are the sounds of beast and bird and everything else fighting or fucking.'

The woman could only blink at him.

'You only have to put your ear to the air, particularly at night. Doesn't take long to tune into the screeching and rustling and squawking and slithering that is breaking and beating all around you. The death and the sex perpetually pound and bite and gnaw away at you from every surface, behind and under every object, and in every damp nook and open space. It's deafening.'

The woman's eyes were welling up, but Claypole could not stop himself.

'The only thing that these fuckers and fighters stop for is the rain. As soon as the rain stops, they're all at it again. A bigger one chasing a smaller one for one reason or another until one or other of their tiny hearts gives out and they get buggered or eaten. Then something smaller still will polish off every last scrap of them before sunrise.'

The woman was staring into her pudding, but Claypole did not notice. 'I tell you, it's a multi-layered cacophony of orgy and murder. Peaceful? Brr.'

Claypole sipped his water and waited for the woman to agree with him. A few seconds passed before she began to cry gently into her lemon posset. He looked around him to see if anyone else had noticed, and went to place a surreptitious hand on her shoulder. She shrank away from him. So Claypole turned to his other side.

Instantly engaged in conversation by a stout and heavily pearled woman, he was asked what he was doing in Loch Garvach, and he told her. But just as she was beginning to give him the benefit of her opinions about wind farming, one of the Americans joined in with an observation about the wind farms in

California. Within seconds, the subject of wind farms engulfed the whole table.

'So, Harry!' bellowed Banfield Haines so that all other conversations were cut short. 'How is the world of wind?' His tone was mocking.

Harry finished his mouthful in a considered way and took a glug of wine before answering.

'Wind farming has changed. It used to be a few crazy people in sandals desperately trying to get tiny projects off the ground in the face of ignorance and suspicion. It was still a bit like that when I started in the business ten years ago.' Here he looked significantly at Claypole. 'Now it is like any other business. There is still ignorance and suspicion, but everyone thinks they know all about it.'

Haines frowned. 'But we *do* know more about it these days. It's in the newspapers all the time.'

Harry snarled, and looked at Marian Pace. 'Mm. Does that mean we are any the wiser?'

Haines scoffed, but his wife took up the baton. 'What do you think of Peregrine's project, Harry? Do you think he'll get the go-ahead to spoil another chunk of Scotland?'

'Ah, you're one of *them*,' Harry muttered darkly.

'I don't know what you mean by that,' said Marian Pace archly, 'but you have to admit, even if you think they're useful, that they are a ghastly scar on some of our most beautiful landscape.'

The words hung in the air. She looked around the table as if no one could possibly disagree with her. Harry stared into his wine.

'Is that it?' he asked of his wine, quietly. The atmosphere suddenly chilled.

'I'm sorry?' Haines knew bare-faced cheek when he

heard it, and could not but react. Claypole didn't know what to think. This was embarrassing, but was it also damaging to his interests? He knew the best policy was to remain quiet.

'Who cares?!' Harry had raised his voice. It had the effect of bringing anyone who was not concentrating absolutely to attention. 'Who cares whether it's beautiful or not?'

There was some harrumphing and shifting in seats. Coky attempted to diffuse.

'Some people think they *are* beautiful, Marian. Me included. I –'

'This could be the ugliest country in the world...' Harry interrupted. 'The ugliest part of the ugliest country... and if wind farming wasn't a good thing to do, then it shouldn't be done. Never mind that there may or may not be a beauty in form and function. But, really... why are we having an aesthetic debate about a power station? No one says they don't like nuclear power because the power stations aren't very pretty!'

'But,' Marian Pace leaned over the table, her face reddening, 'wind farms are ugly!'

Harry smiled grimly. 'Have you actually seen a wind farm?'

'Of course.'

'Where?'

'Coming up here yesterday.'

Harry's smile was sly. 'Oh yes. The one near Moffat, or the one in Cumbria? And the road from which you saw it... the M6... or the M74. Is a motorway a thing of beauty and a joy for ever?'

Marian Pace narrowed her eyes unpleasantly.

'When you build a wind farm,' Harry slurred, 'you have to set aside money to reinstate the land exactly

– exactly – as it was before you built it. You don't have to do that with a housing estate; you don't have to do that with a factory. But you have to do it with a wind farm. It's a very good idea, of course. It's completely unfair, but it is a good idea. If someone finds a better way of making electricity, in twenty-five years the wind farm gets taken down again with no harm done. What we've all got to get used to, and fast, is that we're not in the business of ruining the countryside to the benefit of cities, or the other way around. We are in the business of saving the entire world from total meltdown.'

Claypole wondered whether Harry had lost his audience by being over dramatic.

'Shouldn't we be using less electricity instead of building more power stations?' asked the woman next to Claypole.

'Yes!' Harry was shouting. 'Absolutely. But we should be doing that as well as, not instead of, renewable electricity generation. We have to do everything to combat climate change. Energy efficiency, offshore wind, onshore wind, solar, tidal, the lot. We can't just pick and choose.'

The rest of the table was quiet. No one wanted to be the next target of Harry's righteous ire. He continued.

'Our generation will be asked by the next, "What did you do in the war against global warming?" If the answer is nothing, or not enough, they will be incredulous. They will ask "Why not? You knew there was a problem... you knew that it was up to you... and yet you did nothing." And they will not forgive us. They will hate us, and rightly.'

Claypole looked around. Some of Harry's audience were frowning. A few were leaning back sceptically. Some were trying to think of something else.

'And frankly,' Harry continued, 'if you don't think that's what we are doing, then you can join the cab drivers, the oil and gas lobby, Nigel Lawson and a few disaffected scientists, and you will die in your ignorance and your self-interest.'

With that, he drained his wine.

'You don't have to be a climate change denier,' said Marian Pace in a measured tone, 'to want to question things. That's what a civilised society does.'

'Yes, you can ask questions. But I've answered them. I am an expert, and I'm telling you that this is *the* major threat. Or,' he sneered, 'are you so overweeningly arrogant, so convinced of your own rectitude on all things, that even when faced with an expert on a topic, you are happy to pronounce your views as if they carried equal weight?'

Marian Pace fumed.

'What you think of as your wisdom comes only from what you have read in your ignorant, clod-hopping newspaper.'

'Oh, Harry,' said Marian Pace with a savage laugh. 'I can see now what you are. You're an eco-fascist.'

'And you're a prig, deary.'

Harry sat back in his chair to intakes of breath around the table. The whole table was deathly quiet as they watched him refill his glass. Claypole was utterly torn. He wanted to see Harry embarrassed, and yet he wanted him to win the argument.

Banfield Haines was smooth. 'No one here is saying there is *definitely* no such thing as climate change, I just–'

'Oh, so you're just not sure?' Harry's tone was still challenging, although the volume had come down from fever pitch.

'I just don't think the evidence – '

'Balls. That's like saying you're not sure that the Earth orbits the sun because you haven't yourself been into space and watched it happen. On anything else, you'd take a scientist's word for it.'

Haines gave a supercilious smile. Claypole nearly grinned. Then he saw Coky. She was looking at Harry with pure love.

'And that also means that you can't have Teflon saucepans. Or weather prediction. And you can't have nuclear power either. Because if Copernicus and Galileo hadn't stuck to their guns, there would be no Einstein.'

'Pah,' said Haines and smiled grimly at one of the Americans.

'You don't want to believe all the evidence – the vast amount of evidence – about global warming because it doesn't suit your purposes. You are self-interested. You'd rather things stayed the same because those are the conditions under which you have succeeded. You think the planet is all about you, and you think that the view and the environment are the same thing.'

'OK,' said Marian Pace, her jaw set firm. 'Let's talk about Galileo. Climate change is the scientific orthodoxy of our times. Most scientists believe that global warming is man-made, right?'

'Yes. The vast majority.'

'Well, most philosophers of the time of Galileo, and certainly everyone else, thought that the sun orbited the earth. He was the one who went against the orthodoxy, and has been proved to be right. Just because the majority of people think something is right, doesn't make it so. In fact, most scientific orthodoxies prove themselves to be wrong in the long run.'

'Scientific orthodoxies are not fact. They are the interpretation of the facts. The data don't change. It's how
we read them that changes. The world is getting hotter,
and the weather is getting worse. Interpret that!'

Peregrine stood up. 'Marvellous! I do like a debate,'
he said, with absurd levity but also with a conclusive
slap on the table. 'Now, dancing!'

-+=◎=+-

The MacGilp House ceilidh, it transpired, was open
not just to the dinner guests, but to the inhabitants of
the surrounding countryside. It was now ten o'clock
and there were all ages and varieties of local arriving.
When Claypole came into the ballroom, stocky white-
haired women in quilted waistcoats were dancing with
twenty-year-old farm hands. Girls of six with their
grandfathers. Those not dancing sat on benches that
lined the walls of the ballroom drinking tea, whisky or
lager. A dance was announced, and an excited quickening of conversation enveloped the room. As the accor-
dionist, drummer and fiddler played a few phrases of
a jaunty tune, what had been a milling crowd formed
quickly and effortlessly into lines. Claypole took a step
back towards the wall, as Coky explained to several
men and boys that she was going to sit this dance out.
With an introductory wheeze from the squeezebox,
the band started up and a beat later the dancers set
off, wheeling and whirling and jigging. Claypole
marvelled. This was not the stuffy ballet he had seen
on 'Hogmanay Live!' with po-faced and trussed-up
dancers over-performing for the cameras. These were
grinning and variously dressed folk of all generations,
all dancing in their own styles but to a set pattern

that they all knew. The lines and groups swished and twirled in formation but not in uniform.

'Are you going to dance?'

He had not realised that Coky was next to him.

'Ooh. God. No. God.'

She laughed and touched his arm. It felt to Claypole like a sting.

'My fault,' she said. 'I should have taught you a few basics. It's not as scary as it looks.'

Claypole and Coky watched Harry Lightfoot, just a few feet from them, drunkenly but courteously swinging a nine-year-old in a frilly dress towards a bearded octogenarian in a kilt. The men bowed, and all three were smiling as they clapped in unison.

'So, dinner,' said Claypole. 'Pretty embarrassing.' They both watched Harry joining hands with one of the Americans, who whooped excitedly.

'I thought it was great,' said Coky. 'Harry's pretty wonderful, isn't he?'

Claypole tasted acid in his mouth.

'I suppose lots of women fancy him,' he said, and looked closely for Coky's reaction. It was not what he expected. She giggled. 'You don't think so?'

'I'm sure they do, Gordon.' She turned to him with a grin. 'But they'd have to be a unique kind of chick to have any luck.'

'Eh?'

'You'd have to be a woman with a cock to get anywhere with Harry.'

'Oh,' said Claypole. 'Ah.' And his poor heart soared with hope once more.

'Come and have a drink with me,' she said. 'I noticed you haven't been drinking all evening. Is that for… your health, or… will you have a whisky now?'

If she asked him to, he would drink poison.

'Yeah. OK,' he said, looking out across the dance floor as nonchalantly as he could manage. He saw the man he recognised from the community hall as Kevin Watt, the *Glenmorie Herald* journalist, and they met eyes. There was something about the man's expression that Claypole didn't like, so he looked away quickly and followed Coky outside. The garden was busy. Everyone searched for cool night air when they weren't dancing, and most were smoking. Claypole noticed the wide variety of different smoking apparatus. There were pipes, cigars, cigarillos, roll-ups and ready-made cigarettes of every description, from eclectic luxury to standard budget.

'Scotland really likes a smoke,' he said as they sat on a bench.

'Yup,' she said. 'They make it look fun, don't they?'

He thought for a moment, and then asked her, 'Have you given up?'

She smiled. 'I was wondering when you were going to notice. That's why I've been trying to stay off the booze. Drinking makes me want to smoke, so... Enjoyed the wine tonight, though.'

He nodded. 'That's why I thought...'

'Yeah.'

And the two of them watched the gathering, passing lighters and cans of beer and hipflasks to and fro, and laughing.

'Hey, Gordon.' She took the top off a flask and handed it to him. 'What *does* the "S" stand for?'

Claypole tensed. Did he dare tell her? The one thing he refused to be was ridiculous. And yet, he could hardly demur again. Claypole looked into Coky's eyes. They were not swivelling exactly – but they were drifting gently hither and thither in their sockets. Good, he thought. She might be drunk enough not to remember it later. On the other hand, perhaps she would go and blurt it to anyone who would listen. That's what had happened at school. All those boys in blazers they hadn't bought from Oxfam, whose fathers drove large cars and were still alive, would barge him around in the cold corridors. And even though that was ancient history, it still hurt.

'My middle name is… Sisyphus.'

The silence was edible.

'Yeah. My parents thought it was cool. Sisyphus was the king of Corinth who tried to get one over on the gods of Olympus. He was condemned for eternity to push a boulder up a mountain without ever getting to the top. Brr. My parents thought it was an interesting classical allusion. And because they were such smart-arses, I got called Sissy for ten years.'

Coky nodded gravely.

'That's nothing. I've got a *really* stupid name.'

Claypole looked confused.

'What, Coky? It's a brr… nice name.'

'Thanks, but…' Coky was shaking her head.

'What is it then?' he asked.

'Well, Coky is short for something, for a start…' The knobble on the end of her nose twitched.

'Oh,' said Claypole. 'I thought it was Lithuanian.'

Coky laughed. *'Lithuanian?'*

'That's what you get for Googling,' he said sheepishly.

'The name on my birth certificate is Cocaine.'

Claypole's mouth gently dropped open.

'Yup,' said Coky, her jaw hardening. 'And I have another name… Danger.'

Coky shrugged. Claypole's brow wrinkled. Then he smiled. Then he checked her expression to see if his smile was allowed. She sighed, and Claypole laughed.

'As in...?'

'Yup. Just so I can say... "my middle name is Danger".'

'Cocaine Danger Viveksananda. What idiots,' said Claypole quietly, but with feeling. Then he thought he might have offended Coky, so he apologised.

'No, you're right,' she said. 'They were idiots. But my dad didn't speak much English at the time, and my mum was very young. Nineteen, she *says*.'

They both computed in silence.

'So,' said Claypole. 'We have that in common. Our parents were... Brr...'

Coky looked at him. 'We're a bit more alike than somebody might think,' she said, 'from the outside.'

'Right.'

Claypole was stunned. We are not alike *at all*, he wanted to say. In almost no way similar, we are completely, wonderfully different. But, he wanted also to shout, we could be compatible. We could...

But he said nothing and just looked dumbly at her eyes as she smiled at those who passed by.

Neither Claypole nor Coky saw Kevin Watt approaching them from behind in the semi-darkness.

'Fee. Fi. Fo. Fum,' said the journalist, and Claypole and Coky both looked round. 'You might want to see tomorrow's paper, Mr Claypole.'

There was a dangerous expression on Kevin Watt's face as he produced a slim newspaper from his pocket. 'You should have returned my calls.'

-13-

Gordon is a moron.

'Gordon is a Moron', Jilted John

The Glenmorie Herald

WIND FARM CHIEF IS INTERNET FRAUDSTER

A special investigation by Kevin Watt

MORE controversy has hit the beleaguered Loch
Garvach Wind Farm with the news that its
spokesman, Londoner Gordon Claypole, may be
about to petition for bankruptcy.

Mr Claypole, 35, who is a last-minute addi-
tion to the team trying to get planning
permission for the controversial wind farm
and yet confesses to having no experience of
the energy business, has been discovered to be
in severe financial difficulties. He claims to
be a wealthy internet entrepreneur, but this
reporter has discovered that he is nothing
of the kind.

A credit check on Gordon S. Claypole reveals
that his mortgage payments are nine months in

arrears, he has credit card debts of £40,000, and has exceeded his overdraft at Hunter Chase Bank. When asked whether Mr Claypole was being foreclosed upon over his debts to the bank, a spokesman said, 'We do not comment, on individual bankruptcy cases at the bank.' But this reporter has discovered that there is a petition for bankruptcy pending for a G.S. Claypole at Mr Claypole's last known address. Mr Claypole's internet and television production business, Pumpkin Productions, has a winding-up order pending on it over unpaid business rates at its former headquarters in London's seedy Soho district.

This revelation follows on the heels of an ill-tempered community meeting on Tuesday, where many residents of the Loch Garvach area tried to voice their concerns about the wind farm to the company. Mr Claypole floundered in the face of locals' questioning. Councillor Helen MacDougall told the *Glenmorie Herald*: 'He didn't know, or was unwilling to provide, the detailed answers that this community is entitled to. The plans for the Loch Garvach Wind Farm are clearly in chaos.'

Mr Claypole, who has refused to comment, spoke at the Garvachhead Community Hall, during which he claimed to be about to start a brand of women's underwear with Virgin boss Sir Richard Branson. In front of a packed crowd he said, 'I am not an expert on wind farms. If you want an expert, go and hire your own.'

The Loch Garvach Wind Farm has been beset with problems ever since the development company Aeolectricity Ltd was liquidated in May. Mr Claypole is said to have taken a stake in the venture, but Companies House records indicate that he has as yet paid nothing for his shares and he is not a director of the company.

As at the time of going to press, Mr Claypole was also in breach of contract on a car rental agreement, owing Henderson's Hire of Garvachhead £7,000, and had not yet offered any payment of his bill at the Loch Garvach Hotel.

Editor's comment: If this is the person the Loch Garvach Wind Farm company chooses to defend its planning application, does the council have any option but to reject the wind farm in the strongest possible terms?

With Kevin Watt standing some way off, Claypole and Coky both read the article. When he had finished reading, her blazing eyes were waiting for him.

'Is this…?' Coky choked. She put her hands together in prayer. 'Is it true?'

Claypole's mouth hung stupidly open.

'Course it is,' said the journalist.

Coky turned to him. 'Will you please leave us?'

With a nod that was at once gracious and triumphant, Kevin Watt left them, and she turned to Claypole again.

'Is it true?' she asked again, her blue eyes turning moist.

Claypole blinked slowly and beheld a look of profound disappointment on Coky's face that made his eyes burn.

'Brr,' he said quietly. 'I didn't have any choice.'

She sighed. 'But Gordon, you can always tell the truth.'

He looked at her naïve, imploring face and was suddenly angered. What did Coky know of what he could or couldn't do? She who had never been caught between a rock and a hard place because... well, let's face it, because her family probably owned all the rocks and all the hard places, and if not the Devil too, then certainly a chunk of the Deep Blue Sea.

'Oh yeah?' he snarled offensively. 'And you always tell the truth, do you?'

'What do you mean?' She gulped.

'Gah. Brr. You... you're this great eco-warrior – sorry, eco-*accountant* – right? But you shoot birds like they're fish in a barrel; you have no problem taking flights left, right and centre; and you tool around the hills in a gas-guzzling Land Rover. Funny kind of ecological balance sheet you've managed to draw up for yourself. Why are you really doing the wind farming anyway?'

She was too shocked to speak. He couldn't stop himself.

'You're doing it for the money, aren't you? Everyone does. There's always money at the heart of it. You couldn't hack it doing PR or whatever it was, and now you've run back to the family and wangled a cushy number for yourself. Is that your plan? Get a mug like me to do the dirty work and Uncle Perry will sling you a big bung if it all goes right? Well, cheers. Brr. Now I'm fucked. So thanks very much.'

Tears welled up in her eyes, but Coky fought them back. Instead, she rose slowly from the seat and looked down at him.

'I may not be the world's greenest...' she began. 'But that's not why I... It's got nothing to do with money. It's about something much more important. Things you wouldn't know about. Family.'

'Oh, right,' spat Claypole, also getting up from his seat. 'So just because my family are all... you think I can't understand? Well, fu-'

Seeing the expression on Coky's face, he recalculated. It was not Coky's nature to be unpleasant or hurtful. Perhaps she had meant that he did not understand *her* family, not that he didn't understand families in general, just because he no longer had one.

'What do you mean?' she asked.

'Forget it.' He backed away from her and kicked the ground. He could not look at her. 'I thought... because you said... I thought you were having a dig, because of my mother...'

'What about your mother?'

'Doesn't matter,' he said. 'I think I'd better go.'

He turned around, but did not walk away, hoping Coky would stop him from going. She did not, and was swallowed by the small crowd that had gathered.

Claypole padded away from MacGilp House alone, his footfall heavier than it had ever been. He ambled fatly, weaving from one side of the road to the other. He might have had the appearance of being drunk, should anyone have been watching. But Claypole was horribly, dreadfully, achingly sober.

--➤═◉═◄--

Halfway down the drive to MacGilp House, their camper van hidden from view, the less sober Lachlan and Milky contemplated their motives silently for the crime of kidnap.

Lachlan had no sympathy with the sort of environmentalism that espoused wind farming. Merely making more electricity by slightly better means was

234

no substitute for doing without electricity at all, as he did. Capitalism had caused all the environmental problems the world was currently presented with, and he had no reason to suppose that capitalism could solve them. Lachlan didn't need the economy, and the economy didn't need or want him. But his disapproval of the Loch Garvach Wind Farm had nothing to do with economics. It stemmed entirely from its potential impact on the birds. For it was Lachlan, being both cheap and available, who had performed the ornithology survey for Aeolectricity, and it had become apparent to him that there was a pair of golden eagles nesting above the Giant's Table. There were also two pairs of merlins, and some other raptors nearby. He had informed the company of this impediment to the scheme, by written report because he felt it was more professional, but it had not responded before going bust. His attempts to discuss the matter with Peregrine had been rebuffed, at first with absent-minded giggles, but lately with a threatening silence. Lachlan's care of the grouse on Peregrine's land was in large part because he regarded them as food for the birds of prey that were his true passion. Anything that threatened these birds of prey must be stopped.

Thus, Lachlan reasoned, if Claypole could be stopped from making his spokesmanly speech at the community hall, there would only be those against the wind farm left to speak. The arguments would then clearly swing against planning permission being granted and the councillors, being democratically elected, would have no choice but to vote 'no' to planning permission. All Lachlan and Milky would have to do would be to keep Claypole in the van for the duration of the meeting and the wind farm would be scuppered.

Milky's motives were somewhat simpler. He felt the urgent need to use his seagull-killing bat – the one with the holes in. It was a weapon with which Milky was hauntingly familiar and horribly adept. He knew exactly what sort of blow or series of blows would be merely painful or damaging and what would be critical or fatal. The two of them could easily bundle their target into the back of Lachlan's van and have him bound and gagged in a moment. How much of a struggle there was would be Milky's cue as to how much the bat would be required.

⋯━◉━⋯

Claypole, wandering down the drive to MacGilp House, drew out his wallet and examined it in the pale starlight. He had thirty-five pounds in cash. A pound for each year of his life. This was the only money he had in the world. In fact, he thought, his total worth in the world was something like minus £50,000, and thanks to Kevin Watt of the *Glenmorie Herald,* this fact would shortly be discovered by everyone at the ceilidh. There seemed little point quibbling about the newspaper's slanted reporting and minor inaccuracies, because the salient facts were undeniably true. More importantly, the truth had now been discovered by Coky.

He felt foolish for having pursued her at all. She was celibate, for God's sake. But why? What was the point of that? To Claypole's mind it was incomprehensible. Why, if you *could* have sex with people – if they didn't turn you down with a laugh or a scream – would you not do so, and as much as possible? It was well known to be enjoyable. Oh the irony, he thought. He might have been content to do without sex, if only there had

236

been something in it for his heart. But Coky had no love for him. And now only hate. With that thought, the shame and ache returned again and his shoulders shuddered with one self-pitying sob.

A future with a broken heart, though, was not the foulest horror on his horizon. Yes, he was now walking to London to supervise the dismantling of his life. (The cutting in two of his credit cards; the repossession of his flat that the bank had long been threatening; and presumably then a bankruptcy hearing.) But all this slow and brutal torture was nothing compared to the inevitable and humiliating call to Uncle Jerry.

Jerry would have to fork out for the flight to Australia, and even give him some pocket money while Claypole worked in some spit-and-sawdust bar and lived in Jerry's thunderbox with the snakes and the spiders that would probably kill him before Christmas. The living hell waiting for him in Queensland might be worse than any death. He might find his feet after a while, perhaps becoming an estate agent. After the grinding years of shafting first-time buyers, he would try his hand at property development and make enough money to marry some shrill nightmare with sloping shoulders who didn't shave under her arms, have a couple of fat-faced children and live in a bungalow with last year's Ken and Barbie melting in the scorched back yard. He would learn Aussie Rules Football and go to games on Saturdays, get drunk on brain-aching beer with men he did not like and go home to a house with no books. Was this to be his destiny? He would die in his forties, as his father had done – maybe sooner if he could afford enough drink – and it would be a blessed relief. And yet… perhaps it was not relief enough. How could he short-circuit this living nightmare? A grim smile crossed Claypole's lips as he drifted down the drive of MacGilp House, and an idea struck him that had never struck him before. It was at once appalling, and yet logical and liberating for its simplicity and its finality. His pace down the drive quickened as he tried to think it through.

Claypole had always survived setbacks, but recovery from this one did not seem possible. The reality of the past, having been so opaque, now seemed overwhelmingly real. He had lost sight of what was true and what was not over the last week – over the last month – but it now came over him like a wave. He stumbled on a dried cowpat, and tried to remember the end of his media career not as he had allowed rumour to tell it, but as it had actually happened. Lies had been so easy to tell that they had also been simple for him to believe himself. Tough, unalloyed truth now hit him with full force.

When, after some years at the BBC, Claypole had joined Pumpkin Productions as its only employee, the company's logo was of an animated pumpkin that squeaked amusingly, imitating the famous MGM lion. The sole owner of the company, a Hungarian refugee and illustrator in his seventies called Vidor Vincze, was as jovial and amateurish as the company's logo suggested. For two years, Claypole did little other than drink coffee and have long lunches at Vidor's expense, for many of which Vidor joined him. There seemed to be more conversation to be had than work to do. Claypole was not well paid, but he could hardly be said to have been exploited. One sunny April morning, Vidor informed his employee that bowel cancer was about to end his life, and urged Claypole to continue his legacy. Within four weeks, Vidor was dead and

Claypole had remortgaged his carefully earned flat, taken out a business loan with the bank and paid Vidor's daughter £120,000 for all rights to everything Vidor had ever produced.

For the next two years, there were reissued books of Vidor's beautiful stories, and the cartoons were shown again on some of the digital children's channels, and Claypole and his rapidly appointed staff were busy. Gradually, though, the business had begun to founder. Claypole spent heavily, trying to garner interest in Colin the Calf where it was clearly waning. Soon he halted his own salary, and shortly after that began to renege on bills and to make his staff redundant. The books no longer sold, and eventually went out of print. The cartoons were no longer shown, even in Hungary. And the brand that Vidor had carefully built over thirty years was evaporating. But not before Claypole had taken one huge gamble. Embracing fully the new media, he had launched an App for all tablet computer platforms, with all the cartoons available on it, and all the books in free e-book format. It was his firm conviction that it would revitalise the brand and allow the internet to do the work for him, and he borrowed hugely on his credit cards. When an online community of fans had established itself, he would exploit them by selling advertising. The future for media businesses, as he would tell anyone who would listen, was in communities, not revenue. But no such community existed, and only a tiny and demanding one formed itself. He found that having given away the content for free, he could not even go back to charging for it. He was stuck, broke, and finished.

But, Claypole realised during the sleepless nights and booze-filled days that followed the final demand from the bank, there was one thing he could do to rescue the situation. The one audacious route out from humiliation was to make out that everything had gone as intended, and just see where it took him. He could pretend to have been a success. He would give the impression he had done well. As far as the world was concerned, he would be a wealthy entrepreneur. He could hand the business onto a large and much-hated international media outfit without the world knowing he had done so for free.

After performing this sleight of hand, and receiving payment of £66,180 which would, when cashed, plummet into the black hole of his mortgage account, Claypole should just have joined the massed ranks of the endebted employed. But he had spent five years thinking and acting as a player. An owner, a man of substance, and not just a functionary. So he buried deep within himself the truth: that he had ruined a perfectly good business based on something real and beautiful: the skilled work of a good man. He had sold it short and allowed the buzzwords and bullshit of the internet to lure him into bad decisions. Then he had attempted to prop up his collapsing life by pumping more lies into it. Now, here in Scotland, the whole thing had deflated, and it was suddenly clear to him that there was only one thing he could do to avoid the horror. He smelled the sea, and headed towards it with grim resolve.

⊸≡◉≡⊷

In the fetid camper van's cab, the two would-be kidnappers went about their last-minute preparations.

'Cord?' said Lachlan.

'Aye,' said Milky.

'Can't you say "check"?'

'Why?'

Lachlan folded his arms. 'Just... Never got the hang of having fun, have you, Milks?'

Milky shrugged and began to roll a cigarette.

'So... cord?' Lachlan began again.

'Check.'

'Gag?'

'Check.'

'Rook to Queen Bishop 4?'

If Milky had turned to his childhood friend, he would have seen him grinning idiotically.

'Don't fuck about,' said the bearded and balded Milky.

Lachlan looked at Milky. Not given to humour at the best of times, Milky was being particularly serious. Lachlan had been cracking silly jokes and jiggling in the passenger seat for the ten minutes they had been parked.

'If he's walking, we just grab him, right?'

'Aye,' said Milky.

'And if he's driving, you hail him down and I'll jump in his car.'

Milky exhaled smoke, but was otherwise horribly still. 'No. *You* hail him, and *I'll* get in the car.'

◆━◉━◆

As Claypole continued to trip and stumble down the drive, the night was beginning to chill his sweaty body. Momentarily he was forced to fight down the urge to go back to the house. Might he break through the angry crowds at the ceilidh, find Coky, sit her down,

241

apologise profusely and plead for her to have him, despite everything? If necessary he would beg for it as a favour. Just once. The last wish of a rude dying ginger skinhead bankrupt. But nothing like that happened in real life. Claypole knew he didn't deserve, even after all that had happened to him, to get the girl. He deserved only rejection, humiliation and dishonour. His dreams had turned to dust. Even survival seemed pointless, as long as the end could be painless.

He looked back at the castle, now in the middle distance, his damp eyes stinging with fury and pain. The lights were on all over the ground floor. The music had stopped, but still it looked warm and jolly. A light went on in the east wing's second floor, and then another next to it. Going to bed, he thought. Coky is going to bed. She would soon be between old, smooth linen – her firm brown legs swishing back and forth in a four-poster, the three-bar fire in front of a rusting grate fading from orange to brown.

'Fuck,' he whispered into the night as he turned and resumed his trek. Why is it, he thought, that in Scotland you are never truly warm? He had spent more time in the last few days stumbling through the chilly dark, terrified out of his wits, than one man could reasonably be expected to bear. What relief would shortly come. Soon he would never have to walk down another scary, cold, Scottish road ever again. The sea's freezing embrace would be at first horrible, but then numbing. He snorted as he remembered the irony that he had now taken none of his heart pills for a week. Perhaps, he thought as he stomped through the bushes, the temperature of the sea would stop his feeble heart before he held his head under the murky water and breathed in.

For, what reason did Gordon Claypole now have to choose shame over death? He turned off the road and towards the loch.

-14-

And thus I see among these pleasant things
Each care decays; and yet my sorrow springs.

'Spring', Henry Howard, Earl of Surrey
(?1517–1547)

Early the following evening, chuffing grey smoke into the clear air, Lachlan's ancient camper van came to a stop outside the Loch Garvach Hotel. Milky switched the engine off, and for a full minute the two men did not speak. The tension in the van was even greater than it had been the previous night. It had been a weak plan, perhaps. There could have been any number of reasons why Claypole had not appeared on the driveway of MacGilp House. But now that they had been thwarted, they would have to conduct the kidnap in broad daylight in front of the community hall. This had risks enough to weaken their joint resolve.

Lachlan looked at his watch. 'Do you want chips?' he said.

Milky did not answer.

'Or we could splash out... Let's go to Mackay's and get a veggie Pad Thai.'

'No,' said Milky.

'So we're just going to wait for him here, are we?' He paused. 'This is a mistake. Someone's going to see us.'

Milky did not speak.

'I s'pose,' Lachlan added, 'if he doesn't turn up at all, the problem is solved, right? No fatty, no problem...'

Milky blinked, which Lachlan took as tacit agreement, and the two men once again fell quiet.

⊷══◉══⊶

Inside the community hall, Coky had been alone for some time. She was about to stand up in front of seventy or eighty people, most of whom had known her since birth, and address them on a topic on which she was very far from being an expert. She had not tried to ingest so much information in so short a period of time since A-levels, and it was a shock to her system. How was she supposed to represent the case for the wind farm when she had so little grasp of the detail? What had Peregrine said? 'Claypole's not only PNG, he's also AWOL, and everybody around here hates me. It's got to be you. Go to it, my girl, and bring us home some bacon.'

She had agreed, of course. Not because she felt so strongly about renewable energy, or wind farms in particular, and her uncle's money worries were his own affair. But the long and horrible war between Peregrine and his sisters had its origins many years in the past – ever since Peregrine's disgraceful actions at his mother's deathbed – and it was high time they all put it behind them. That was Coky's opinion, but it was not one that she could voice to any of the combatants in this war. To varying degrees, they treated her like the child she had (very nearly) been when her grandmother had died. She was counsel to none of them. So Coky had had to go about her task of reuniting her fractured family with great stealth, telling no one of her intentions. She just knew that if they could get through the wind farm problem there might be a greater than zero chance of peace breaking out among the MacGilps. Not, she couldn't help feeling, that the stupid buggers deserved it.

Coky was angry with Peregrine. He knew more about the Loch Garvach Wind Farm than anyone, and yet he refused to stand up and make the critical speech. He had let Claypole take the heat in the last meeting, but why on earth was the old man still hedging his bets? Perhaps if planning permission were refused, Peregrine wanted to be in a position to deny that he had pushed for it. He could pretend that he was just the landowner on whose land the putative wind farm might have been built, and that it had been nothing to do with him if it either did or didn't happen. But this was no time to be cowardly. It should be him sitting in her seat.

Coky was also angry with her mother. Bonnie had gone out of her way, and beyond the normal course of logic, to be against the wind farm, simply because it was to Peregrine's advantage if it went ahead. If there had been some principle underlying her reaction, it had long been superseded by simple spite. Bonnie was abusing her position as a voice in the community (or long-standing pain in the neck, to put it another way) to poison public opinion and ensure an atmosphere of hostility towards the wind farm. She had certainly lobbied Councillor Helen MacDougall successfully. So it was not only spiteful and annoying. It was corrupt.

Apparently even her only child's advocacy in favour of the wind farm was not enough for Bonnie to keep an open mind. How Coky wished for the steady voice of reason of the late Angus Straughan.

Coky was even angry with Dorcas. Her lovely, wise aunt had stayed in the background while the politics of the wind farm had played out with increasing animosity. Dorcas had made protestations to Coky that she no longer held a grudge against her brother. But if that were true, why had Dorcas stood idly by when his scheme, with its environmental benefit, needed her support? Normally Dorcas would have championed a good cause. Dorcas shouldn't be hiding like a hermit. She should be the one influencing local opinion, with her learning and her erudition and her infinitely subtle intellectual balance.

Coky's anger towards Claypole, though, had different, more complicated flavours to it. He had lied to her – lied to everyone – about his past, and his capabilities. He had also insulted her and then deserted her at exactly the hour he was most needed. Some friend he was. And yet she couldn't help feeling sympathy for him. Peregrine had most brazenly used Claypole as a fall guy, allowing him to be demonised and burned at the stake of public opinion. She also could see, as a result of the revelations that had so horribly been brought to her attention, that Claypole's motives were not simple. He wasn't just another plutocratic opportunist, as she had originally thought, although he had portrayed himself as such, and if environmental considerations made up any of his interest, it was only a small part. In the main, it had been a desperate man's last throw of the dice. He had come up to Scotland to try and save himself from bankruptcy. Much as that might have been a foolish gamble, it was at least under-standable. People do the strangest things *in extremis*. Certainly there could be no other explanation for his actions. Could there?

But Coky was unaccustomed to anger, and she tried to dismiss these unwelcome thoughts while she tried to read about projected wind speeds and the capacity factors of industrial turbines.

The second person to arrive in the hall was chairman of the planning committee Tommy Thompson. He approached Coky, but seeing she was so ensconced in her reading, he backed off and started laying out chairs. The third and fourth persons were the other council-lors – Helen MacDougall and the strange-looking John Bruce. MacDougall played with her smartphone, and Bruce sat scratching his greasy scalp and rocking back and forth metronomically while reading a copy of the *Glenmorie Herald*. Soon others began to file through the door and take their places. The noise built further, and Coky was forced to abandon her attempts to concentrate.

When Peregrine MacGilp arrived, wearing a maroon tie that matched his hangover complexion, Tommy Thompson took him off into a corner of the room.

'I heard about Mr Claypole's departure,' said Tommy Thompson quietly.

'Bloody fool,' tutted Peregrine.

'Yes, well,' Tommy Thompson said, also smiling. 'It doesn't matter. I did what you asked. John Bruce is in favour, so that makes two to one on the committee.' Tommy Thompson gave a wink to his old friend. 'It's in the bag.'

Peregrine took his seat with a sly smile playing on his lips.

The hall was nearly half full now, and Coky felt a presence by her side. She turned to see her mother.

'You know that little Johnnie Bruce is against it, don't you, darling? Helen MacDougall and I met him yesterday and he's definitely going to vote against the wind farm.'

Coky looked at her mother and gave a painful sigh.

'You've never given me an inch, have you, Mum? Not one inch.'

Bonnie looked at her daughter with surprise. 'There's no need to take it personally, darling. I'm only doing what I think is best. You chose to...'

'To what...?' said Coky after a pause.

'Well, to side with Peregrine.'

'Oh God,' said Coky, suddenly riled. 'Is that what you think this is? Now who's taking it personally?'

'Oh, darling –'

'No, you just listen for a change,' Coky whispered furiously, shaking. But she couldn't continue. She was near tears, and did not want to be. Not now.

'You didn't think,' said Bonnie, her moon eyes widening, 'that this was about *family*, did you?'

Coky took a breath. 'I'm not defending what Peregrine did over the house and estate for a moment. But it was ages ago, and it's not as if he's had it easy...' Coky stopped abruptly. This argument could be conducted another time. 'I need to prepare,' she said. But she could not stop herself from asking one further question of her mother.

'Mum, why did you give your consent to the right of way if you knew we would be defeated today?'

To Coky's surprise, her mother looked pained. The hall was nearly full. Tommy Thompson was looking at his watch as Bonnie whispered to her daughter.

'I'll tell you why,' said Bonnie without her usual shrill tone. 'I think Gordon Claypole, for all his bumbling weirdness, is quite a class act. It takes some balls to try and do what he did. He's funny too, even if he is a crook. Do you know what he said when I asked him to produce one reason why I should vote in favour of the wind farm? He said, "money".'

Coky smiled weakly. 'Aye. I thought I liked him too,' she said.

'There's another reason, though. I...' Bonnie paused for a moment, during which Coky wondered if she had ever seen her mother like this. 'I once did the Claypole family a... disservice, shall we say...'

Coky screwed her face in confusion, but remained silent.

'It was before I met Angus. I was having a strange time, and I didn't behave well... So... Well, we'll leave it at that.'

Bonnie smiled sheepishly as she took a seat among the building audience. Tommy Thompson banged his gavel.

'Good evening, everyone,' said Tommy Thompson, and the room hushed in a moment. 'First tonight is Tony Ponder, the council's Acting Planning Officer.'

A small man in a blue suit, whom no one had noticed, stood and gave a highly technical speech to which no one listened. Although his recommendation was that the scheme be turned down, it was entirely clear to everyone in the hall that he had no power. When Ponder had finished, Tommy Thompson stood again.

'Thank you, Tony,' he said without enthusiasm, and turned to the hall. 'It has been a dramatic week in the life of our community, I think you'll all agree. The questions we asked of the Wind Farm Company at the last meeting a week ago have kindly been answered, and copies of that document are on some of the chairs in this hall as you can see.'

He coughed, as did some others.

'It seems that we will have to do without the spokesman for the wind farm, as he has been indisposed.'

There were some titters from the assembly.

'But Coky Viveksananda has kindly agreed to step in at the last moment and read a statement by the company. So we should give our thanks to her.'

There was silence in the hall as Coky rose from her chair and prepared to pronounce the last rites over what she was sure was the dead body of the Loch Garvach Wind Farm. She had decided, as her one and only tactic, to give the facts very formally and drily, in the hope that anyone speaking against the wind farm might sound hysterical and illogical by comparison. Her voice as she began was quieter than Tommy Thompson's professional boom, but it was steady and gently confident. Her small presence on the stage was attended to closely by the whole hall, and even those at the back found that they could hear her well.

As she went through her statement on behalf of the wind farm, correcting certain misconceptions that had surfaced at the previous meeting, and logically presenting the case in favour, she noticed certain people in the audience. In the front row of the audience was Peregrine. His beaming grin was intended, she knew, to provide her with confidence, but it was the same smugness that Coky had been ignoring in her uncle all her life in order to try and love him. She glanced at the back of the hall. There was Lachlan, brooding and looking at the floor. Milky, standing next to him, had been the last person into the hall. He looked distracted. There was Kevin Watt from the *Glenmorie Herald*. And there, right at the back, with the door swinging silently shut behind him, was Gordon Claypole.

Coky stuttered slightly, but managed to continue her speech despite the storm raging in her head, once or twice looking back at Claypole to check that her eyes were not deceiving her.

'In conclusion, then, we say change should be given a chance. The Loch Garvach Wind Farm will improve the environment and enhance our community. Thank you.'

She sat down, and a ripple of applause began around the hall. It couldn't be said to be much more than respectful, except from the wind farm's known supporters. Coky's eyes directed a questioning look at Claypole. He smiled awkwardly.

John Bruce, seeing Claypole, leaned across to Tommy Thompson and whispered. The chairman also looked at the back of the hall and raised his eyebrows when he too saw Claypole. When the applause died down, Tommy Thompson spoke.

'Thank you, Coky. At this point there may be questions from the floor.' A few hands were raised. 'I should remind you that this is not a time to express your opinions. That time has gone. This is to explore last-minute questions of fact.'

Tommy Thompson smiled as he saw that several people with their hands raised had put them down again. But of the hands that remained in the air, the most noticeable was that of Claypole. Tommy Thompson seemed to hesitate for a moment before he said, 'Well, ladies and gentlemen, I had been led to believe before this meeting that the spokesman for the

Loch Garvach Wind Farm was not due to be present at this meeting, but I see now that he is. So, the chair recognises Gordon Claypole.'

There were a few mutterings, and some of the audience turned their heads in the direction of the chairman's eyeline. But the biggest reaction came from Peregrine, who bolted out of his chair and swivelled on his heels to see Claypole making his way through the audience and coming to the front of the stage. Peregrine's face had turned beetroot. He gathered his thoughts, and then blurted, 'A point of order, Mr Chairman!'

'Yes,' said Tommy Thompson in a tone of measured surprise. 'Peregrine MacGilp.'

'Claypole no longer represents Loch Garvach Wind Farm Limited.' And turning to Claypole, he snarled, 'You're fired, matey.'

Tommy Thompson looked at Claypole, who reached the stage and stood coolly beside the fuming Peregrine. 'Brr. What if I were here in a personal capacity?'

There were mutterings from the audience. Peregrine huffed triumphantly. 'Nothing entitles you to be here, in that case. You're not even a resident of Loch Garvach...' And he added with a cruel twist of his lips, 'or anywhere else, apparently.'

No one laughed. They were waiting for Tommy Thompson's reaction.

'This is a public meeting,' began Tommy Thompson thoughtfully, 'and as such can be attended by any member of the public. The chair has recognised Mr Claypole.'

Peregrine's eyes darted furiously from Tommy Thompson to Claypole and back again.

'Perhaps,' began Claypole, 'I could be allowed a

moment in private with my coll–... Sorry, my former colleague?'

Tommy Thompson looked at Peregrine, and Peregrine looked at Claypole, who looked at Coky and smiled.

'Guh,' said Peregrine, and pointed at the back of the stage.

'Thank you, Mr Chairman,' said Claypole, and waddled off after Peregrine.

'While they are... um, perhaps I could answer a few questions from the floor?' said Coky, facing the front.

Next to a large cardboard shark, Peregrine turned to Claypole. They could still be seen by the audience, but not heard by them.

'That's a very good idea,' said Tommy Thompson, glancing behind him at the two men at the back of the stage. 'Does anyone have any questions?'

No hands were raised, and Tommy Thompson could see that all eyes were fixed on the silent drama unfolding behind him. Peregrine was poking Claypole in the chest, but the younger man was not reacting.

'Well, perhaps I'll ask one,' said Tommy Thompson, also unable to tear his eyes away from Peregrine and Claypole. Claypole had drawn some papers out of his pocket and handed them to Peregrine. 'Could you remind us of when building might begin on the wind farm, should it, er... should it be given planning permission?'

'Yes, I, er...' Coky looked behind her as surreptitiously as she could to see Claypole, his hands in his pockets, talking quietly, while Peregrine leafed through the papers he had been given. The old man clearly did not like what he saw, or heard. 'Initial works on the foundations could begin in about nine months, but...'

Coky had ground to a halt. Peregrine was running his hands through his hair, and his shoulders had dropped. Claypole was continuing to speak to the old man.

'... And, er... yes, if everything goes... If everything goes well, then, er...' Coky looked back at the audience, and saw that no one was listening to her, so she gave up and stopped talking.

All the eyes in the hall watched as Claypole gave Peregrine a pat on the shoulder and walked confidently back to the front of the stage. Peregrine followed him a couple of seconds later, grim defeat on his face.

As he reached the front of the stage, Coky searched Claypole's eyes but he looked nothing other than completely collected as he planted himself in the middle of the stage.

'It seems that... Brr... I am happy to say that I have been rehired as the spokesman for the Loch Garvach Wind Farm.'

Everyone's attention switched from Claypole to Peregrine, who nodded before sitting heavily in his chair at the front of the audience. Then all eyes were back on Claypole.

'First, I'd like to say a little something about myself, just for the record... Brr. Got any water?'

Coky offered him the glass that stood in front of her.

'Thanks,' said Claypole, and drained the glass. Coky noticed that he was dressed in the same clothes he had on the previous night, and found herself wondering where, or whether, he had slept. Like everyone else in the hall, she was also wondering what on earth had just taken place between Claypole and Peregrine.

'So. Yeah. You've probably read the *Glenmorie Herald*,

and... I'm not a rich and successful entrepreneur. Actually I never said I was. But I didn't deny it, so... that was foolish, and I did it, I suppose, because the fact is that I'm really in the sh–... Er...'

He looked at an old woman in the front row, whose eyes were narrowed. He inclined his head slightly in her direction.

'I am in a *jam*,' he continued. The old woman nodded graciously. 'But I've spent a week here now, immersed fully, um, in the area... and I've got a bit to say about the place.'

He cleared his throat gently and glanced down at his hands. The audience was now completely still, attending closely to every word.

'Let's deal with the big picture first. Anyone who doesn't think that climate change by human cause is scientific fact beyond reasonable doubt is either an idiot or being deliberately obtuse. But even if you insist that it is still a matter of opinion, there remains the simple reason that it is now government policy. Our governments, both UK and Scottish, have decided that generating electricity using wind turbines must happen.'

Claypole looked up. Every eye was on him.

'The question before us – and every other wind farm – is not "should there be wind farms?" but "should there be a wind farm *here*?"'

Claypole looked at his left palm, and stared at it. Then he looked at his right. Coky could see now that both hands were covered in blue biro.

'Sorry, brr,' he said, looking on the sleeve of his shirt, where there was more biroed scrawl. 'Wrote this in a bus shelter. Ah, yeah. So... no one likes the idea of suddenly living next to a power station, of whatever kind. Some don't like the idea of a power station that moves, and moves in what may be a beautiful setting. And we fear the unknown. Who can say from a map or a drawing what they will really feel when they see a 125-metre-high turbine across the valley? But really, none of this matters.'

There were murmurs from the audience, but Claypole ignored them, rolling up his sleeves to reveal more biro.

'We all go through life thinking that the nasty things get done somewhere else. Modern life is designed this way. You might never see the inside of a morgue, but sure as Christmas you will die. You might never go to an oil processing plant, but you still drive your car. And you will probably use a hundred megawatt hours of electricity in your life without ever going near a power station. Most of us are completely disconnected from the consequences of our actions.'

There was a hiss from somewhere, but Claypole ploughed on.

'But "why here?", you say. Here in Loch Garvach, where there are no traffic jams, no sirens, no pollution to contend with, although all of those things happen in the cities that make your lives possible. Government and crime and mail order distribution centres barely impinge on your lives, and yet you have roads and police and you can buy anything you like on the internet. Wind farming is the one thing of inconvenience that society at large is now asking of the country dweller. Is that so bad?

'I've listened to the fears of a lot of people in the last week. I have spoken to shepherds and ghillies and people who rely on tourism, and I'm convinced there will be no impact on their livelihoods. The forests and the fisheries will be unaffected, and your house will still be worth what it is today.'

Claypole paused and looked at the faces in the hall. Some wore grimaces, set firm. Some smiled curiously. Some had mild frowns. All were paying full attention. Tommy Thompson interrupted him. 'Could you stick to matters of fact, Mr Claypole? Your opinion as to the value of my house is not relevant.'

Claypole smiled at Tommy Thompson.

'Sure,' he said calmly. He rolled his sleeves down and put his note-ridden hands in his pockets. 'I'll give you some facts. Wind farming is a professional business. People with MBAs and electrical engineering degrees operate a multi-billion-pound industry. Very rarely do the little guys – the amateurs like the Loch Garvach Wind Farm Company – get a large wind farm through planning successfully. But in the rare cases that they do, it is because they give something special to the communities in which they exist. My final word, therefore, is this...'

Claypole paused, looked at Coky briefly and raised his voice suddenly – almost shouting – so that some in the audience jumped.

'If you're going to have a wind farm, for God's sake get it right! Why are you only getting £2,000 per turbine? Ask for ten. Or twenty. Peregrine MacGilp will still make millions out of it, but so will you. At the moment it's like someone's found gold in your hills and you lot are all standing around wondering why anyone would want the shiny yellow rocks. An opportunity like this comes along once a century, and if you don't grab it with both hands, you will have spectacularly missed out, and you'll only have yourselves to blame.'

Claypole's hands were held out to the audience as if grasping it collectively by the elbows. The community hall was completely still except for Peregrine, who was shaking his head and grinding his teeth. But he said nothing.

'If I were in charge... and let's face it, I'm not... In fact, I hearby resign as the spokesman for the wind farm... But if I were in charge, I would make Peregrine do all the environmental survey work again. But this time make him accountable. Do it together! Maybe you could even pay for some of the survey work that clearly still needs to be done. Then you can see that it's all done correctly and reap more of the reward. Perry gets his wind farm, all aspects of the environment are protected, and not only does the community make money, you can make sure that none of you resents it without being properly heard first.'

Claypole sighed. 'Well, that's it. Don't say "no", and don't say "yes". Say "maybe". Say "give us a better deal". That's my advice. I wish you all good luck, and goodbye.'

Claypole walked off the stage, the only sound his own footsteps on the lino. He walked through the hall and out through the double doors. Lachlan and Milky slipped out behind him.

Only when the doors had stopped swinging did the room begin to stir. A grim-faced Tommy Thompson leaned over to Helen MacDougall and John Bruce. There was intense whispering between them as some in the audience began to talk. The noise of discussion was loud by the time the councillors emerged from their huddle. It was John Bruce who spoke. He did not stand, nor did he look at the crowd, which shut up instantly, and he addressed a point some four feet in front of his toes.

'We are required to give an answer today to the

request for planning permission for the Loch Garvach Wind Farm. Much as Mr Claypole might advocate it, the answer "maybe" is not an option. There is only "yes", or "no", and it has become apparent that I have the casting vote. Councillor MacDougall has been implacably opposed to the wind farm since it was first suggested. She disliked the idea on principle, and her mind has not changed. Chairman Thompson, on the other hand, is convinced in the other direction. It is his view that any commercial activity for an area of this kind should not be passed up merely because it may be an inconvenience for a few individuals.'

Tommy Thompson did not demur.

'I respect both of those points of view, and have taken them into account in forming my own opinion. In fact' – Bruce straightened up – 'so firmly held are these views that I have been lobbied by both sides in this debate, and very heavily in the last couple of days. So heavily, in fact, that I'm afraid I have had to pretend to agree with both sides...'

Eyebrows were raised from both his fellow councillors, but they did not interrupt. Tommy Thompson looked at Peregrine, who sank lower in his chair.

'... for which I apologise to both of them. I think it is a matter for judgement, not dogma. I can see the advantages, and I can also see that there will be some damage and some inconveniences. I must weigh those considerations and make my decision.'

John Bruce chewed his lip. There were no sounds in the auditorium.

'In my mind, it comes down to this. Do I safeguard the immediate local environment, and vote against? Or do I try and safeguard the wider environment, and vote in favour?'

He took a breath. There was a cough from somewhere in the audience.

'Well, I am a little man. I am concerned with little things. That's why I became a local councillor. Because I like little problems. And yet here I am faced with a big decision. And I cannot say "maybe", as Mr Claypole advocated. There is only "yes" or "no".'

He sighed.

'Here it is. If I am wrong, then I'll have to be forgiven...'

He looked around the hall, blinking seriously behind his thick spectacles.

'I would like to vote in favour of the application.'

On this lonely road, trying to make it home.
Doing it by my lonesome – pissed off – who wants
some?
I see them long hard times to come.

'Long Hard Times To Come',
Gangstagrass (feat. T.O.N.E.-z)

Inside the Loch Garvach community hall, the news that the wind farm had obtained planning permission was greeted with a set of differently intended yelps. Peregrine's hand curled into a tennis player's victory fist, and he muttered 'yes, sir' as he pumped his elbow tightly; Coky, whose initial reaction was more of surprise than celebration, uttered an 'oh'; and one or two other supporters muttered 'good', or 'whoa', depending on the relative triumphs of expectation and hope. Those against the wind farm gave whimpers that were more deflatory, naturally. Bonnie just puffed her cheeks and made a 'puh' noise as if she had been punched in the stomach; some of the audience could be heard 'oh no-ing'; and an overtired ten-year-old began to cry along with her mother. But whether they were pleased, disappointed or indifferent, they almost all shared in common the urgent need to get over the road to the bar of the Loch Garvach Hotel as soon as possible.

In every old-fashioned bar in Scotland – the ones that haven't yet substituted focaccia and Pinot Grigio for the traditional 'heavy' and crisps – there is Daddy-Drunk's Chair. Nearest the till for easy pestering of the bar staff, in a corner with plenty of bar to lean on, and normally with arms to the chair to pin the encumbent in, Daddy-Drunk's Chair is where the oldest and baddest alcoholic in the neighbourhood sits, or leans, during the sociable (and very often also the unsociable) hours of opening. He must be a particular kind of drunk, of course. He must have money for a start. A worker's injury compensation cheque, a scratchcard lottery win, or a life insurance policy on the late wife normally suffices. When this man's liver gives out with a violent pop, or the use of a motility scooter means he must choose a spot nearer the door, Daddy-Drunk's Chair is inherited by the next-worst drunk in the place, who inherits the title of Daddy-Drunk, and all the regulars move up the line of succession.

Perhaps the Loch Garvach Hotel bar was in a period of interregnum, because this night it was Claypole's pleasure to occupy Daddy-Drunk's Chair. Despite theoretically staying in the hotel, he had never been into its bar. Now he slumped as if he had been there fifty years, wearing an indelible frown that would not be erased by either a positive or a negative result for the wind farm. He had done his best to be truthful, and without betraying anyone. Thus, assuming he'd shortly be cursed by antis and pros alike, he was in the pub to drown his sorrows with the last of his cash. Having spent all night writing his speech, he needed the caffeine and sugar provided by a pint of Coca-Cola. He was just contemplating, if he could afford it, adding a measure of the hotel's cheapest brandy, when celebratory voices outside announced the arrival of the victors in the Loch Garvach Wind Farm war. Claypole listened. Was it the ayes or the noes chirruping? He heard Peregrine's raking laugh, breathed a sigh and slumped further in the chair. Peregrine, Coky and Tommy Thompson came into the saloon bar. Peregrine's guffawing, and his long stride, were checked somewhat when he caught sight of Claypole, but he saw that he could not avoid the occupant of the Daddy-Drunk's Chair if he wanted to order a drink.

'Evening, partner,' said Peregrine, pronouncing the words with sodden irony. The old man's face was a filthy cocktail of triumph and disgust. Claypole regarded him with weariness. He caught Coky's expression out of the corner of his eye – he could not bear to look at her directly – and saw that she too thought her uncle's swagger distasteful.

Peregrine bent towards Claypole and whispered, for his ears only, 'You're a bankrupt and a blackmailer.'

'Yup,' said Claypole, also *sotto voce*, 'and you're a fraud and a thief.'

Peregrine's grey eyes were icy, but he chortled as he slapped Claypole on the back for everyone to see. 'Ha! Never mind the hiccups now.' But he leaned in again to Claypole and whispered, 'I win, old boy. Ker-ching!' Then he shouted, for the whole bar to hear, 'Champagne, I say!'

The other occupants of the bar turned to look at Peregrine, some with surprise, but most with silent irritation. But the hotelier and barman, a bumptious

Glaswegian with teeth like a freshly creosoted fence, came scurrying over.

'Did I hear the magic word?' he said.

'You certainly did, Gareth,' said Peregrine. 'A magnum of your finest, and as many flutes as you can fit on the bar.'

The bar was beginning to fill, and Gareth's smile was broad as he scuttled away into a back room with a feudal duck of his head. Peregrine pronounced, to no one in particular, 'God knows what this'll be, or what we'll have to drink it out of. I don't imagine he's got a magnum of anything, or any champagne flutes. Bloody Scots. So joyless.' Tommy Thompson gave the weakest of possible smiles.

'Perry,' said Coky, and raised her eyes to heaven. This simple gesture diffused the tension. They all watched in awkward silence as Gareth poured some very fizzy wine into some wine glasses with laborious and inexpert care. Peregrine turned to Tommy Thompson and began to mutter inaudibly and giggle.

Coky approached Claypole as the bar began to fill up with people coming from the community hall. He could not look at her. 'Listen, I just wanted to say' – she was blushing – 'that I think what you did in there was brave.'

Claypole nodded carefully. 'Fanks.'

'But what did you say to Perry to shut him up?'

'I… It's all… It doesn't matter.'

'Hm. Well. Anyway, there's some detail that you might find interesting…' Coky continued, but was interrupted.

'Cheers!' barked Peregrine at everyone, and they all dutifully sipped the urine-coloured fizz, grimacing or raising eyebrows.

'What detail?' Claypole asked Coky quietly.

'Christ,' barked Peregrine, eyeing his glass. 'Smells like furniture polish. Tastes of old fish.' Gareth frowned, but was not paying attention to Peregrine. His gaze was fixed on Claypole.

'Are you Mr Claypole?' asked Gareth.

'Yes,' said Claypole, still looking at Coky.

'Could I have a word in the lounge, sir?'

'Awright,' said Claypole, but there was something in the man's tone, and the paleness of his face, that put Claypole on alert.

In fact, as Claypole made his way through the building crowd, he detected the pungent odour of Impending Punch-Up. The snatches of conversation he was able to pick up told him that the subject of the wind farm was allowing the pent-up tensions and suppressed animosities that had formed over the last few months – or the last few decades, for all he knew – to ferment quickly. They would shortly bubble over. It could not, Claypole calculated, be longer than another half-hour before a fight broke out. Worse, someone might turn their attention to him with a grievance to air. He needed to be far away and alone. Since he had first been able to get into pubs aged sixteen, he had always managed to be targeted early during bar fights, and had never yet talked his way out of one. After several beatings, he had learned to smell when they were imminent and to be somewhere else when it all kicked off.

Gareth was waiting for him in the lounge, and was holding Claypole's rucksack.

'Oh, er, thanks,' said Claypole, reaching for the rucksack.

'Not so fast, sir,' said Gareth, placing the bag on the

floor and stepping in front of it. The hotelier smiled threateningly. 'You can have your bag back when you pay the bill for your room.'

⋅→═◉═←⋅

Lachlan and Milky had sat in the airless camper van and watched the steady stream of people crossing the road into the hotel. What they were engaged in could not be said to have reached anything so lofty as debate, but they were taking different perspectives on Claypole's speech in the community hall.

'Nothing's changed,' said Milky in his gloomy drawl.

'Yeah, it *has*, Milky,' said Lachlan, observing that Milky's fingers were shaking as he rolled a cigarette.

'Hasn't.'

'Has.'

'No. We still need to fuck him up,' said Milky as Lachlan stared at the lights going on around the harbour.

'Why are you talking like a gangster?' Lachlan said with a snort, and looked at his old friend in confusion. 'Milks, the game's off.'

Milky lit his cigarette and inhaled sharply. 'When I was shaving his stupid ginger head, I should have cut his throat.'

'Whoa,' said Lachlan in genuine shock. 'Don't be daft.'

Milky reddened. Lachlan had always been able to cheer Milky up or to change his mind, but this was a struggle.

'We've got the wrong guy here,' Lachlan continued. 'Claypole's not the villain. He's an idiot, and he can't tie his shoelaces outside a city, but... didn't you think that was quite a speech in there? Anyway, we were supposed to do it *before* the meeting. It's too late now. There's going to be a wind farm whether we like it or not. Eh? Milky?'

Lachlan opened the door to the van, ignoring the expression of fury on Milky's face.

'I'm going to get some air. Just stay here,' said Lachlan, 'and don't play with the handbrake.'

Milky watched Lachlan heading towards the harbour wall. Milky was in turmoil, trying to understand why the resolve had disappeared from his friend and idol. They had seen the wicked fat man going into the Loch Garvach Hotel. Why didn't they just have him away when he went for a piss? He looked in the wing mirror of the old van, saw the doors of the hotel, and fumed. He watched as the last of the attendees of the public meeting emerged from the community hall, texting and phoning. He cursed and punched the steering wheel a glancing blow.

At Milky's feet was the bat with holes in that had been his weapon for the dispatch of many seagulls. He picked it up. 'The wrong guy', Lachlan had said. Well, Milky could think for himself. He played with the bat in his hand. Suddenly he sat up, stunned both by the arrival and the brilliance of an idea. With complete clarity, Milky suddenly knew what he must do. It was simple, and perfect, and required little adaptation of their previous plan. His frustration was replaced with excitement. Milky would show Lachlan that he could be useful and righteous. The rest of the world would never know. He smiled, showing his blackened teeth. Never mind what Lachlan said, he thought. There would be violence tonight yet.

⊷≡◉≡⊶

Outside the Loch Garvach Hotel's back door, the wind was salty. A soupy westerly had got up, but Claypole pulled his suit jacket around him as he emerged onto Harbour Street at the front of the town and regretted that he had not pleaded with Gareth the hotelier to at least let him have a jumper from the sequestered ruck-sack. He headed towards the hill, past Peregrine's boat moored in its usual spot. He heard a burst of laughter coming from the hotel behind him and turned round to see Peregrine emerging with a cigarette in his mouth. Peregrine lit it and caught sight of Claypole simultane-ously, quickly stepping back away from the light and into the shadows. The smoke billowed out from the darkness, and Claypole snorted wrily.

He turned and began to make his slow way up the hill that led out of Garvachhead. He had a notion that he would take a walk into the woods, which no longer held any fear for him, before turning back and getting the midnight bus to London. Eighteen pounds, one way – although he would have to beg some of the money from Coky. Perhaps in the forest he would find a nice spot to sit down, rest his head against a tree and sleep for a few hours.

As he walked, he began to hear the low dieselly whine of a van behind him, coming up the hill. As it got closer, he could tell that it was travelling in a high gear, in a hurry, and he instinctively turned to look at it as it came up on him. At the wheel he saw Milky, and the expression on that willowy shaven head with its black beard chilled him. As the van sped past him, and despite the fading daylight, Claypole could see that there was something desperate in Milky's eyes, and they were reddened. He backed away into the shadow of a shop awning – the last shop on Harbour Street – and did not resume walking for a moment. The expression on Milky's face puzzled Claypole. Could the depressed hippy be so saddened by the planning permission given to the wind farm that he had wept? Was it anger that made him drive so fast? Perhaps he was just stoned.

He took up walking again. The next sound he heard, apart from the sea, the wind and the gulls, were footsteps. Fast footsteps hold no alarm if they are those of children. But these were of a man, running at full tilt, and that is never good news. He turned to see Lachlan Black heading his way, his donkey jacket flapping wildly around him and his steelcapped boots pounding on the pavement as if to break it. Claypole wondered whether he could be seen and realised with horror that he was now underneath a streetlight – one of only two on the whole of Harbour Street. Lachlan looked up and directly at Claypole.

'Claypole!' he shouted, and Claypole jumped. He was Lachlan's target, and would surely be got unless he could think of something, fast. So he thought as he turned and ran up the hill. Why had he not taken the threat – the finger across the throat – seriously? Why was he not in the safety of the hotel instead of out in a deserted town about to be murdered? Did he deserve to get spatchcocked on a gloomy housing estate by the militant wing of the RSPB?

Claypole found himself running down an alley behind a pebble-dashed terrace. He hadn't tried to sprint in fifteen years, and his body objected most strongly. His stomach seemed to be swishing absurdly from side to side at the moment when he needed it just to propel forward. His legs had stiffened after just twenty yards, and his lungs ached almost instantly. His heart too was galloping nastily. He looked back. Lachlan was catching up to him far more quickly than he expected. Well, of course he was, thought Claypole. That should be no great surprise. Lachlan was probably eighty times fitter than he was. So Claypole gave up running. If there was going to be a fight, and there was every sign that it would be to the death, it was better for Claypole not to be completely exhausted. That was the only way he stood a chance. That and possessing weaponry to rival the eight-inch hunting knife that Lachlan probably had concealed in his coat. Claypole looked around him and saw a plastic recycling box out for collection. He grabbed a large bottle, opened the knife that Dorcas had given him and stood in plain sight, ready for the last fight of his life. If Lachlan was going to slit Claypole's throat, as he had promised to do, he was going to have to do it with at least a few bruises and gashes of his own.

When Lachlan saw Claypole baring what remained of his teeth in a snarl and with his ginger nut glistening with sweat, brandishing an empty bottle of Newcastle Brown Ale and a tiny Swiss Army penknife, Lachlan's instinct was to laugh. But he knew there wasn't time to be amused by the fat man's fear and ineptitude.

'You've got to come with me,' said Lachlan, panting.

It was a relief not to be instantly murdered, and Claypole wondered how long he could postpone his imminent death by talking.

'You're going to kill me somewhere else?'

'What?' said Lachlan frowning. 'No. Look, I haven't got time to explain.'

'Bollocks,' said Claypole simply. He was going to

need a good deal more reassurance. 'Not moving an inch. You threatened me.'

'Oh, aye. But that was before... Look, everything's changed.'

'Oh, pray, do tell.' Claypole impressed himself by summoning sarcasm.

'Oh God, you're a prick,' said Lachlan with feeling.

But Claypole just curled his lip and shrugged.

'Oh, for fu–... Look, Milky's got Peregrine in the back of the van,' said Lachlan quickly, and his thumb gestured to the road out of town, along which Milky had sped in the camper. Claypole didn't know whether to be alarmed or amused.

'What?' Claypole snorted. 'He's...'

'Kidnapped him, aye.'

Claypole lowered the bottle and the knife.

'We were going to take you, but... that all changed when you... Anyway, I reckon Milky's lost his shit and I think I know where he's going.'

'The beach?'

'No. The old church at Glen Drum.'

'Were you going to...?' Claypole gulped.

'No, don't be daft. We were just going to keep you out of the picture until the wind farm was voted down.' Claypole nodded. He could see the logic. Lachlan continued. 'But now that the wind farm is going ahead, Milky might be going to... Well, it might be more in the way of a punishment...'

Claypole examined the face of Lachlan Black and found it to be genuine.

'Sorry, anyway,' said Lachlan quickly. 'Look, if you won't help me, just lend me your car.'

'Haven't got one. Twatted it into an elk.'

'Oh.'

The two men both thought.

'Look, if Peregrine's in Milky's van –' Claypole began.

'My van.'

'Your van... then why don't you take Peregrine's boat? It's quicker, apparently.'

Lachlan brightened instantly. 'Brilliant!'

'Thanks,' said Claypole nonchalantly, and put the beer bottle back in the recycling box and folded the knife away. When he had done so, he found that Lachlan, to his surprise, was still there.

'I can't sail it on my own!' said Lachlan.

'Well, I'm not... Brr. Find someone else to help you,' said Claypole.

Lachlan swallowed hard. 'I haven't got time.'

Claypole closed his eyes with dread. Then he looked puzzled.

'Hang on. Why do you care if Peregrine gets beaten up? I thought you and Peregrine had fallen out.'

'I think Milky might do more than just give Peregrine a kicking...' Lachlan looked at the ground while Claypole watched him sceptically. While Claypole was assuring himself that no one, even strange Milky, would actually murder a man because of planning permission, Lachlan was making a calculation in his head. There was nobody alive – except Milky, of course – who knew what he was about to tell Claypole. But, he thought, he could tell Claypole because shortly Claypole would be gone from Loch Garvach. Anyway, what choice did he have? It would sound strange to voice out loud that which had only been in his head for two years.

'And anyway... Peregrine is my father.'

-16-

GRIFFITH: Men's evil manners live in brass; their virtues
we write in water.

Henry VIII, Act IV, scene ii,
William Shakespeare

As Lachlan and Claypole jogged to the harbour and towards Peregrine's boat, Lachlan indulged Claypole's curiosity with short bursts of information. Lachlan was a fit man, for his age. But he was also a smoker, so his answers were necessarily staccato. He knew that he should feel disinclined to give Claypole more information than was absolutely necessary, and yet telling someone provided a release that he had long needed, so he talked.

'Mam used to work with old Mrs MacGilp's horses,' said Lachlan, accompanied by the rhythm of his boots pounding the road. Claypole nodded, reserving his breath for the appalling task of running. In between heavy breaths, Lachlan continued.

'Peregrine was home from boarding school over the summer... Mam got pregnant... He paid for her to go to Glasgow and have an abortion... She went to Glasgow, but kept the money, and kept me... Then one day she came back to Garvach... I don't remember it... I was five, and she took me to see him... We walked up the drive. Knocked on the door. Is young Mr MacGilp in? He's in the south parlour, miss. You can imagine the scene... She says, "Hello, Perry. This is your son."...'

Lachlan looked at the ground and wheezed painfully.

'Only thing he said was that I wasn't very good-looking, so I couldn't possibly be his son. Too short, he said... I was fuckin' five years old. Of course I was short... Anyway, he denied the whole thing. She didn't want money. She just wanted him to squirm. I dunno what she expected, but she didn't expect him to be such a... What a...'

After a pause, Claypole suggested 'Wanker?'

Lachlan gave a sad smile. 'I was going to say something worse.'

'Right,' said Claypole. They were about to reach the boat. 'So you're after a bit of payback?'

Lachlan stopped. With relief, so did Claypole. Lachlan looked very serious, and pointed at Claypole. 'Absolutely not. I don't want anything from him.'

Claypole shrugged. 'It would be fair enough –'

'I just want him to own up. Or even... just to acknowledge it to *me*.'

When they had arrived at the boat, the two men immediately set about casting off. Lachlan began unwinding the bow painter from a cleat on the harbour wall, and Claypole did the same at the stern. They threw the ropes onto the deck and hastily jumped on board the boat themselves. They looked at each other as they caught their breath. Both standing in the helmsman's position, they continued to look at each other

275

expectantly. The boat drifted slowly away from the harbour wall. Claypole was the first to speak. 'What do we do now?'

Lachlan looked surprised. 'You mean you don't know how to sail this thing?'

'No idea.'

'But all posh people know how to sail.'

Claypole would have found the idea that he was posh amusing if he had stopped to think about it, and if he were not distracted by the fact that they were now on a very expensive fifty-foot yacht, drifting towards the open sea with increasing speed.

'You grew up by the sea,' Claypole protested. 'You must know how to sail.'

'I grew up in Garvachhead. Till I left school I didn't know how to do anything except watch telly and take drugs.'

They both looked around for inspiration as the horizon began to twist and rock in the current. Claypole regarded the dials, switches and gimbles in front of the captain's wheel.

'Can we drive it? You know, use the engine?'

'No keys,' said Lachlan. 'But... isn't there a *little* boat somewhere?'

They looked at each other before both running to the back of the boat and peering over the stern. There was a small dinghy with a small outboard motor being bobbed and bumped by the hull of the bigger boat.

'There you go,' said Lachlan.

'I'm not going in *that*,' said Claypole with feeling.

Lachlan sighed. 'You have to. Milky's going to do something terrible to Peregrine, and I might not be able to stop him on my own.'

'Why don't we... call the police?'

Lachlan's laugh was hollow. 'Great idea. They might even arrive before the end of the weekend.'

'But the police station's just next to the community hall,' Claypole protested.

'Turned into flats. Nearest police is forty miles away.'

'Oh,' said Claypole, feeling suddenly horribly tired. 'What do we do about this thing?' He pointed at the deck they were standing on. The yacht was now moving at the full pace of the current.

'Bollocks to it,' said Lachlan simply. 'Does Peregrine want his boat saved, or himself?'

⊷══◉═⊶

Whether Peregrine would rather have taken his chances with Milky than have the *Lady of the Isles* given even the mildest scratch was a question that Claypole and Lachlan could not answer. Even if Peregrine would rather have sacrificed himself than the boat, Peregrine would not have been able to confirm this owing to having, at that moment, a long-life hessian shopping bag over his head, his hands tied with the cord from a Moulinex Falafel King 2000, and a child's vest stuffed in his mouth. It was most strange for him to be one moment enjoying a celebratory cigarette outside the Loch Garvach Hotel, and the next minute being tossed about in the back of a filthy camper van on his way to God knew where. He had recognised his attacker as Lachlan's weird sidekick from the camp, which is why he had agreed to look inside the van. If it really did contain Beyoncé, his beloved black Labrador, injured but still living, as the tall streak of piss with the beard/ shaved head combo had claimed, he wanted to tend to the animal immediately, his only thought whether the poor bitch could survive the loss of another leg. How could he have known that the van contained nothing more animal than the smell of farts and body odour, and that he would be bundled inside and tied up at the hands of a crazed vegetarian?

While Lachlan was straining the tiny outboard motor on the dinghy which had until recently been attached to the *Lady of the Isles* somewhere on the Garvach headland, Milky was taking Lachlan's camper van along a barely used dirt track towards an old ruined church at a handsome gallop. After two minutes of furious bumping and lurching about, Milky finally halted the bruised vehicle. When he turned the engine off, he could hear muffled but heartfelt swearing coming from Peregrine, trussed up in the back of the van.

Milky got out and opened the back doors. Peregrine was now still, listening.

'Right, fucker,' said Milky, 'when I take that bag off and untie your legs and let you out, either you can struggle, or do something stupid like run away – we will fight and I will win... or you can just behave yourself and do what I tell you... What's it to be?'

Peregrine mumbled clear assent even though no words could be divined.

Milky took the bag off Peregrine and squinted at him in the dim light of the van's tail lights. He smiled to see the old man's distress, but took the child's vest out of his mouth. Immediately, Peregrine screamed.

'Help!' he yelled into the wind. Other than wincing from the volume of the scream, Milky did nothing.

Peregrine yelled again, 'Help me!' at a slightly higher pitch and even louder, but Milky merely gestured towards the darkness. Although Peregrine could not see further than a few yards, he knew that Milky was indicating the futility of shouting into the wind and the wilderness. With bitterness, Peregrine was forced to give up all thoughts of rescue.

'Bugger off,' said Peregrine with feeling, and spat unpleasantly.

'That's better,' said Milky darkly. 'Now, if you would be so kind as to walk into that graveyard. You and I are going to have a wee chat.'

Lachlan and Claypole had not spoken for the first four minutes of the boat ride from Garvachhead to Glen Drum beach. But Lachlan now shouted in order to be heard above the noise of the engine and the sea angrily slapping the hull of the dinghy.

'What did you say to Peregrine at the community hall?'

'Brr,' said Claypole.

'One minute he was all for having you thrown out of the meeting, but after your little conference, he didn't say another word. What did you say to him?'

Claypole calculated before answering. He could not have told Coky, but perhaps he could tell Lachlan. Lachlan had, after all, confessed to him.

'I blackmailed him.'

'What?' Lachlan had either not heard, or was astonished.

'I blackmailed him. I found a bird survey that said there was a pair of nesting golden eagles above the Giant's Table, which Perry had tried to destroy. I told him I would tell everyone about his fraud if he didn't let me have my say.'

'That was my survey!' Lachlan seemed pleased, and then realised that his work had been ignored. 'Oh. Did he keep the bit about the merlins, and the ospreys?'

'He buried the whole thing. Would have shredded it if I hadn't... nicked it.'

Lachlan thought again. 'But why didn't you trash the whole project, then?'

'Because,' Claypole shouted, 'if Peregrine were actually proved to have been fraudulent, the whole wind farm would have been thrown out. I didn't want to do that to Coky. But I did want it postponed. I meant what I said in there. It could be a good wind farm, if the environmental survey were done properly and if given a little more time. If there are rare birds up at the Giant's Table, the turbines near them should be removed from the plans. But it doesn't mean that the whole thing should be trashed. I realised all this while I was standing in the sea last night.'

'Hm', said Lachlan, now deep in thought. They focused on the horizon and the approaching beach at Glen Drum.

The two men wordlessly dragged the boat onto the beach, and Claypole looked around while Lachlan secured the boat. He had been looking forward to landing at the beach, not just because bobbing around on a dark and forbidding ocean was not his idea of fun, but because it was a familiar place. It appeared so different from the friendly venue for Lochstock. It was so vast and forbidding, and the little camp, with only one light on in a teepee, looked so tiny and desolate.

They scrambled up some rocks at the back of the beach and headed into the dark forest at a brisk trot. Claypole remembered the small torch that Peregrine had lent him along with the Land Rover, and felt for it in his jacket pocket. It proved to be worse than useless. It cast a thin light, sure enough, but it created shadows that gave false impressions of what to avoid and what was air.

'Best just get your eyes used to the dark,' Lachlan said, and Claypole chucked the torch away. Any excess weight might hold him back, he thought. But once again, Claypole had cause to remember that he was not a slick machine, the forward movement of which might be improved by being lighter. Lachlan was now scampering through the woods, ducking branches and skipping over fallen trees. Even if he had not been hit by, or had not tripped over every one of these obstacles, he would still have found it impossible to keep up.

'Come on, Claypole,' Lachlan would call behind him every few seconds, but received no response. Claypole had been too out of breath to reply after a minute. They had been running for ten minutes and it took all Claypole's effort to muster a one-finger salute, unseen as it was in the darkness. Then Lachlan whispered, 'We're nearly there,' and Claypole managed to grunt with relief.

Then there came a weird call from out of the darkness ahead of them. It sounded to Claypole's ear like a wolf, and both men halted. They looked at each other, and Claypole felt a new dread. He wondered briefly if there were any coyotes in Scotland, and decided that there probably were not. So, a cat maybe. Or a badger. Just as he was debating in his mind whether badgers made any noise, they heard the noise again. Louder and more prolonged, it chilled them both instantly. It was a human, in distress.

'Come on,' said Lachlan, and dived further into the brush.

'Oh, God,' muttered Claypole. The idea of rescuing Peregrine had in the previous half-hour amused more than frightened him. He had allowed his mind to play several fantasies out. First, he imagined Milky and Lachlan undergoing some sort of boxing match with Claypole acting as referee. The second fantasy involved the appearance of Coky playing the role of mewling damsel, and had a more convoluted rescue that ended in a kiss. The third, quite Gothic and blood-strewn, involved Claypole bouncing from the undergrowth like Rambo and single-handedly disarming Milky and (it was a fantasy) laying waste to an additional half-dozen Nazis using only a Swiss Army penknife, before a grateful Peregrine forgave him and paid off all his debts. But the reality that Peregrine might actually have been physically harmed by the encounter with a genuinely crazed and bloodthirsty Milky had been brought home to Claypole all too well by the real horror contained in the scream he had just heard. He no longer felt merely out of place and uneasy. He was properly scared now.

Claypole slowed as Lachlan darted forward and out of sight. The moon was hiding, and although he could see that there was a clearing coming up in the dense wood, he could make out little else.

'Lachlan,' he whispered, but there was no reply.

The scream came again, this time more agonised and prolonged, and at its end it had a self-pitying tremor that was gut-churning. Suddenly, Claypole could feel his chest tighten, as if in the grip of a fist. He bent over and breathed deeply, feeling a metallic taste in his mouth. His body was in crisis, and his mind turned

again to the unswallowed pills in his ransomed rucksack at the Loch Garvach Hotel. He looked up again to
locate Lachlan, but Claypole could see nothing except
a few branches, and felt utterly alone.

As he inched forward, crouching, the air changed.
From being just the outward breath of trees, close and
muggy, Claypole felt the salt wind gently on his face.
As he approached the clearing, Claypole suddenly
wanted more than anything not to be there. All confidence evapor-ated, he would have turned round and
crawled off in the opposite direction if he thought
he had a greater chance of survival. But he inched
forward again. Then he saw what he most feared, and
he gagged.

The clearing was a long-ruined churchyard, and
by one of the larger grey headstones was a tall dark
figure knelt over a body that was partly white. Was that
a disarranged shirt or pale skin? Another figure that
Claypole recognised as Lachlan appeared, walking
with purpose towards this scene. Lachlan hesitated
as he got nearer, but then rushed towards the man on
the ground. Lachlan said something terse and direct.
There was protest from the standing figure which, as
it turned, Claypole could see was the shaven-headed
Milky.

Claypole crawled further forward and squinted
at the man on the ground. His face was pale and his
white shirt was torn open to the navel. The man's wide
dry eyes stared deeply into nothingness. Peregrine
MacGilp was dead.

Lachlan quickly straddled Peregrine's body. He
pounded at the dead man's chest, slapped his face
and puffed into his mouth. Milky watched and paced
while yanking stupidly at his own fingers and saying

'fuck, fuck, fuck'. When Lachlan finally realised his actions were pointless he sat back on the ground and spat. Then he tucked his head into his chest and was still, his arms limply hanging by his sides.

'Oh shit, oh Christ,' said Milky, backing off a couple of yards. Lachlan turned to look at him wordlessly.

'I didn't do anything,' protested Milky in a childlike wheedle.

Lachlan said nothing. He just looked empty.

'I didn't touch him,' said Milky, in the same whine.

'Is he...?' This was Claypole, now standing behind the two men. They turned to him. Lachlan nodded.

'Did you...?' This was Claypole again, directing the half-question at Milky, and backing away.

'I only wanted to scare him,' said Milky pathetically.

Claypole edged backwards.

'Don't go anywhere, Claypole,' said Lachlan, with a tone of exasperation, and Claypole stopped.

Milky looked at Lachlan, who got up from the ground as if exhausted.

'What do we do, Lachy?' The use of the diminutive name, in that childish whisper, jarred Lachlan.

'Claypole,' said Lachlan quietly. 'Don't go anywhere.' Claypole, who had begun to move backwards again, stopped once more.

'Lachy, I didn't...' said Milky, back to his monotone drawl. 'It's the truth. I tied him up and just wanted to get him to talk, and he just... went.'

'What about the screaming?' Lachlan's voice was level.

'That was *me*, man.'

They both looked at Peregrine's too-still body, its face contorted in horror.

'OK, Milky,' sighed Lachlan.

There was silence between the three men, and Claypole took this as his cue. He turned and ran.

For a moment, Milky and Lachlan just looked at Claypole hoofing his way through the clearing and away from them. In no particular hurry, they looked at each other.

'Where on earth does that fat fuck think he's going?' asked Milky in a tone of wonderment.

Lachlan sighed. 'Just get after him or we'll all be for it.'

Claypole thundered away from the scene of death in a hideous daze. His legs were quickly wobbly and uncommandable. There was a pounding of blood in his ears and each swish and sting of branch and bracken felt like a lash as he ran through the trees. But there was the echo of that scream and the image of poor Peregrine's body, white and lifeless, flashing horribly in his mind to urge him on. He stumbled on and found that the forest was becoming less dense. But then he heard Milky's massive thudding steps bearing down on him. His heart gave a skip and a lurch. Claypole tried to shout something but found that he had no voice. He tripped just before Milky reached him, and Claypole was as certain as he could be – as certain as the last time he had fallen over, voiceless, in a café in London, in the presence of the woman he loved – that he was about to die.

–Epilogue–

Se vogliamo che tutto rimanga com'è bisogna che tutto
cambi.
If we want things to stay the same, things will have to
change.
The Leopard, Giuseppe Tomasi de Lampedusa

A thousand hooded crows were barracking each other in the huge cypress trees above MacGilp House on the morning of the first day of September. Jim Fry, the Minister of the Loch Garvach kirk, looked up at the black birds, wheeling and cavorting noisily, and hugged his anorak tightly around him. He knew that there was an unusual collective noun for crows, and had whimsically been trying to remember it for the last five minutes. He turned his mind to the peroration he must now perform. He got up slowly and thoughtfully, minutely adjusted his dog collar and stepped in front of his audience of no more than a dozen souls. Just before he began to speak, he remembered the collective noun for crows and smiled to himself. A murder. That was it. A murder of crows.

Fry felt uneasy about conducting a funeral in such circumstances. It was not that they were not in a church, although having an event outdoors in Scotland in autumn has obvious weather risks. But the rain had as yet held off, and the wind, although it had something to say in the matter of the changing season, was not yet biting. What irked Fry was the fact that he had been asked to conduct a service that, at the request of the MacGilps, was to contain no reference to God. This was not liturgical fussiness on his part. He did not mind that the casket was wicker. He did not mind that, rather than a headstone, a tree was to mark the last resting place of the departed. And he did not object, for he knew them well and liked them, to being given instruction by George and Vesper, the 'green' funeral directors. He felt sure that the Almighty paid scant attention to these things. But Jim Fry had his suspicions that the man in the casket would have preferred a church service, having taken part in one of his services only the Sunday before his death. Nonetheless, the minister thought to himself, a funeral service is for the living, not the dead. The modern clergyman must compromise and adapt to the wishes of his congregation. So he examined the individuals in the assembly with his stern stare, attempting to transmit solemnity rather than rebuke.

Notable among the mourners were Coky Viveksananda and her mother, the redoubtable Bonnie Straughan, along with Dorcas MacGilp. They made a handsome coven, thought the Minister, all in smart black dresses and dark overcoats. Bonnie even sported an elaborate black hat, pinned invisibly in place with what to Jim Fry was mysterious female know-how in defiance of the wind. There was Councillor Tommy Thompson, his eyes pleasingly closed in reverence, and either side of him the farmers and their families from the Loch Garvach estate. Lachlan Black held the hand of Jade, his heavily pregnant girlfriend. (Or was it wife? Fry could not remember having married them.) The only absentee that Jim Fry considered worthy of note was Ronald 'Milky' Duffy. But rumour had it that Milky had gone to County Antrim to visit a friend, and it was not known when, or whether, he would be back.

'Welcome, everyone,' said Jim Fry, and paused. 'We are here to celebrate the life of –'

The Minister broke off, hearing a small crash behind him. He followed the eyes of his congregation, and turned to see a fat man in a deerstalker hat re-erecting a lawn chair that he had just knocked over. The man looked up at him and smiled weakly.

'Sorry,' said Gordon Claypole, reddening. 'Sorry I'm late. Brr. The bloody Land Rover wouldn't... Sorry.'

'No matter,' said Jim Fry beneficently as Claypole squeezed into a seat as quickly as he could. 'Claypole, isn't it?'

'Gordon,' said Claypole.

'Gordon, yes. I'm so glad you could make it.'

Claypole, or rather Gordon, nodded weakly.

'As I was saying,' Jim Fry continued. 'Let us now give thanks for the life of Peregrine MacGilp.'

Gordon, as he tried not to breathe lest he draw further attention, cursed himself that he had, for one last time, contrived to arrive late for Peregrine. He had in fact elected to walk to the funeral, and should have called an earlier halt to his raking of the first of the autumn leaves on the lower lawn of MacGilp House. Perhaps, he thought now, it was pride. He wanted the raking job finished so that he could start work on the out-of-control rhododendrons in earnest the next day. But perhaps it was the fact that, since he had been doing a few odd jobs around the gardens, he had started to lose a bit of weight and felt so much better for it. Gordon went to touch his head and realised that he still had a hat on. He whipped off his deerstalker to reveal the beginnings of patchy ginger curls and tried to focus on Jim Fry's words.

'The last ten days have been a difficult time for all of us in Loch Garvach, and particularly for Peregrine's family and friends,' Jim Fry pronounced.

There was an extra gust of wind, and Gordon shivered as he thought of all the jumpers in his chest of drawers in London. Had the jumpers, the chest of drawers and the flat itself not been about to be sold to pay off some of his whopping debts, he would now be wearing something with a smart designer's name neatly sown into the collar. Instead, he wore a shirt that had belonged to Peregrine, and an ancient waxed jacket that could have belonged to any number of the dead relatives whose portraits no longer hung in the dining room of the big house, and sported a pair of wellingtons that were three sizes too large and made comfortable only by the wearing of multiple pairs of kilt hose.

'Before I hand over to Peregrine's older sister,' the Minister was saying, 'I feel there are some thanks we should give. We should thank the North-Western Constabulary for establishing so efficiently the circumstances of Peregrine's untimely death, sparing the family more distress than was absolutely necessary.'

Gordon glanced across at Lachlan before focusing severely on the Minister. Jim Fry himself seemed unaware of the growing wrinkles of disapproval on the brows of his congregation.

'Indeed, it was only following the coroner's report

that the Procurator Fiscal could be absolutely satisfied that the bruises on our late friend's torso had been caused by the attempts of Lachlan Black to revive Peregrine following his heartattack. And we are so very grateful to Lachlan for that.'

Fry inclined his head graciously, but Lachlan had his head bowed.

'There are those in the community,' continued Fry with a frown, 'who have cruelly wondered what three grown men were doing in an abandoned churchyard in the middle of the Loch Garvach forest at midnight. But it is no business of ours if a man wishes to celebrate the granting of planning permission for his wind farm with some of the "superskunk" to which he was so partial.'

One of the farmers coughed into a handkerchief.

'Nor is it our business to speculate on, or to judge, the quantity of alcohol to be found in Peregrine's blood. But alas for those he has left behind, the precipitous climb to the old church, the champagne, and the forty cigarettes a day for fifty years, must have concatenated to precipitate his massive and fatal myocardial infarction.'

Dorcas emitted a 'tsk', but Fry gave a supercilious smile.

'But there is another person to whom we must all be particularly grateful. Peregrine himself. For, without him, we would not have the Loch Garvach Wind Farm. In due course, when the wind farm has been built, Garvachhead School can have its new technology centre and its playing fields, and the parish council may be in a position, for example, to renovate my own church, or… whatever other purpose it may see fit… with its extra… funds. So thank you, Peregrine MacGilp, from us all.'

Fry smiled, folded his notes and nodded to Dorcas. She rose without looking at the Minister and took her place in front of the assembled mourners. She looked at the wicker coffin thoughtfully and sniffed once before she proceeded to give a perfectly measured eulogy. She spoke of her brother's attachment to MacGilp House and the Loch Garvach estate, and his love of travel, of sailing the *Lady of the Isles* and of 'the fun things in life'. He avoided doctors and paid employment, but 'said no to little else'. She was glad that he had lived to see his wind project through, if not to completion, at least to a more certain future. When it was eventually built, it would see his beloved estate funded for the next twenty-five years and become a huge contributor to the local community. Dorcas ended with a heartfelt regret that Peregrine and his sisters had not been better friends in their late middle age, but asserted that he had loved his niece Coky most sincerely. It was only right and proper that she should inherit the estate.

After Coky had read a poem by Ted Hughes about foxes going to ground, to more discreet sniffs they all stood while George and Vesper put Peregrine MacGilp of MacGilp in the ground with touching simplicity. Everyone was invited to throw a handful of earth on top of him, and a healthy-looking three-year-old pear tree stood by, waiting to be planted in the loose earth. Whisky was handed round, received in solemn gratitude. Coky, looking pale and dignified, raised her glass.

'To Peregrine,' she said.

'Peregrine,' they all said, and drank deeply.

Later, while the mourners sombrely drank tea and ate sandwiches in MacGilp House, Gordon went through the papers in Peregrine's library office, as requested by

Coky. In the evening, when all the guests at the wake had gone, he confirmed to Coky and Dorcas what they already suspected, viz. that Peregrine had no money.

'He wasn't just, you know, poor for a rich guy. He really had absolutely no dosh,' said Gordon. He had sold pictures, furniture and books for years to meet the gap between the estate's income and its expenses. But Peregrine had never got into debt – a principle that Gordon could admire, it being one that he had found so impossible to follow.

'Thank goodness for the insurance money, then,' said Coky.

'Huh?' This was Gordon.

'From Perry's boat,' added Dorcas, and then her eyebrows furrowed. 'You know, I still find it odd that Peregrine managed to get so drunk that he unmoored his own yacht in the harbour with the result that it wrecked itself on the bridge at Glenmorie, and yet he was sober enough to take a dinghy across the loch and walk through a forest and up a hill. Don't you think that's odd?'

Gordon addressed Coky, ignoring Dorcas. 'Yeah, but... brr... that money won't last long, and even if you get the wind farm built in three years' time, the estate is going to need to pull its socks up well before then. You'll need some income.'

Dorcas and Coky nodded gravely, and the three of them sat down to have some ideas.

Getting MacGilp House into a state in which it might be a tourist attraction would take too long and cost too much, and it was Coky who suggested regenerating the Victorian walled garden. Gordon approved, but thought that the plan needed an extra twist. He suggested a model organic garden, comprising the walled garden and the upper field next to it. Produce could be sold almost all year round to local restaurants, and the public could be charged to visit. This would need everyone to pitch in, they decided. Aside from an enormous amount of energy and determination from Coky, and Lachlan working more or less full time just keeping the buildings from falling down, Dorcas would need to advise on the gardening aspect. While she was willing, Dorcas was of the view that the project would need an under-gardener who could also help Coky to manage the estate. While the beach-dwellers might be a source of casual employment, if they wanted it, the estate needed someone permanent with a business head on them who could also use a spade. This was quite a demand, considering that the money available to pay this person was small. They all tapped their chins as they wondered who might fill this role, or whether such a person existed.

When Dorcas had gone home, Gordon had a question for Coky.

'Does all this make you feel guilty, at all?' he said.

'What?' She poured herself some more mint tea, and pushed the bottle of Knockenglachgach towards Gordon. In answer, he swept his hand around the room grandly.

Coky said, 'I don't know a lot of people who inherit a 3,000-acre estate and then spend a lot of time feeling guilty. It wouldn't look good, would it? And anyway, there isn't time.'

Claypole shrugged. 'I don't know many people who inherit anything.'

Coky nodded, and they were silent for a moment.

'So are you going to help me do this?' She smiled as

he frowned. 'You know, run the place… as a full-time job?'

'Me? But…'

'I can't pay you much,' she said. 'But I can put a roof over your head. And there's the wind farm to sort out.'

'But,' Gordon protested, 'I've got to go to London and dismantle my life. I don't…' He trailed off.

'You've been well educated. You can do all the numbers and stuff.'

'Pff,' he said.

'My education was rubbish, considering what it must have cost. All my school taught me was how to shoot, dance and paint a lovely picture of hollyhocks. But someone's got to talk to the accountant.'

He crinkled his mouth into a smile. 'Just because I know the causes of the First World War, doesn't mean I can run a Scottish estate.'

'Well, I know a bit about that. You have certain other skills and characteristics that I don't, and… you know, we might be a team.'

Gordon thought. He knew that it would require a lot more than talk to get the Loch Garvach estate into decent and sustainable order, especially when they had so little capital. It would require what real entrepreneurs have. Unquenchable zeal, ingenuity and adaptability. Whether he could find these qualities in himself he did not know, but it was possible that her flair, personability and local knowledge would compliment his logic, attention to detail, and his business experience… or rather, his experience in getting it all so wrong. He might have questioned whether he was the ideal candidate for the job of getting the wind farm straightened out, but he found himself saying, 'Perhaps I can learn.'

'That's the spirit,' she said, and they put the dinner things in the dishwasher.

⊷╾⊚╼⊶

At first, Gordon had started work as factor of the Loch Garvach estate and part-time under-gardener with a heavy heart. He felt he had missed his opportunity to confess to Coky. The memory of the episode twenty-five years ago still burdened him. It had haunted him over the weeks since Peregrine's death, and every time he remembered it, it stung afresh. But he couldn't tell Coky now that she was his employer. It might jeopardise his accommodation, apart from anything else.

His initial disappointment at not being given one of the two beautiful if dilapidated Victorian gate lodges at the bottom of the drive, and instead being billeted in a caravan, turned unexpectedly to joy. The caravan was not, as he had expected, some 1970s horror that rocked perilously when you went from one side to the other. It was a sturdy Edwardian showman's caravan, extravagantly painted in the traditional gaudy colours by Coky herself the previous summer. A log-fired stove got the place from icy to snug in ten minutes, and all the gilded mirrors gave the impression of space. The bed was deep if narrow and as long as he didn't move much, he slept well. And these days, he never moved when sleeping. He was simply too physically tired.

For a time, while his bankruptcy was going through, Gordon would slip into the crib of a bed in the caravan, turn out the lights and *then* get drunk, three swift bolts of supermarket whisky to catapult him into the land of nod. But he soon realised that the hangovers weren't worth it. Of his new friends, who generally worked outdoors, only the very young ones could work on a hangover, and they didn't tend to drink because they were all saving up for something. Surfing in Cornwall, New Year in Goa, or just to buy mojitos and caipiriñhas at the weekend for Fiona or Keira or Mairi. Gordon quickly realised that he could not be a gardener knocking on the door of forty years old and be hung over. When the last of the bankruptcy hearings was over and he had made his last coach trip to London, he gave up drinking altogether.

Gradually – at a tectonic pace, it sometimes seemed – the estate under the new chatelaine and her manager began to transform. In the Peregrine Era, the place had become ossified, immune or allergic to change. Peregrine had somehow contrived to repel the world. No longer was this the case. In what remained of the autumn, it was seriously a-buzz. There was no greater symbol of this than the selling of the wrought-iron gates to the main drive, allowing unfettered access to the estate from the public road. Things were being fixed; plans being put into action; and people coming to check things and make assessments and give quotations. Every morning there was Gordon or Coky, and sometimes both of them, on the front lawn or the gravel, shaking hands and initiating action or further planning.

Then winter drew in, and there were fewer people. Only Lachlan remained, gradually making the upper floors of the old house safe. Next year he would make them habitable, the year after that comfortable. (Coky's insistence on using only the most environmentally friendly materials and methods might have frustrated another builder, but Lachlan only approved.) During the dark and glowering mornings, Gordon worked on the wind farm. The plans, Coky and Gordon had privately agreed, needed to be revised in the light of the revelations about the bird surveys. The wind farm's planning application would be resubmitted, this time stripped of the three controversial turbines, and there was a heap of financial work to do, not least to express the community's increased share of the profits. This paperwork was not simple, even with Harry Lightfoot available on the phone for consultation. Gordon spent his afternoons working in the garden, Beyoncé the Labrador always nearby. Dorcas would drop by periodically, and he absorbed horticultural knowledge from her by osmosis rather than actively learning. He reserved his mental energy for his 'grand plan' for the estate, about which he would think as he worked away at the burgeoning veg patch, or turning the compost, or doing whatever was required, losing weight and gaining muscle by the week.

In the evenings, he would chew over some idea or other with Coky, and they would show each other budgets, research and plans. Dorcas would very often join them, usually bringing supper from her house. They didn't discuss plans for the estate or the wind farm when Bonnie came to dinner, but those occasions were polite enough – and when they weren't, they were usually funny. Gordon had developed a good line in teasing Bonnie when she became pompous or daft, and this kept Coky in the cheery mood she might not have otherwise been in when in the presence of her mother.

It was on a December afternoon with the rain sweeping from the west in drowning horizontal drifts that Gordon found himself playing snooker with

Lachlan. The pink and three reds were missing, and there was a large tear in the baize, but this did not reduce their enjoyment. They hadn't been talking about anything very much, until Lachlan raised the topic of his new living arrangements. Coky had told Lachlan that Peregrine had made an amendment to his will to give Lachlan and Jade the flat above the stables, and the couple had just sold the camper van and moved in. Lachlan was pleased to be away from the beach before winter, and Jade had certainly been relieved now that the birth of her child was imminent. But something was making Lachlan uneasy. As Gordon lined up a difficult blue to the corner pocket, Lachlan unburdened himself.

'D'you think Peregrine really...?' Lachlan inhaled deeply. 'Did he really give me the flat, or has Coky...? Is she just being... well, sisterly?'

'She knows about the whole half-brother thing, then?'

'Mm-hm. Said she'd suspected it for years.'

Gordon thought before answering. 'Brr. I don't know, but I wouldn't be surprised if she was just being nice. Sort of thing she does. If you ask me, there shouldn't be any more secrets. There's been enough truth buried around this place – facts and feelings – and, it's not healthy to...' He trailed off.

'Aye,' said Lachlan, and silence descended for a moment. Then he said with sudden gravity, 'Some things should always be a secret, though, eh?'

Gordon looked at Lachlan, and the two men's eyes met sincerely. 'Oh, that's definitely true,' said Gordon.

'Just between us, aye?'

Gordon nodded, chalking his cue.

'The *whole* truth can hurt,' added Lachlan. 'But... I've

been meaning to thank you.'

'Yeah?' Gordon played the blue, and missed by a foot and a half.

'In the old churchyard that night... you made everything... fit. Told us what to say to the police and how it would all work out, after you'd, you know, got yourself together and stopped screaming. God knows I wasn't thinking straight. Milky was even more of a mess.'

Gordon shrugged modestly. 'Years of watching crap telly,' he said. 'Everything's got to tie up.'

'But, you know, Gordon,' Lachlan began, making no effort to take his next shot. 'You're right about secrets. And if there's anything you need to tell somebody... Coky, for instance... Anything you might *feel*... you should tell her.'

A worried expression played on Gordon's face.

'Brr,' he said, and the two men played the rest of the frame in silence.

-◆==◉==◆-

It was only the following morning that Gordon and Coky were next alone together, walking down to the walled garden. The rain had stayed away long enough for him to have planted the beech whips that would form a hedge going all the way down one side of the drive, as they had discussed. They had stood and stared at the wobbly line of new plants for a moment before moving off down the Old Walk.

As the wind whipped his uncut ginger curls about his frayed collar, he said, 'Why do you keep me around?'

'Well, you're such an ace gardener,' she said, and they both sniggered.

They were walking now on the soaked and mossy

lawn through the yew trees, a limping Beyoncé their only company.

'Hm,' she said, her lips turned up in a smile. 'Honestly, I think it's because you're the only man I've ever known who actually gets nicer when he's drunk.'

He gave a hollow snort. 'Oh. Well … you may not have noticed, but I'm not actually drinking at the moment.'

Then she looked at him with wide, serious eyes. 'Yeah, and that's OK too.'

They walked on a short way. The wind was getting up, and she shivered.

'Shall we start the lessons tonight?' she said with the uncertain smile.

'Oh. Yes.' He too was nervous. 'You mean… the dancing?'

'Aye.' She smiled her fangy smile.

The wind suddenly dropped as they entered a clearing, and he turned to her. 'There's something I need to confess,' he said.

She was still smiling as she looked at him. But seeing how serious he was, she said, 'OK. What's up?'

They sat down on a stone bench and he told her. He told of his memory, jogged by degrees over that dreadful first week in Loch Garvach, and reassembled since, of what had happened in the gardens at MacGilp House all those years ago. He told of his shame at having lied so unpleasantly, and the horrible guilt he felt, not just that he had hurt an innocent Coky and a blameless Harry, but that he had unwittingly begun the break-down of his parents' marriage. He told her too that for years he had blamed an unknown woman for splitting up what his mother had thought was a happy home, and that he had colluded unquestioningly with that convenient half-truth, little knowing that he would eventually find this woman to be Bonnie Straughan, and to find that she had probably been as unhappy as his father had been. He told her of his dread fear that this knowledge might have saved his mother from the long horror of never understanding the truth, and from the imprisonment of tortuous self-sacrifice with Gordon himself as the ironic beneficiary. It might have made her life more bearable, if not longer.

What Gordon did not say was that, while he felt he must tell her these feelings, his biggest fear was that Coky's opinion of him would almost certainly be reduced if not destroyed as a result.

Coky listened in still silence. When Gordon had finished, he looked at her, his eyes pink and moist, and prepared for the worst.

And so it was there, in the windless clearing, that the future changed so utterly. The girl took the boy's hand, and softly kissed it.

–*Acknowledgements*–

For encouragement and critical eyes I owe my readers Jez Butterworth, Tom Butterworth, Mary Bowers, Ben Macintyre, Kate Macintyre and Daniel Toledano. Other advisers were Dr Jan Toledano on medicine, Sir John Becher on shooting, Andy Wightman on land owner-ship, and Mike Davies and other colleagues provided wind industry background. I hope I do not embar-rass any of them by having bent or ignored reality in favour of story. My agent Jon Elek at AP Watt, my editor David Isaacs and publisher Rebecca Nicolson at Short Books all need to be thanked for their faith and congratulated on their expertise. Minnie and Wilf, the occupants of 'the pram in the hall', have been nothing but a hindrance and distraction in this context, but might be pleased, when they learn to read, to know that I wouldn't have had it any other way. My greatest thanks, though, go to my wife Lucie Donahue, provider of patience, fine editorial advice and love, with whom I jointly do almost everything except this.

I like to hear from readers via Wordpress, Twitter, Linked-In or Facebook.

Magnus Macintyre grew up in suburban Oxford and rural Argyll, and then read History at Jesus College, Cambridge. He has been a serial entrepreneur in magazine publishing, film, television, and wind farming, with varying degrees of success. Only once has he had a proper job, as managing director of the *New Statesman*. He now lives in Somerset with his wife Lucie and their two children, and writes full time. *Whirligig* is his first novel.